HEARTS
Of Ice

HEARTS
Of Ice

'One's real life isn't the one one lives.'

HALLA CAWKFIELD

ISBN: 978-1-72105-665-1

CONTENTS

ACKNOWLEDGEMENTS

To my beautiful daughters. My love for them has saved me, though they do not know the true extent. Their lust for life kept me going through my darkest days. They are my reason for being.

My family are a disappointment to me on the whole. They have found it easier to label me as mentally ill, rather than support me. They have been more of a hindrance than a help – but all is forgiven. Karma will prevail.

To Women's Aid and the Freedom Programme, both of which opened my eyes to domestic abuse and covert control. They are my unsung heroes.

To the friends who have stuck by me… and for the friends I have lost along the way, I give my love and gratitude.

To the thousands of people, both female and male, who are daily trapped in abusive relationships, I hope this book gives faith and courage – and the knowledge that the power of love can give you strength. You have to dig deep within yourself to overcome great obstacles and bring about positive changes.

Finally, to Emily, Lorna and Rob – without you, this book wouldn't have been published.

'Justice cannot be for one side alone,
but must be for both.'

– ELEANOR ROOSEVELT –

CHAPTER 1

A Mirror Sea

Force 1 on the Beaufort Scale

A sudden gust of wind yanked the taxi door as Jenny stepped out, wrenching it from her hand and tearing off one of her freshly manicured nails. Another flurry joined by a spattering of rain then ruffled her hair, unpinning wisps of her perfectly coiffured chignon, plastering strands to her face before sending a draught billowing up her dress, ballooning it out. Unfortunately, the result was less Marilyn Monroe and more crinolined toilet-roll cover.

Typical! Jenny thought. *Here I am, making a grand entrance to my 25th wedding anniversary party and I'm a tousled, harried mess before I've even walked into the restaurant.*

That was the trouble with living on the North Devon coast. It's picture-postcard pretty, until a leaden cloud comes scudding off the Atlantic and suddenly you're in a tornado… Moving to somewhere less wild and unpredictable never crossed her mind because she always thought the weather would improve; that things were bound to get better.

Jenny carefully smoothed her hair back into place and deflated her dress whilst pasting on a smile. They'd arrived early but there were already several guests milling around who would have enjoyed this pre-party entertainment, including Rachael, their Finance Manager, who was always immaculately dressed, her shiny brown hair perfect despite the weather.

'All right, my darling?' asked her husband Mark, walking around to her side of the car to offer his arm. 'Look at my little Birdy, all in a tizz,' he said softly. Ever solicitous, ever thoughtful was Mark, especially when he was out in public. She knew everyone at the party thought she was a lucky woman to have him by her side. He didn't have a hair out of place and his tailored Canali suit – well, it suited him. The only impact the weather was having on him was that the petals of his buttonhole carnation were quivering slightly. It was just like the cream carnation he'd worn at their wedding.

Mark was good at the little details of life. His memory was astounding. Jenny had always been in awe of it – he could recall names, places, even whole conversations word-perfectly from years before. She often found herself boggling at this ability, becoming speechless when he challenged her recollection of events with his own. Sometimes she'd be sure of a certain fact, only to be firmly corrected by Mark who seemed to take great pleasure in proving her wrong, one way or another. Like that time when she'd mentioned the black leather seats in his first car and he'd searched high and low for a photo to show her that actually, they were navy blue. He'd proved his point so often that now she deferred to him as their joint memory bank, not because it was easier but because she couldn't bear to always be in the wrong.

They crunched over the gravel towards Chez Joy, an expensive French restaurant where 100 friends and family were gathering. Their friend Tony owned it, and there he was, standing in front of the entrance, ever the genial host.

'All right, squire, how are you doing?' asked Tony. 'Oh, and Jenny too – mustn't forget little Jenny must we,' he added, flicking a glance at her.

'All the better for seeing you, Tone. Thanks for sorting this out for me – much obliged,' said Mark, just as Jenny was opening her mouth to reply.

'Not at all, Mark. Any time, mate.'

Mark had worked out some sort of deal with Tony to hire the whole restaurant for the night. Jenny wasn't sure quite what the deal entailed as she wasn't party to that kind of information any more. Mark had his finger in so many pies – business-wise – that Jenny couldn't keep up with it all, and it was years since she had tried to. Early on in their marriage, Mark made it clear that he needed autonomy in his decision-making and that he didn't want to discuss everything with her.

'You can trust me to keep a tight rein on our finances,' he'd once said, and she did trust him, but as the years passed he'd become very evasive about the specifics. He hadn't exactly said, 'Don't worry your pretty little head over it,' but he may just as well have done. Back then though, his masterful handling of every area of their life felt kind and loving; like she was his princess and she didn't need to worry about a thing – he was taking care of her. It was only as the years passed that she began to sense that his micro-managing wasn't always in her best interests. What did her friend Liz call it the other day…? Disempowering.

Jenny gingerly picked her way up the wide entrance steps, made slippery from the rain, raising the hem of her evening dress to avoid tripping over it, still clinging-on to Mark's steadying arm. She admired the shiny damson nail polish on her toes, which were wedged into silver stiletto sandals. She wondered if the one ragged nail on her ring finger was some kind of bad omen. It wasn't often that she dressed up like this – it wasn't often that she went out at all these days, to be honest.

When Mark and Jenny had met, over a quarter of a century ago, Jenny was a different person. She was a vibrant 20-something running her own design business, Truscott Interiors – oh, how she loved her business. She'd always had a flare for colour and could instantly visualise how a room could look its best. Growing up by the coast had been inspirational for Jenny; the vivid blues and greens of the Atlantic were her go-to palette. Even on an overcast day, the greys and fawns of the pebbles contrasted so starkly with the steely sea and sharp knife-edge of the horizon that they seemed to pop out at her. Jenny would often find herself on the shore, eyes half-closed, imagining the different colour stripes of the landscape translated into flooring, fabrics and wallpaper. Surrounded by swatches and paint charts made her very happy. She was creative, spontaneous, perhaps a little scatter-brained, but a successful businesswoman. Back then, Jenny was an attractive proposition.

Mark had been just another contractor on the project she was working on – he was property-managing the renovation of an old barn that was to be turned into holiday lets. She'd been hired to bring a fresh new identity to the place. One look at the high wooden beams and she knew that white walls and accents of azure blue would be the perfect foil. Cream curtains with a pale print of cows on them was a cheeky nod to the previous incarnation of the place as a milking parlour. She knew the client probably wouldn't appreciate this connection but it amused her, and also seemed to respect the barn's history. Jenny's talent rested on her intuition. Something had to feel right for her to be comfortable working on it. If they had insisted on tangerine walls and burgundy carpets Jenny would have baulked, but she would have found a way to make it work.

Mark and Jenny bonded over a tin of spilt paint. Jenny had been up a stepladder, measuring the windows for curtains when she heard a crash.

'Oh dear, what have you done?' came the comment from directly behind her. She whipped round, nearly overbalancing, to see a smiling face looking up at her, one hand on the steps to steady her.

'What? Oh my god, no!' Jenny's eyes widened as she took in the scene below. A tin of expensive paint had fallen off the table and white gloss was slowly forming a puddle on the wooden floor. Jenny hopped down the stepladder and dashed to grab a cleaning rag, tentatively mopping-up the mess, trying not to make it worse than it already was.

'Thank god it was only half a litre,' she murmured. 'Gloss though – what a nightmare.' Luckily most of it had spilt on the protective sheeting Jenny always made sure the decorators used, and so the paint had not yet soaked into the wooden boards below. Mark knelt beside her, despite wearing a suit and hard hat (the classic project manager's outfit), and began to help. Jenny sneaked a glance at him and took in his dark eyes and wavy chestnut hair poking out from under the yellow plastic. She couldn't help but admire what she saw.

'I left that tin perfectly safely on the table. How has it just jumped onto the floor?'

'Maybe it was bewitched?' replied Mark teasingly. 'I'm Mark Damerell by the way, the new project manager. I'm taking over from… Bob, is it?'

'What's happened to Bob?' asked Jenny, now opening a bottle of white spirit to wipe off the rogue splashes of paint that had found their way onto the skirting boards. 'I hope he's okay.' Bob had been a rock to her. He'd given Jenny her first break in the design business and they'd regularly worked together ever since.

'Who knows?' replied Mark. 'Ah, look – here's your culprit. This newel post cap must have rolled over and knocked the tin off.' He held up the offending large oak sphere, due to be attached to the bottom of the bannister.

Jenny was secretly impressed with his use of the correct terminology, where most would have called it a wooden ball, but she wasn't going to reveal this to him. He was so self-assured, so composed that *of course* he knew the right word.

'Yes, it must have,' Jenny replied. 'Silly of me to leave it there.' She flashed a smile at him, her green eyes sparkling.

'I think we probably need a drink to calm down after all this excitement, don't you?' said Mark, standing up now that all the paint had been dealt with, and brushing an imaginary speck of dirt off his trousers. Somehow, he'd managed to remain spotless.

'We probably do, yes,' replied Jenny, using another rag to clean the white gloss off her hands.

'And look, it's nearly wine o'clock,' said Mark, glancing at his watch.

Jenny checked her own large, vintage watch, the strap spattered with years of dried paint. 'Half-past four?'

'Yup, clocking-off time every first Thursday of the month – project managers and interior designers only,' replied Mark, straight-faced.

Jenny laughed. This sudden flash of humour was irresistible to her and she found herself packing up her things despite normally being so conscientious. And so, the pair sneaked off to the country pub just down the road and shared a bottle of very good wine that Mark selected.

This was the beginning of their relationship and Jenny didn't know it yet but she was about to be totally mesmerised by this charming, charismatic man. Her life was to change beyond all recognition.

The following week, Mark called her and suggested that they look around the nearby stately home, Lynscott Manor, that weekend. 'You can get ideas for your next project,' he said, 'and I can daydream about the day that I'll own a place as big as that. I love old houses – they have so much dignity and yet they still yield enough so you can really stamp your identity on them.'

Jenny was happy to go along though she wasn't quite sure where she stood with him. Nothing had happened in the pub – they'd chatted about all sorts and had parted on friendly terms – but she was sure there'd been a spark between them. The way that he devoted all his attention to her when they were talking, how he really listened to what she was saying and seemed interested in her opinions was all rather addictive. Whereas most men divided their time between ogling her cleavage and planning how to get into her knickers, Mark seemed to be interested in her as a person, asking questions about her parents and family and being sensitive and perceptive, reflecting her own feelings so wonderfully that she was bowled over. At the end of the date, he gave her a lift back to her cottage but didn't make any attempt to come in.

'Thanks for a lovely evening, Jenny,' he said, looking at her with a gentle smile.

'Yes, we should do it again some time,' Jenny replied and she meant it. Being with Mark was so exhilarating. She felt like a moon orbiting around his sun; the gravitational pull was palpable. She tilted her chin up for a kiss but he leant to one side and brushed her cheek softly with his lips. She turned to open the car door, saying a breezy, 'Bye then!' to hide her blushes and disappointment, and let herself into her home, not watching as he drove off.

Jenny decided to let Mark take the lead after that. It was so tantalising to spend the following weekends with him but as the weeks passed, things never progressed further than a dry peck, and she continued to feel confused. Was he interested, or wasn't he? Did he fancy her or not? She wasn't sure. Mark would choose where to go and they visited mansions and disused tin mines with equal fascination. Jenny had never met anyone who shared her interests before – most boyfriends had heaved a sigh of reluctance about visiting decrepit old buildings – but Mark seemed to be actively excited about them. Sharing this common bond drew them closer together until finally, as they left a tiny vicarage tearoom one Sunday afternoon, Mark held her close and kissed her lips, his arm cradled around her protectively. Jenny smelt his spiced cologne and felt a jolt run through her from the warmth of his touch.

'That was as good as I knew it would be,' said Mark. 'You really are rather extraordinary, you know that?'

'So are you,' replied Jenny, leaning in for another kiss.

'Naughty, naughty, wait your time,' said Mark, pulling back. Jenny refastened the clip in her strawberry-blonde curls to hide her embarrassment. He was a conundrum, this man. Jenny was sure that there was chemistry between them but why was he so resistant? *There's taking things slowly and there's dragging your feet,* she thought. She wasn't used to such self-control.

'Six weeks and you *still* haven't done it?' cried her friend Liz when they met up later in the week for a coffee. 'What's wrong with you guys? You're supposed to be all over each other like a rash, after all, this is the 'honeymoon period' for god's sake. I prefer the term "shag fest" personally.' Jenny spurted her coffee between her teeth and almost choked as Liz continued, 'So, has there been some heavy petting then?'

'Heavy petting! That sounds like something you'd see on those noticeboards at swimming pools. *No Running, No Jumping, No Heavy Petting!* No, no heavy petting either. It's weird,' said Jenny, 'it's like he really likes me, but he's not quite sure if he fancies me.'

'Don't be daft, Jen – of course he fancies you – look at you, you're gorgeous! He'd be mad not to give you one!'

They both chuckled into their coffee at that but Jenny deftly changed the subject, not wanting to delve further into the whys and wherefores of Mark Damerell.

That weekend, Jenny was determined to progress further than just kissing. Despite her patience, she needed to know if this relationship was going anywhere or not. She invited Mark over for a meal and when she answered the door, he immediately noticed that she had left the three top buttons of her blouse open so a glimpse of her lace bra peeped out.

'Hello gorgeous, you look ravishing,' he said, hanging his coat on the hook in the hall, and catching a glimpse of himself in the mirror.

'So, ravish me,' she replied provocatively, gazing directly at him.

He raised an eyebrow and then caught Jenny's arm, pulling her towards him and kissing her deeply. They shimmied backwards to the dining table, eyes locked, arms entwined. He swept aside the cutlery from the table and lifted her onto it.

'Oh, and I'd set the table so neatly…' Jenny joked feeling slightly alarmed at his sudden intensity.

'Shut up,' he whispered. Shoving her skirt out of the way and pulling off her underwear, he sunk a finger inside her. Jenny gasped at how sudden it was – she didn't feel ready, she wanted to take things a bit more slowly – but then, hadn't she wanted this? Longed for this? Wasn't he doing exactly what she'd asked for and was ravishing her? She saw the tent of his erection and went to unzip his trousers but he brushed her hand aside and did it himself. He pushed himself into her and began forcefully thrusting. Jenny clasped her arms around his neck and closed her eyes, trying to focus on the moment. She felt elated that they were finally making love, but was that the right term for it?

'Your first shag was on the kitchen table? Hilarious!' said Liz when they met for a breakfast summit. 'I wholeheartedly approve.'

Jenny decided not to mention the fact that the salad servers had dug into her back or that she would have preferred some foreplay. She knew she didn't want to tell her best friend about the candle either. She didn't quite know how she felt about it herself, to be honest. After they'd had sex, Jenny expected them to cuddle up on the sofa and maybe have a glass of wine, but no, Mark had other ideas. Still on the table, Mark undid the rest of the buttons on her blouse, reached over for one of the candles Jenny had lit to create a romantic atmosphere and tipped it so drops of wax fell on her pale stomach. All the while he kept his eyes locked on hers. Jenny winced at the sudden heat but didn't say anything. He drew a finger through the wax as it solidified: the letter M.

Jenny felt like she was being branded and was struggling to find it erotic but she could see from the intensity of Mark's gaze that he was. He then peeled off the wax, holding the fragile, translucent letter up to the light. 'M for magical, marvellous, mind-blowing,' he said.

'Or Mark,' Jenny ventured, then instantly regretted it as it seemed to shatter his mood. Mark crumbled the letter between his fingers and walked off to the bathroom. She could hear the shower being turned on so she got herself up and dressed, resetting the table and pouring herself a large glass of wine.

So that was our first time, she thought. It was not what she had expected at all. There was a faint red M on her stomach and her skin felt a little sore. Her hand kept straying there throughout the evening, checking it, checking that it really had happened. Even days later, she still felt a strange sensation right in the core of her and she couldn't stop thinking about Mark's intensity – almost distraction – during sex. It was as if the hot wax had burnt an image of him into her mind. He was mystifying to her and she spent much of her time trying to work him out. He was charming, intelligent, spontaneous, handsome, and undoubtedly, he ticked a lot of boxes, but she also felt that there was something more to him that he wasn't revealing. This was like a moth to the flame for Jenny. She could usually read people like a book, but here was one volume that wasn't easily opened.

Soon they were spending every evening and weekend together. Jenny discovered that there wasn't anything Mark couldn't do – he bent over backwards to make her happy. He tinkered under the bonnet of her old Morris Minor and cured it of its annoying rattle, he reprogrammed her central heating so it came on automatically, rather than her usual method of just firing it up when she was chilly. And the first night they spent together signalled the beginning of a whole new chapter in Jenny's love life.

Previously, she would have described her erotic tastes as 'vanilla' – enthusiastically vanilla but still pretty conventional. Now Mark was introducing her to a veritable ice-cream parlour of sexual experiences. Each time he came around he had a new sex toy with him, things she didn't even know existed – leather bondage gear, love eggs, teasers – and she grew to recognise his expression as he revealed that evening's activities. Eyes glittering, mouth in an enigmatic smile, the only word to describe him at these times was *masterful*. She felt helpless, like putty in his hands; it wasn't that she didn't like it exactly, it was more that she felt utterly detached from him. Jenny didn't feel their sex was loving, although Mark was definitely loved-up afterwards, hugging her, chatty and glowing from his exertions. Jenny always felt half-anxious, half-aroused at the thought of what each evening would bring, but she banished far from her mind the lingering question mark that hung over Mark's previous partners. Did they like what he liked to do? He would never talk about them when she asked and she didn't want to dwell on whether this unusual equipment had been used before, and on whom. The thought crossed her mind that maybe she should bring something to the party too, but she didn't know where on earth to buy that stuff from. When she asked Mark he said, 'Don't worry about it. I know what I like, and I know what you'll like too.'

'Jenny!' Mark elbowed her in the ribs. 'The least you could do is mingle with the guests. What are you doing staring into space? *Circulate*,' he hissed.

Jenny roused herself and headed towards the safety of her old friend Liz, who had been a rock for her over the years, despite Liz having had more than her own share of hardship. Her son was born with cerebral palsy and wasn't expected to live. He did, but the illness was more than her husband Clifford could bear and he left Liz and their son when the little boy was just eighteen months old. As a single parent, it was hard for Liz to make ends meet and look after Joe on her own, but she coped.

'Great party, kiddo,' said Liz, putting a reassuring arm round her friend.

'Yes, Mark's gone to a lot of trouble,' Jenny replied.

'Or paid someone to.' Liz arched her eyebrows. 'He's not exactly folded the napkins himself, has he?'

The two women sniggered into their champagne, but over the speeches – given at length, first by her father and then by Mark – Jenny found her mind wandering again, back to those early days of their life together.

Mark's dominating attitude in the bedroom slowly but surely, translated itself into all areas of Jenny's life, but because he was always so attentive and considerate, on the whole, Jenny was happy to go with the flow. Life was easy when she was with Mark, she didn't have to think about a thing and having run her own business for several years it was nice to have someone else making the decisions for a change. She felt fortunate, almost content.

One thing Mark wouldn't help with was her beloved, ancient ginger tom, Smudge, when he needed deworming.

'Not so keen on moggies, to be honest,' he said, eyeing the marmalade cat as Jenny struggled to get a tablet down his throat. The feeling was mutual and Smudge always disappeared whenever Mark was around. Mark was happy to help when the cat went missing though, and plastered the village with posters offering a generous reward. No one came forward and after a few weeks Jenny had to accept that Smudge had gone. She was heartbroken – she'd only had him for a few years, since he'd turned up on her door-step one day and decided to stay. Before Mark, he'd been her only company most evenings.

When she told Liz at their regular Tuesday meet-up, she knew just how Jenny felt, being devoted to animals of all shapes and sizes herself, and one of those people who would nurture a fledgling that had fallen out of a nest, despite the poor thing doing its best to die. 'Oh no, not Smudgy-boy… He was a darling. What could have happened to him?'

'I've no idea. It's like he's just vanished. I hope he's taken up residence somewhere else like he did with me. Who knows, he may be a serial monogamist kitty with a string of broken-hearted owners behind him.'

'He'll never find an owner as good as you though,' said Liz, patting Jenny's arm affectionately. 'Talking of the men in your life, when am I going to meet Mr Wonderful then?'

'Soon, I promise. He's just so busy with work…' Jenny replied. She didn't mention that Mark had shrugged off her suggestion of meeting up with friends. No, he just wanted to stay at home with her and she loved that she was enough for him – it was intoxicating. 'You'll like him though. He's gorgeous and so easy to talk to. I've never felt this way about anyone before.' Jenny also didn't mention that she'd never felt this way about sex before. She was vaguely aware that she'd started to keep secrets from her best friend.

'He sounds like a catch, that's for sure,' said Liz, thought-fully stirring her cappuccino. She decided to reserve judgment until she met Mark. Liz was a shrewd judge of character and had seen Jenny's romantic forays before – one minute they were flavour of the month, the next, past their sell-by date.

Liz's wish was granted over the bank holiday week-end when Mark organised a barbecue for Jenny's birthday. 'Invite who you like – Liz, is it? And your mum and dad… Your brother… I'd love to meet them all,' said Mark as they cleared away the breakfast things one morning.

'Are you sure about meeting them all at once? Baptism of fire or what?' said Jenny as she loaded the dishwasher.

'I prefer to think of it as the next step in our relation-ship, darling. I want to know all about you, what makes you tick. How you became this incredible person who I just can't get enough of,' said Mark, reaching to fondle her breasts as she was sorting out the cutlery.

'You're right, Mark,' replied Jenny, craning around awkwardly to give him a kiss. 'It is the next step in our rela-tionship, and they're all dying to meet you. I'll ring round today. What about your family – shall we invite them too?'

Mark visibly stiffened. 'We don't keep in contact much.'

'But I'd like to meet them, Mark… Maybe now's the time to reconnect, y'know, break the ice and all that?'

'I said we don't keep in touch, alright. My mother's… not our sort.'

'Oh.' Jenny knew better than to pursue the subject. She could read that closed look on his face and it would not end well if she persisted, but what on earth did he mean by 'our sort'? What 'sort' did he think they were? She knew he was impressed that her parents lived at Trethorne Manor, but they weren't exactly 'gentry', and he liked the fact that she went to a private school, but that didn't make her any different from anyone else. She let it drop, but made a mental note to try and find out more on his family life and background.

Just as she'd predicted, everyone was as curious as Liz to meet Mark, and all jumped at the invitation to the barbecue, offering to bring a plate of food or bottle of wine, but Jenny explained that Mark had it all covered.

'Not even my famous potato salad?' asked her mum, Eleanor.

'Not even that, Mum.'

'God save us from your bloody potato salad,' said Jenny's father grumpily.

Jenny ignored him and his habit of belittling her mother. 'Mark just wants to treat everyone – y'know, to make a good impression. I know you're going to love him.'

'Okay, if you're sure…' Eleanor wasn't used to Jenny's boyfriends being so organised. At previous gatherings, she would generally arrive with a carful of food and spend the entire party cooking. Eleanor was interested to meet this new breed of boyfriend.

The day of the barbecue arrived and as Jenny drove over to Mark's place, she could see a storm cloud gathering out at sea. She hurried to his beautifully renovated Victorian terrace just as the first drops of rain landed, polka-dotting the path up to his front door.

'Hello, darling,' said Mark, enveloping Jenny in a hug. He was wearing a beautiful pale grey linen shirt and tan chinos, hitting exactly the right style note as usual.

'Shame about the weather,' said Jenny, thrusting two bottles of good champagne into Mark's hands. She was feeling jittery about him meeting her family and friends and wanted everything to go to plan.

'Veuve Clicquot, good girl,' he nodded approvingly. 'Well, I always say prepare for the unexpected and that includes North Devon weather.' He added her contribution to a tub full of ice already crammed with bottles and poured them both a glass from an open one. 'It may be rainy, but you're my ray of sunshine.'

'He's a virtual rainbow himself, aren't you, Marco?' said a voice emerging from the conservatory.

'I'm sure I don't know what you mean, Guy,' said Mark smoothly.

Jenny was taking a sip of champagne and nearly choked when she saw Guy walk over to them. He was medium height, very muscular, like a scrum-half, and gorgeous.

'Oh, ignore me,' Guy said. 'Now, this must be the fragrant Jenny. I've heard so much about you.'

'Hi Guy – oh, that rhymes…' faltered Jenny, feeling a blush rise up her throat. 'I mean, it's nice to meet you…' She couldn't think of what to say in the face of this godlike creature. Mark had told her that Guy had just returned from South Africa after a brief marriage and painful divorce, but she didn't think now was the time to mention it. She downed her champagne and Mark promptly topped it up.

'Any for me? I've a raging thirst,' said Guy. 'I've been working up a lather in Marco's orangerie,' he added to Jenny.

Before Jenny could ask what he meant, the doorbell rang and she went to answer it. She was feeling rather discombobulated and it wasn't just the champagne – for a start, what was all this 'Marco' business. Liz's silhouette showed through the stained-glass panels in the front door and Jenny heaved a sigh of relief. Liz was always a tonic in any situation. She flung the door open to be greeted with a bunch of sunflowers, Liz's face peeping from behind them.

'Happy birthday m'dear! Now, where's the prosecco? I'm gasping.'

'Champagne, I'll have you know,' answered Jenny, 'and it's this way.'

'Ooh, look at this hallway. Isn't it… tasteful?' commented Liz, taking in the olive fleur-de-lis wallpaper and black-framed watercolours.

'The whole house is like this. He's a better interior designer than me!' replied Jenny.

'No one's better than you,' said Liz, protectively.

'You're right, Jenny is the best there is,' said Mark, appearing suddenly, linking his hands around Jenny's waist and pulling her gently towards him. 'You must be Liz,' he added, and you've brought sunflowers. How cheerful.'

'Hi Mark – good to finally meet you in the flesh. I was beginning to think Jenny had made you up.'

'Oh no, I'm real all right,' said Mark as the doorbell rang again. 'Excuse me, I'll just get that.' As he headed off, Liz and Jenny walked into the living room.

'Christ on a bike, who on earth is THAT?' whispered

Liz, tilting her head towards Guy, who was standing examining the bookcase.

'It's Guy. He's amazing looking, isn't he? He's *look but don't touch* though Lizzie – he's getting over a painful divorce. He's just got a job in the upper echelons of South West Water.'

'He can fix my pipes any day,' shot back Liz, and as Jenny burst out laughing her mum, dad and her brother Paul walked in.

'What's so funny, Sis?' asked Paul as they all gave Jenny a kiss and handed her a pile of presents and cards.

'I'll tell you later,' she replied as she set about putting her gifts safely on the sideboard, but not before she saw Guy approach Paul. Paul had just come back from travelling and his red hair had been turned bronze by the sun. He looked gorgeous in a deep indigo shirt. Jenny joined them and they'd just begun to chat when Mark came up to them.

'Hi Paul, nice to see you again after all these years,' said Mark. Paul's face was inscrutable. Mark continued, 'Don't I recognise you from university – you were in the rugby team, weren't you?'

'What?' asked Jenny incredulously, 'you guys know each other? That's one spooky coincidence, don't you think?'

'It's a small world Jenny, darling,' replied Mark. 'We never really moved in the same circles, did we Paul?'

'No, we didn't,' said Paul, seemingly as surprised as Jenny at this turn of events.

Then several more of Mark's friends turned up, all armed with bottles of fizz, and the volume in the room cranked-up, the noise of voices competing with the music. Party noise.

Just then there was the deep boom of thunder and the rain began to sheet down, rattling the windows.

'Perfect barbecue weather!' called Mark to the crowd, to much laughter. 'Now I've got your attention, I wanted to let you in on a little surprise for Jenny. I suspected that the elements might attempt to thwart our barbecue, so I decided to bring the outdoors in. Jenny, everyone, follow me.'

He took Jenny by the hand, led her to the conservatory and flicked a switch. The spacious room was filled with the glow of a thousand fairy lights, reflected in all the windows against the blackening sky, and woven in and out of them were flowers – lilies, peonies, freesias, all scenting the air. *Happy Birthday Jenny* was spelt out in deep red roses on the far wall.

There was a collective 'ooh' from everyone and a, 'Must have cost a fortune,' muttered by Liz, then a cheer went up as Jenny stood on her tiptoes to give Mark a kiss.

'Oh Marco, it's wonderful,' she whispered.

'Don't call me Marco, darling' he hissed in her ear, but to the throng he said, 'I knew you'd love it.' He then pressed a chic white box into her hand. It was a bottle of Chanel No. 5.

Before she had a chance to thank him, he raised his voice again to address the crowd. 'Now, we've got a mountain of food to eat, so please can everyone help themselves.' Turning to Jenny's mum, he said, 'Mrs Truscott, it would be an honour if you would try my potato salad. I'm hoping you'll approve.'

'Oh, call me Eleanor,' she replied and Jenny was sure she detected a flirtatious smile from her mother. 'Certainly, Mark, I'd love to try your potato salad,' and she let herself be led away by this charming man.

'Well, happy birthday, Jenny,' said her father George, gruffly. 'This is all quite jolly, isn't it? Good show. So, what did you say this Mark fellow does?'

'He's a project manager, Dad, but he's got his own portfolio of properties too. He wants to build it up. You should talk to him about it. Maybe you could invest?'

'Hmmm – don't know about that,' replied George who liked to play his cards close to his chest. 'What about his family? Are they local?'

'I'm not sure, Dad, you'll have to ask him.'

'What do you mean, *you're not sure*? Haven't you asked him, girl?'

'Well, he doesn't like to talk about it Dad. Don't make a scene, please.'

'I'm not making a scene. Good god. Relax and enjoy your party Jenny.' George looked at his daughter disdainfully and eyed a bevy of men in the corner – Mark's friends – with whom he was sure he'd have a more interesting conversation.

Why was it that Jenny always seemed to rub her dad up the wrong way? They could rarely say three words without them turning into an argument. He was always so abrasive, so judgemental, or so it seemed to her.

Jenny sighed. She could see Mark working his magic on her mother and felt a swell of pride to be his girl. He was perfect and, unlike her father, he utterly adored her.

This was the best birthday ever. She almost swooned with joy, like some sort of Victorian heroine as Mark returned to top up their glasses.

'Mr Truscott, I'm so glad you could make it. I wanted to ask your opinion on the housing stock around Bideford.'

Jenny saw her father's eyes light up, delighted to have the chance to talk about his pet projects. Although he was nearing retirement George was still one of the county's most established and successful property developers and loved nothing more than talking shop.

What a charmer, Jenny thought. *Mark knows exactly how to get into people's good books.*

As the afternoon turned to early evening and the rain continued to hammer down, the party inside gradually dispersed, Jenny's parents leaving last, with her dad giving the parting shot.

'Mark's really rather special, Jenny. I'm quite taken with him. Good work.' His colour was high, as if he'd had too much to drink.

You're not in the Army now, Dad, she thought. *Good work? Honestly...* But she didn't say anything, instead choosing to keep the peace. She hugged them both as they left, her father palpably stiffening as she insisted on giving him a peck on the cheek.

Jenny was feeling rather wobbly but still radiant as she started to gather up plates and glasses. Mark came up behind her and wrapped her up in a bear hug.

'Trapped! Can't breathe!' joked Jenny, a glass dangling from one of her pinned hands.

'You're wearing Chanel No. 5,' said Mark, nuzzling her neck and inhaling deeply. 'I'm never going to let you go.'

Jenny wriggled around to face him. 'Promise me you won't.'

'I won't.'

CHAPTER 2

White Horses

Force 3 on the Beaufort Scale

'So, 25 years…' The crowd in the restaurant gave a great cheer as Mark tapped his champagne glass to conclude his speech. 'Since the day we met I've never looked back. They always say that behind every successful man is a strong woman and I know that's true.' Mark looked out at their guests as Jenny once again roused herself from her reverie, noticing that his gaze lingered on Rachael and in the glow of the candlelight her eyes seemed to be twinkling back at him. But everyone else was looking at Jenny, smiling and acknowledging the success of their marriage.

'It may be our 25th wedding anniversary, but it took nearly five years to persuade Jenny to marry me, so I consider it our 30th.' Lots of oohs from the party.

'And 30 years is celebrated with pearls, so happy 30th anniversary, my darling Birdy,' said Mark, reaching down to fetch a jewellery box from below his seat. He raised it up to show the crowd, who all made the appropriate oohing sounds.

'What's this?' said Jenny opening the box, remembering to smile. It was a necklace made up of two strings of freshwater pearls, fastened with a diamond clasp. They gleamed with that iridescence of quality. She removed her simple gold pendant and replaced it with the pearls, her 'thank you' drowned out by cheers and clapping.

'May I propose a toast to my wife, Jenny,' said Mark.

'To Jenny!' roared the crowd. Then, just as Jenny was about to say something, their son Marcus stood up.

'Hang on a moment, Dad, this party is to celebrate both of you so I'd like to propose a toast too – to Dad and Mum, I mean Mark and Jenny.' Amidst laughter glasses were raised again and Marcus' toast echoed around the room.

Jenny could hear murmurs all around her: 'Such a lovely family…' 'Jenny is so lucky…' 'Isn't Mark generous…'

'When did you get this?' Jenny asked Mark, gesturing to her pearls.

'Oh, back in April during our trip to Australia. You were having a nap. Completely oblivious.'

'Oh… well thank you, it's absolutely gorgeous, but you shouldn't have.'

'No, I shouldn't have,' replied Mark taking a sip of champagne and looking away. Jenny slipped out of her seat and went to the Ladies.

As she locked the cubicle door and sank down on the seat, she tore off a length of loo-roll to blot her tears.

Is this party just one big charade? she asked herself. *Should our marriage really be celebrated, when Mark is stone cold to me in private?* Jenny sighed, wondering how things had gone so wrong after the euphoria of their early years. As usual, she was tired and aching all over, and yearned to be away from this party and back in the comfort of her bedroom, preferably under the duvet. Just as she was popping out some tablets from her blister pack she heard the door to the Ladies open.

'That pearl necklace is gorgeous! It must have cost a bomb,' came an unfamiliar voice. 'Can I borrow your lipstick?'

'Sure, here. Mark's such a nice chap isn't he – and not short of a few bob either,' replied another voice. 'But pearls? I don't think they're going to make their actual 30th wedding anniversary to be honest.'

'I know what you mean. Jenny's not looking so great these days, is she? What's wrong with her? And what's with the Birdy nickname? Hardly – unless it's an ostrich!'

Jenny heard laughter as two cubicle doors slammed shut and she rushed to leave before they re-emerged. In the foyer, she felt like she was going to faint, so she unfolded her collapsible flowery walking stick and slowly made her way back to the party, trying to block out what she'd just heard.

Come on, Jenny, buck up. Listen to Mark. You are strong. You may feel inadequate but you're not a victim, she said to herself. *But what did they mean, an ostrich? Am I burying my head in the sand?*

As she passed through the restaurant and the seats furthest away from the top table, she felt a tug at her arm. It was Liz, with Joy, Tony's wife, sitting next to her: Jenny's two dearest friends. Both their lovely, kind faces shined up at her, brows knitted in concern.

'You okay, darling?' Joy asked. 'I've got some painkillers if you need any.'

'Thanks, but I've got some,' replied Jenny opening her palm to reveal the two tablets nestled there. 'Give us a swig of your water though.' Jenny swallowed the tablets down. 'Let's catch up properly in the week. I suppose I should put on a good show now,' she is nodding towards the main party throng. Liz and Joy grimaced in sympathy as she went back to her table.

'You know, I always wondered why it took them five years to tie the knot,' Liz whispered to Joy. 'It seemed to me that Mark was more interested in schmoozing with George than marrying Jenny. It was like a *ménage à trois* at times.'

'Oh, don't be daft, Liz,' Joy quipped, 'you've got too much of a fertile imagination.'

'You think so? You didn't see what was going on. At first I thought Mark was just gold-digging, you know? Getting on with the old man to worm his way into the family business, but sometimes, the way George and Mark would work a party, hitting on the women and the men too… it was creepy.'

'Maybe he was just trying to prove himself to his prospective father-in-law? Show that he was a good catch?'

'Well, Jen did tell me once that he was embarrassed about growing up on one of those rough council estates in Ilfracombe… but it's more than that, Joy. Mark, he's a… he… oh, forget it.'

'You read too much into things, Liz. You've just never liked Mark, that's your trouble, but he's helped Tony out with the business a lot over the years.'

'Well, that's as may be, but you're right, I don't like the man. I never have.'

By 10pm the volume at the party had trebled as Mark and his cronies started singing rugby songs. Faces red and sweaty, shirts open, they'd swapped champagne for pints which were slopping as they swayed arm in arm in full song. The cronies' wives were all sitting around one table, whispering together and Jenny spotted Rachael in the midst of them. She felt happy to leave them to it.

'Can you give me a lift home, Jessica?' she asked her daughter.

'Don't you think you should stay a while, Mum?' Jessica questioned. 'Dad's gone to a lot of trouble with this party, you know.'

'I know love, but I'm getting a bit tired.'

Her daughter huffed. 'You're always tired, Mum.' Jessica had finished her degree and had been home for a few months, saying she wanted to earn some money and then go travelling. *I'm going to miss her*, Jenny thought as she gathered her things. Her children were the one source of pride in her life.

Marcus, who'd always got one eye on the tension between his parents, noticed his mother readying to leave and came over to say goodbye. He hadn't passed his test yet, much to Mark's annoyance. He'd been all set to pick out a vintage car for Marcus to celebrate getting his driving licence, but when Marcus failed his test, Mark spat, 'Call yourself a man?'

Back at home at The Rectory, Jenny sighed with relief as she slipped out of her strappy heels and into sheepskin slippers. *Heaven is a pair of brushed cotton pyjamas*, she thought, as she sank into her bed a few minutes later. She lay back and listened to the wind howling outside, with the dull roar of crashing waves in the background. Jenny felt relieved that the ancient sash windows had been replaced by sturdy modern ones as gusts buffeted the glass. She had always been happiest tucked up in her nest, and this was why Mark first came to call her Birdy, all those years ago.

Jenny had been asleep for a few hours when she was awoken by her door making a popping noise. It was the air whooshing up the stairs from the front door opening. *Mark's back*, she thought. She listened as he crashed around the kitchen, making himself his typical snack of cheese on toast. *I hope he remembers to turn the grill off.* She waited for the pipes to gurgle, but there was only silence. *He hasn't flushed.* Mark's heavy footsteps on the landing and then the sound of the spare room door closing. He slept there most nights now, and especially after a night out – he said he didn't want to disturb her in her nest. It hadn't always been that way. Jenny remembered when Mark had always wanted to be with her. She had felt completely consumed by him once upon a time and she felt a pang of nostalgia for the days when she was the centre of his universe.

Jenny's thoughts turned to how Mark proposed and it made her instinctively curl up. It wasn't the happiest of memories.

'I've been thinking. It makes financial sense to get married, so how about it?' asked Mark walking back into the bedroom after a shower.

'Erm…' said Jenny from the bed.

'There are tax breaks for married couples so it's silly not to take advantage,' he added, towelling his hair.

'I suppose you're right,' replied Jenny.

'That's sorted then,' said Mark. He opened a can of Carling Black Label and gave her the ring-pull. 'There's your ring until we can get a proper one,' he said with a smirk.

Jenny snapped off the metal tongue and slipped the flimsy ring on her finger. 'You charmer,' she said smiling lightly, but deep down, Jenny wasn't sure how she felt about marriage to Mark. Certainly not over the moon or head-over-heels or any of those other clichés you're expected to feel when proposed to. Her uppermost feeling was of discomfort about what had just happened in bed.

Mark had suggested some 'afternoon delight' and they'd headed to the bedroom, Mark slapping her rear as she climbed the stairs. The word 'delight' was a misnomer though. As soon as Jenny got through the door, Mark had tugged down her trousers and got to work. There was no tenderness, not even any eye contact. She didn't feel connected to him, rather that she was just a vessel. She thought of the phrase that summed it up: 'he's doing his business on me'. And the usual leather paraphernalia had come out too. She'd never really warmed to this aspect of their sex life, but as Mark obviously did, she went along with it. She didn't feel violated so much as isolated – who was this man in her bed?

Jenny had learned the hard way not to question the motives of others. As a young girl, her sense of curiosity constantly got her into trouble with her father. When asking why mummy was crying again, he'd barked at her to keep her nose out of other people's business. When she asked why he had burned a pile of letters in the garden, he'd ranted about, 'fucking privacy in my own home' and slapped her across the face. As an ex-Army man, George was keen on discipline and part of that was to 'Do As You're Told'. It was a mantra in her childhood home.

'Dad – why do I have to wash-up again?'

'Don't question me girl! Just do as you're told.'

But when she did do as she was told, it paid off. 'You're a good girl Jenny,' he'd once said when she'd polished his Jaguar XJ6 to a high shine for his birthday. 'Thank you poppet,' if she'd got up and cleared the table without being asked. And so, to keep the peace, Jenny did as she was told, all her life, until she no longer questioned it.

So, after Mark had finished his business, even though she felt shaken and sore, she didn't say anything, but that didn't stop her trying to rationalise what was going on. She knew that after a while, the sex in any relationship grew to be routine, but that word implied some sort of mundanity and boredom. Jenny certainly didn't feel bored – no that's not the word – she felt punished. It was as if Mark vented some unknowable emotions in the act of sex; anger and frustration were part of the mix and it seemed they were directed at her. So, as was her wont, she tried to figure out what was going on for Mark, because understanding him would help her accept his behaviour.

The metaphorical portcullis that clanged down when she'd tried to ask about his family was a big clue. She had gleaned that he was an only child, and that his father and mother were divorced, but she knew no more than that. She realised that it was too painful for him to talk about. This made the question-mark that hung over Mark's sexual behaviour dissolve into sympathy and compassion. Maybe he'd been neglected as a child, or dominated – or worse… abused. But she would heal him. She would take that pain away and make him better. It might be hard work in the interim, but it would be worth it.

Jenny rang her mum later and held the receiver away from her ear as Eleanor screamed in delight. 'Oh Jenny, that's wonderful news! We must all go out so we can toast the happy couple. What are you doing this evening?'

So, Jenny and Mark found themselves at the local pub with her parents. Jenny hurriedly took off the lager ring-pull and slipped it in her pocket as she didn't think they'd appreciate the joke. 'Mark's taking me shopping this weekend,' she explained when they asked where the engagement ring was.

'One month's salary. That's what it's supposed to cost,' said George, adding, 'it's supposed to hurt.'

'Don't worry, George, I have something in mind,' replied Mark. 'I'm good at making people happy.'

'I know you are, young man,' said George, beaming approvingly. 'My little girl needs looking after and you're just the man for the job. I realised that when you asked me for her hand in marriage last week. We'll have to look at your future in the family firm too…'

Eleanor took Jenny to one side as the two men's conversation turned to business.

'From the moment I saw him, I knew Mark was right for you. The way he makes such an effort, and he's such a gentleman too, just like your father. Remember that room full of flowers he did for your birthday, when you first met? Oh, it was wonderful.'

'You're right, Mum, he is lovely.' Hearing her mother's excitement helped cement in Jenny's mind that she was making the right decision and that any worries about their love-life could be overcome in time. And to hear her mother speak affectionately about her father after enduring so much denigration from him, well, it gave her hope. Hope that love conquers all. Hope that her feelings for Mark could melt the ice in his heart. And of course, the fact that her parents approved of Mark was another vote in his favour.

As she was buying a round at the bar, she felt a tap on her shoulder.

'Jenny, isn't it? Jenny Truscott?' said a voice behind her.

Turning around she struggled to recollect where she knew this smiling man from until it clicked. 'Oh, hi James!' she replied, smiling at him. 'Good to see you again. How's the house?' James was a client she'd worked for a year or so previously.

'Marvellous, thank you. What you did to it was nothing less than miraculous. Anyway, I can see you're busy so I'll let you get back, but it's so nice to see you again.' He gave her a warm smile and squeezed her hand briefly, a friendly gesture that Jenny hoped might mean more work in the future. After all, he liked what she'd done to his house.

Jenny returned to the table with the drinks and thought nothing of this exchange until she and Mark got home later.

'What do you think you were playing at tonight?' said Mark calmly, the moment he had bolted the door behind them.

'Hmmm? What are you on about?'

'Humiliating me in public like that, and in front of your parents too.'

'Mark? Sorry, but I haven't an inkling what you're going on about...' Jenny said, searching Mark's face for clues. His eyes were flat and cold. The only visible sign of emotion were his slightly flared nostrils.

'Flirting with that man at the bar, right under my nose.'

Jenny laughed, but instantly regretted it as anger flashed in his eyes. 'James? Oh, he's just an old client. And he's twice my age. Honestly, Mark – relax.' But Jenny didn't know if Mark had heard, as he was walking upstairs in silence, the knuckles on his hand white as he grasped the bannisters.

Jenny felt the same surge of panic as she did during her childhood when her father was furious with her. As an adult, she knew she needed to stand up for herself, but the old triggers made her freeze. *Christ on a bike*, she muttered under her breath. *What's wrong with him. Can't I even have friends now?*

Later that night Jenny had a repeat performance from Mark in bed, but this time he drew blood. It felt like punishment.

'Mark… be careful,' Jenny winced. But he didn't stop.

Afterwards, he stroked her back. 'It's because I love you so much, Jenny,' he whispered.

'I love you too, Mark,' she replied. 'Mark…'

'Uh-oh,' Mark said, rolling away from her. 'I know that tone of voice.'

'Remember when you told me about that horrendous bully at your school?'

'Elizabeth Bartlett? What about her?'

'Well, you said that she used to beat the smaller boys and that she really enjoyed humiliating them.'

'Yes, the cow, and she'd make us all watch. Poor brats, but I was never the one on the receiving end. What of it?'

'Could it be… tell me if I'm wrong, but… maybe part of you *enjoyed* watching?'

'What the fuck are you on about now? Of course not, it was awful, Jen,' replied Mark, sitting up in bed and switching the bedside lamp on.

'I mean, subconsciously,' Jenny persisted, knowing she was on thin ice. 'The six-year-old you saw what pleasure it was giving the bully, and it imprinted something in you. Does that make any sense? I'm just trying to get my head around why you enjoy…' Jenny hesitated, unsure how to phrase it. 'When we play in the bedroom,' she finished.

'Christ knows… maybe,' Mark replied sharply. 'You just carry on with your bullshit mumbo-jumbo analysis if it helps. I don't care about Elizabeth fucking Bartlett and I don't know why you're bringing this up now.'

'Don't get angry with me, Mark, I'm just trying to understand why you…'

'I mean, basically, you're calling me a bully, Jenny. Is that what you're getting at?'

'No, no… I just want to, I mean…'

'Oh, shut up and go to sleep for god's sake. I've a meeting in the morning and I could really do without this,' he said, snapping off the light and plumping his pillows with a fist.

Mark may not have wanted to engage in the conversation, but Jenny felt that maybe, just maybe, she'd hit upon something. Maybe, subconsciously, he related dominance with pleasure. A wave of compassion washed over her. Poor boy, struggling in a loveless home and a bullying school environment. No wonder he failed at times to show his deeper emotions. She knew she loved him, even his darker side. She knew there were worrying shadows in his personality but she yearned to shine a light on them, to be the bright morning sunshine to his twilight. Yes, she would heal him with her love.

The next day after work, Mark produced a small box. Inside was a large solitaire diamond ring.

'Happy now?' he asked.

'Yes, it's gorgeous,' Jenny replied, although it wasn't what she would have chosen. She had thought that they were going to choose a ring together – preferably at the antiques market in Barnstaple – but she didn't want to spoil the mood.

'Now you can start planning the wedding, that's what you ladies love to do, isn't it? Fussing over whether the napkins should match the flowers and suchlike.'

Of course, Jenny *had* already thought about the colour scheme. That was as natural to her as breathing. All white, with green accents, to go with her simple, elegant white dress and bouquet, but in fact, the wedding didn't happen for over two years after their engagement. Work commitments, her parents' pre-planned trip to see cousins in Canada and other events just kept getting in the way – and perhaps Jenny did drag her heels a bit.

When the wedding day eventually came around, to a casual observer it was like a fairy-tale. Just as Mark was 'perfect on paper', according to the wedding album, the day was too. Two beautiful people surrounded by family and friends. But the smiling faces didn't reveal any of what was going on under the surface. Such as how Mark had done absolutely zero to help, but had then taken the credit during a moving speech about, 'Mr and Mrs Damerell being a team for life'. Or, how Mark got completely wrecked with his cronies at the reception and spent their wedding night AWOL.

Even the exotic honeymoon was a disappointment. Jenny had been scrupulous about not drinking the local water but she still managed to get a terrible sickness and diarrhoea bug.

'You muppet, how have you managed that?' asked Mark.

'Oh darling,' she sobbed between bouts of retching, 'I'm so sorry for ruining the honeymoon.' Her body was wracked with another set of cramps. 'I thought I'd done everything to avoid it, but obviously not.'

'Ugh, I can't stand the smell of vomit,' replied Mark, wrinkling his nose. Instead of looking after her he made himself scarce, taking advantage of the all-inclusive hotel.

'It's a waste not to,' he explained, standing in the doorway with a tinkling G&T. And Jenny understood. Why would he want to spend all day holding her hair out of the sick-bowl when he could be by the pool?

Back at home and feeling better, Jenny reminded Mark that they should use condoms for a week as the sickness bug meant her contraceptive pills wouldn't be reliable.

'But you'll be throwing those away now, surely?' he exclaimed. 'Kids are definitely the next logical step. The Damerell empire needs to expand you know.' He smiled, ruffling her hair. They had talked about having children but Jenny didn't realise he meant before the confetti had been swept up. The next day she couldn't find her pills.

'Mark, do you know where they are?'

'Try the bin,' he replied without turning around from brushing his teeth.

'Hang on a minute, they're where? I'm not ready to have children.'

Mark spat the toothpaste into the basin and turned to face her. 'But I am, and you do want to make me happy, don't you?'

'Oh, Mark! This isn't the Middle Ages you know. I do have a say in the matter. Of course I want to make you happy, but it's such a big step. I'm still in my twenties, so there's no rush.'

'Oh for god's sake, get over yourself,' Mark snarled. 'I know how fucking old you are.' Then he instantly softened. 'Sorry darling, it's just that you'll be a fantastic mother, I know you will. You're so caring and thoughtful. You're the dictionary definition of nurturing. It's a no-brainer.'

Jenny still wasn't convinced – she just didn't feel ready for kids yet, and what about Truscott Interiors? She had her career to think about, she had responsibilities. She tried to speak to him about it again, but he was having none of it, so she got a coil fitted, much to Mark's chagrin.

A few days later, she drove into town to buy a pair of boots stopping first to go into the bank to withdraw some cash.

'Sorry Mrs Damerell,' said the bored young cashier. 'Your account's got a stop on it. You're overdrawn.'

'What? How can this b-be?' Jenny stuttered, feeling embarrassed as an interested queue of locals formed behind her.

She drove home without her new boots and marched over to the flash modern office building that Mark had installed at the bottom of the garden. She needed to ask him what the hell was going on, seeing as he oversaw the finances for both their businesses and now, also for the 'family firm' as George called it, having made Mark a Director, a wedding present from father-in-law to son-in-law.

Mark didn't seem at all surprised when Jenny told him what had happened and explained that Rachael, their new Finance Manager, (who Jenny thought looked way too young for such a title) must have, 'moved some money around'.

'Well she's not doing a very good job, is she?' demanded Jenny. 'And why has she got access to my personal account?'

'Oh, don't fret, Birdy, it's just business. You wouldn't understand.'

'Don't patronise me, Mark Damerell,' she hissed, surprising herself with her level of outrage. 'My business, is *my business*. I'm going to sort this out.' She stalked over to Rachael's office, just as she was coming out of it, carrying a tray loaded with cups.

'Oh, hi Jenny. Have you got any cream in your fridge? Mark prefers it in his coffee.'

'Er, no, I haven't. He'll have to have milk like the rest of us. Actually, I wanted to ask you about why I'm overdrawn…'

'Oh, don't worry about that. It's all about cash flow, you're not actually overdrawn,' Rachael explained airily.

'I AM overdrawn,' Jenny corrected, 'and I don't like being overdrawn. Please arrange for my drawings to be paid back into my account this afternoon, and do not let this happen again. In fact, if you need to move my money about, consult me first next time. Is that clear?'

Rachael's neck blotched red as she attempted to keep a lid on her annoyance. 'Of course, Mrs Damerell. I do apologise.'

Jenny turned to leave, pleased that she'd got the upper-hand, but she clocked the smirk on Mark's face and realised that actually, he'd achieved his goal: Jenny and Rachael were now sworn enemies.

As the months went by, she sensed that something had changed. It was like she'd crossed a rubicon with her refusal to get pregnant and then for standing up to Rachael. She felt shut-out, conspired against. She knew that Rachael and Mark were not involving her in business decisions that she really needed to know about. When she asked, she was stonewalled. There was a chilliness about Mark now. He was making her pay for her defiance, for not doing as she was told. So soon after their marriage, the sunny skies of their early relationship had diminished and there were storm clouds gathering on the horizon.

It was not all bad though. Jenny secured a great contract for Truscott Interiors refurbishing a courtyard of holiday homes near Bude, just on the border between Devon and Cornwall. It was a beautiful part of the world, unspoilt and tranquil and there were six cottages for her to play with. The budget was generous and the client wanted 'contemporary chic' which gave her the opportunity to visit exhibitions, galleries and shows in London and Exeter, for inspiration.

The more absorbed she became in her work, the more petulant Mark became in their relationship. He sulked for days if she needed to travel to a show and on one occasion insisted that the car had engine trouble (despite him driving to Bristol and back in it the previous day), meaning that she missed her train connection; then he would show up at the cottages with a champagne picnic just as she was about to sit down with the client to look at fabric swatches. Embarrassing, or what?

'Honestly, he's like a big kid sometimes,' Jenny moaned to Liz, on her way home from work one night. Quite often Jenny would make a detour and have a cup of tea with her bestie, just to delay going home to a chilly atmosphere. Even though Liz was coping with her baby son's many needs and was going through a rough patch with her husband, Liz always found time for Jenny.

It took her about eighteen months all told to complete the Meadow Barns contract and towards the end of her time there, she started to feel a little flat and a sensation of longing would overcome her when she least expected it. The only problem was, she couldn't work out what it was she was longing for. She would find herself feeling bereft and tearful for no particular reason. When she spoke to Liz about it, her friend's intuition shocked her to the core.

'Sounds like you're getting broody to me, girl. Sounds just like how I felt.'

He just couldn't get enough of her, once she told him she wanted to have a baby; it worked like human antifreeze. She became his princess again and he adored her. During her fertile times, that was. When she was ovulating, he pretty much had a permanent erection and was ready to impregnate her any time, any place. And interestingly, Jenny noted, the sex-toys were nowhere to be seen. This kind of sex was different. To Mark, this was making babies.

'Potent, aren't I?' said Mark when Jenny became pregnant after just two months of trying. 'Super-sperm, that's what I've got.'

Jenny smiled and tried not to make too much of a fuss over her morning sickness. She remembered how Mark didn't like vomit. When they were out having lunch with friends, Mark was every bit the expectant father, reminding Jenny what she could and couldn't eat and making sure she had a cushion for her back, even though she was barely showing.

At the scan, Jenny felt her eyes pricking with tears when she saw the fuzzy black and white profile of her baby.

'Perfect. Baby's growing as he should be,' said the sonographer.

'He? So, it's a boy then?' asked Mark.

'Well no, I haven't checked. It was just a turn of phrase, but I can see if you want to?'

Mark and Jenny replied simultaneously, Mark with: 'Yes, definitely.'

As Jenny said: 'No, thanks.'

The sonographer looked at them, eyebrows raised.

'Go on darling, it will help us prepare,' said Mark and Jenny recognised the determined look on his face, daring her to disagree.

'Okay, then,' agreed Jenny and the sonographer swooshed the scanner around on Jenny's belly some more.

'Ah yes, nice and clear. You're having a baby girl.'

'A girl?' echoed Mark. 'Right.'

As they walked back to the car park, Jenny wondered aloud about names. 'Maisy's pretty. Or what about Beatrix?' But Mark was pensive. When they got back to the car, Mark just slammed the door shut and started the engine, staring ahead in silence.

He needs time to process it, thought Jenny. *I think he had his heart set on a boy, an heir apparent.*

'What the…? He should just be grateful she's healthy!' exclaimed Liz when Jenny confided in her. Liz was outraged. Here she was, coping with a baby with cerebral palsy… she would give her life for her own child to be healthy. 'Jen, listen to me, it's ridiculously old-fashioned to want the first-born to be a boy, it's positively medieval. You just focus on growing that gorgeous bubba inside you, and don't think about Mark's antediluvian attitude.'

'Okay, I will, once I've looked up antediluvian,' replied Jenny, laughing. Liz always made her feel better. 'I was wondering Liz… would you consider being my birth partner?'

Me? Are you kidding? Oh, Jenny, I'd love to! I need to square it with Clifford, but it would be an honour. But what about He Who Must Be Obeyed? Won't he want to do it? I don't want to put his darling little nose out of joint.'

'Mark, you mean? Oh, I'm sure he'll be there,' replied Jenny quickly, but her hesitation was not lost on Liz. She knew they'd recently bought a doer-upper, a crumbling old

Victorian Rectory that 'was an absolute steal' according to Mark, (but to Jenny it just seemed to have turned into a dust factory with the constant renovation). Currently, if Mark wasn't at work, he was busy knocking down walls in the Rectory and thinking about the fortune he was going to make when they sold it.

'I just thought you could be back-up, in case of any problems' continued Jenny. 'He's so busy with the new house, you know how he is, so I thought maybe you could come along with me to some of the antenatal classes. That's if you didn't mind…'

'Mind? I'm in there. Ooh, how modern, we can pretend to be a lesbian couple!'

'Don't let Mark hear you say that – he's got some pretty antidelu-whatsit views on that as well,' said Jenny.

'You don't say? The man's a Neanderthal' said Liz.

They doubled-up with laughter. Jenny loved how irreverent Liz was about Mark. She didn't seem to be either charmed or intimidated by him like most people she knew – she seemed to have an innate awareness that Mark was a bully, without Jenny having to say it and feel like she'd betrayed him somehow. When they first met, Mark tried to work his usual magic on Liz, but she seemed to be coated in Teflon, as the compliments just bounced right off her.

'Right old smoothie isn't he?' she'd remarked afterwards.

'Mark thinks you're great too,' replied Jenny, even though he had said nothing of the sort. He'd actually called her a, 'silly bitch.'

Two weeks before the baby was due, Mark started to pack an overnight bag.

'Where are you going?' asked Jenny, alarmed.

'Oh, just to scout out some properties up-country. Your dad wants us to consider expanding into Dorset and Hampshire. I shouldn't be more than a couple of nights,' replied Mark, neatly folding a cashmere sweater.

'A couple of nights? But what if the baby comes?'

Mark bent over her bump. 'Don't come out yet!' he called. 'There, sorted. I wouldn't worry about it – when have you ever done anything on time?'

'Mark, it's really inconsiderate of you to do this, when the baby's so close. I need your support.'

It was like she'd waved a red rag at a bull.

'What the *fuck* to you think I'm doing, woman? This isn't a weekend break you know, this is work. To keep you and that brat in there,' he stabbed a finger at her belly, 'in the lap of luxury.'

Jenny's eyes filled with tears.

'Oh, don't start blubbing, for god's sake, Jen. It's no big deal, it's just work.'

'But I need you here. I can't do this on my own.'

'Well, I can't do this one for you Jenny, so really, you are on your own.'

He stalked out, leaving her wretched on the bed. *How could he do that? How could he abandon us like that…?*

Jenny felt the lowest she'd ever felt in her life. At a time when they should be joyfully anticipating the birth of their first child, he'd put work and money first. Usually the eternal optimist, a little spark of light in her heart was extinguished that night.

That evening as she sat and watched TV, she felt a dull ache low in her abdomen.

'Just hang in there, baby, not yet,' she whispered, stroking her tummy. But later after an awful nightmare about drowning, Jenny woke up with the bed soaked. When she looked down. It was blood. She reached over for the phone and dialled the number he had left on the table for the brick-sized, new-fangled mobile telephone thing Mark had bought himself for Christmas. 'All the best businessmen have them,' he'd explained.

'Hi, this is Mark Damerell. I can't take your call right now but...'

Damn it! Answerphone. She left a message pleading for him to come home, then rang her parents, hoping to get hold of them instead, but remembered they too were having a weekend away. Bad timing, or what? She rang Liz who answered on the second ring. 'Don't worry babe, I'll just sort a few things out with Clifford and I'll be right over.'

At the hospital, the obstetrician explained that the bleeding may indicate a problem with the placenta. 'You need an emergency caesarean,' she said.

Oh Mark, where are you? thought Jenny as Liz helped her into a surgical gown. She left another hurried message for him and then waddled into theatre.

As the sunrise bathed the hospital in a rosy glow, inside the operating theatre the glare of the overhead lamps illuminated the birth of a perfect baby girl. As she was brought over the partition and rested on Jenny's chest, she looked up at her mother, perfectly at peace.

'My little angel, welcome to the world,' whispered Jenny, overcome with emotion.

Liz brushed away tears and kissed Jenny's forehead. 'You absolute marvel, what a beautiful daughter you've made.'

A couple of hours later, mother and baby were settled in the maternity ward, cuddled in a nest of blankets. Liz had left, promising to return later.

Jenny was gazing down at her sleeping girl when her parents walked in.

'We came as quickly as we could,' said her mother. 'You poor thing, what an ordeal for you but thank goodness baby's all right. Isn't she precious?' As she moved the blanket to get a closer look at the exquisite, wrinkled face, she whispered, 'It's a shame Mark couldn't have been there.'

'Yes, he had to go away apparently. Couldn't be helped. Dad wanted him in Dorset looking for bargains.'

'Oh, your father is good at sniffing out potential goldmines alright, but dreadful as always with his timing' replied Eleanor giving her daughter a knowing look. Jenny felt infinitely better that her mother knew how she was feeling.

At that moment, Mark walked in with a huge bunch of white roses.

'Oh Birdy, look at you, you clever thing, giving birth without me! And let's take a look at the baby then.' He peered at the tiny bundle. 'Oh yes, she takes after me, I can see that already,' he said, pecking the top of the baby's head. 'I thought the name Jessica would suit her,' he said decisively. 'And congratulations to the proud grandparents too, although you don't look old enough to be a granny, Eleanor!' he said, giving her a kiss. He rummaged in his bag and brought out a small velvet box. 'A little something for Mummy.'

Jenny opened the box to see a pair of emerald earrings, perfect with her colouring.

'Thank you, Mark,' she said quietly, her father nodding approvingly.

'I can see you're tired so why don't we leave you in peace and grab a coffee?' said Mark, ushering everyone out of the ward. 'George, I have something interesting to tell you…'

George gave Mark a knowing look and took Eleanor's arm. 'Come on Grandma,' he said, pecking his wife on the cheek, an affectionate gesture that Jenny hadn't seen her father bestow upon her mother in a long while. Having a grandchild had put him in a good mood for once.

Jenny sighed and carefully lowered her baby into the cot by her bed, and sank her head back on the pillow. Every atom of her being was wrung out and she gratefully drifted into a deep sleep.

In the following weeks, Jenny gradually became accustomed to motherhood. It dominated her life and overwhelmed her utterly, changing everything she had previously known. Jenny the attractive, dynamic interior designer was replaced by Jenny the exhausted, bleary-eyed, leaking servant. Jessica wasn't a difficult baby but it was certainly a shock to discover that she had no time for herself – not even time to wash her hair – and no choice but to surrender to her new role. Mark didn't seem to be troubled by the same identity crisis. He pushed the pram around the park a couple of times but wasn't keen on anything more hands-on than that. Jessica was quite a possety baby and he didn't want his clothes to smell of baby sick.

It wasn't long after Jessie was born that Clifford, Liz's husband, left her for a younger model. Jenny was appalled, knowing how hard it was to look after a baby, even with a hands-off husband – but to be left on your own with an eighteen-month-old… it was criminal. Jenny's heart went out to her friend, and she resolved to count her blessings, even if Mark wasn't exactly the model husband and father.

As Jessica grew into toddlerhood, Mark started to make noises about a brother for her, seemingly oblivious to the fact that Jenny could have another baby girl.

'When did you last have your period?' he demanded one day.

'Why?'

'I want to know when you'll be fertile, darling. Don't you think it's time?'

'Christ Mark, I'm exhausted with Jess,' Jenny replied irritably.

'I can see that,' he snarled. 'Look at the state of you. Why would anyone want to shag you?'

'Oh Mark, don't be cruel. I'm not saying "no", I'm saying not yet.'

But he wasn't to be deterred. What Mark wanted, Mark usually got. He started being demanding in the bedroom, but the sex-toys once again had disappeared. She knew he was determined and despite her protestations, it was only a matter of time. She hadn't gone back to taking the pill after Jess and she just couldn't keep saying no to Mark's demands. It was just too tiring. She gave in and he got his way.

She became pregnant with baby number two, and this time the ultrasound confirmed that it was a boy. Mark was delighted, 'My son and heir' he took to saying. Jenny secretly wondered what might have happened if it was a girl. Would he have demanded an abortion? She would never have acquiesced, but his desire for a son was all-consuming.

Like Jessica, baby Marcus arrived early, several weeks premature.

'He looks like a skinned rabbit,' observed Mark disappointedly, although at least he had made it to the birth this time.

As Marcus grew, he was often sickly and struggled to put on weight. Jenny did all she could to build him up, doubling-up breast feeding with a bottle, but even though this meant Mark could help with night feeds, he showed no inclination.

'You get on with doing what you do best and I'll do the same,' he said.

Jenny felt like she was going to buckle under the strain of having two babies under two. Several loads of washing a day barely made a dent in the laundry basket and the twin demands of a teething Jessica who was cutting her molars and a new-born made every night a trial. Since Mark was out all day, he didn't see what a monumental effort it was, and how grindingly monotonous too. He'd come home at the end of the day, stride into the kitchen and lift the lids on the pans on the cooker, asking what was for tea. Jenny tried to make a hot meal every night, even though she was so tired she was seeing double. After they'd eaten, it was all Jenny could do to keep her eyes open long enough to wash up and tidy the bombsite that was the kitchen, whilst Mark usually made himself scarce. He was too restless to join her and had no time for his children. Rarely did he register their presence, let alone pick either of them up for a cuddle or heaven forefend, change a nappy.

'Where's my blue checked shirt? I need it for a meeting,' asked Mark one morning.

'Ummm, it's on the line, I think. I'll get it,' replied Jenny, who was simultaneously trying to breastfeed Marcus whilst persuading Jessica to eat her Weetabix.

'No, no, don't trouble yourself,' he hissed and marched outside, slamming the door behind him with such force that both children started to cry.

Jenny followed him, baby on hip, to help pick-in the rest of the washing as she noticed it had started to spit with rain, but just as she opened the garden gate, she saw Rachael walking towards Mark from the office.

'Well, look at you, Mr Domesticity,' she said, her black jacket with padded shoulders and pencil skirt with a slit at the back making her look decidedly sexy and professional. Jenny felt a pang of jealousy.

'Oh, I do my bit Rache – Jenny simply can't cope otherwise,' he replied with a wink as he threw the last of the washing from the line into the wicker basket.

Rache… that's a bit pally, Jenny thought.

'Here, I've brought in your washing for you,' he said as he brushed past Jenny, dumping it on the overflowing kitchen table.

As Marcus took his first tentative steps, he became a little less needy, but still spent most of his time clinging to Jenny's leg. She grew used to having a thigh-level tidemark of snot and crusted food on her jeans. When he hit three, Marcus started nursery and came home one day dressed in a little pink tutu.

'I love it!' said Liz, who was having a coffee in the kitchen, her son Joe well enough today to play with Jessie and Marcus in the garden.

'Yes, it's very fashion forward,' replied Jenny laughing.

But when Mark came home from work, he didn't agree. 'Why on earth is my son dressed like that?' he thundered when he saw Marcus pirouetting in the garden, with Joe trying to copy his moves.

'Oh, relax Mark. It was pirates and fairies day at Rainbows Nursery, and Marcus wanted to be a fairy,' shrugged Jenny.

'Absolutely not! No son of mine is going to dress up as a fairy, it's not natural,' said Mark.

Jenny bristled. 'Oh, he's a son of yours now, is he – now that you don't like something. Well it's a bloody miracle you've even noticed what he's wearing, you pay so little attention to him.'

Liz paled and put her mug on the kitchen counter. 'I'd best be going Jen,' she said. 'It's been a long day for Joe and he'll be getting tired.' She picked up her handbag and kissed her friend on the cheek – ignoring Mark – and went out into the garden to extricate her son from what looked like a fabulous tickling game. *Do you ever laugh quite so wholeheartedly as an adult, as you do when a child?* Liz thought.

'Don't ever, EVER talk to me like that in front of some-one again. Do you hear me?' Mark raged.

'Oh do FUCK OFF!' Jenny screamed. 'You come home demanding your dinner and laying down the rules and do nothing – absolutely *nothing* – to help me. How dare you? How dare you!'

Mark scowled at her, hatred sparking in his eyes. He marched outside and stripped the tutu off Marcus, who started to wail.

The atmosphere between Mark and Jenny was decid-edly frosty for some time after that, and he chose to sleep in the guest room, which was absolutely fine with her, in fact it made life much easier because she was always so tired, and she didn't have to put up with his constant petty vindictiveness and demands in the bedroom. However, this didn't apply to poor little Marcus who was at the mercy of Mark's random parenting decisions, the latest of which being his determination that Marcus was going to learn to 'be a man.'

'He's a toddler, Mark. There's plenty of time for him to learn to be a man in later life.'

'What would you know about that?' Mark demanded. 'What would you know about being called a cissy in the playground?'

Jenny thought that this was a telling comment, but decided to let it lie, and watched with exhausted disapproval as her husband attempted to teach her son some life lessons. Marcus had his heart set on a new bike for his fourth birthday but Mark decided that he could only have one if he learned to ride his old bike without stabilisers.

'But Mark, he's only little.' Jenny couldn't help but intervene as she watched Marcus perilously wobbling around the patio.

'He's got to learn sometime,' Mark replied. 'I think now's as good a time as any. Give him a head start in front of the other little oiks at nursery.'

Just then there came a crash and a wail as Jenny rushed out to find Marcus and bike in a tangled heap, Marcus' knee bleeding.

'Idiot,' muttered Mark from the doorstep. He strode over to the bike and flung it in the wheelie bin.

'My bike!' screamed Marcus.

As Jenny took a sobbing Marcus indoors to patch him up, he asked, 'Mummy, will I still get a new bike for my birthday?'

'We'll see, my darling,' she said. 'I'll get your old bike out of the wheelie bin, and you and me can have a go at riding it again, shall we? Just us, and I'll push you. I won't let go unless you want me to.'

When she asked Mark whether he could pop into town on his way home from work and get Marcus his birthday bike, he didn't reply. She hoped that this meant he would come around to the idea, because she sure as hell wasn't going to be able to find time to go and get one. But, she just couldn't read Mark these days. In fact, she wondered if she had ever been able to.

On the day of Marcus' birthday, they had a tea party with a few friends and family. Marcus kept tugging at Jenny's sleeve.

'Mummy, what about my bike, what about my bike?'

Mark stood up and said loudly, 'So Jenny, you'd better bring out the main present now.'

As Marcus screamed delightedly she looked at her husband, confused.

Mark didn't miss a beat. 'Oops, it looks like silly Mummy has forgotten to buy you a bike, Marcus,' he said, watching as Marcus' face crumpled.

The group looked at Jenny, an awkward silence only broken by Marcus' tears.

'Oh, dear me,' Jenny said, then looking pointedly at her husband she continued, 'I'm sorry Marcus, I thought Daddy said he would get it for you. Don't worry, we'll go out and buy it tomorrow and you can choose a special bell to go on it, okay?'

Marcus nodded slowly, his tears abating. He was such a good boy.

The awkward atmosphere lifted slightly and people began to chat again, but Mark threw dagger looks at Jenny. She would pay later for getting one over on him. And she did. She found her bottle of Chanel No. 5 smashed on the bedroom floor. He must've taken a hammer to it.

The trouble was, these days, everything was such hard work. Jenny had hoped that the heavy cloud of exhaustion would lift as the children grew up, but she was still as tired, as broken as ever. She felt like she was at such a low ebb that all she wanted to do was sleep and never wake up.

Jenny confided in Liz who persuaded her to have a check-up. 'God knows, being a mum is knackering enough, but you look beyond tired.'

The GP did some blood tests and then referred her to a specialist, 'Just to be on the safe side – it's probably nothing.'

Jenny went along to the appointment, expecting to be given some iron tablets, but was instead put through yet more blood tests and a very painful lumbar puncture.

She had only just got home when the medical secretary rang her up for another urgent appointment. 'It's best if you bring someone in with you,' she advised.

'Why, what is it?' asked Jenny, her mouth dry.

'I can't say over the phone. The consultant will talk to you tomorrow.'

CHAPTER 3

A Whistling in the Telegraph Wires

Force 6 on the Beaufort Scale

'Jenny Damerell?' Jenny's heart lurched as she followed the nurse into the consulting room, Mark following behind her. The consultant stopped peering at her computer screen to shake their hands.

'Ah, Mrs Damerell, good to see you again. I'm afraid it's not good news. The MRI scan has revealed two areas of damage in your central nervous system, which point towards multiple sclerosis.'

Silence.

'Oh, my god, no!' Mark looked stricken. 'Oh Jenny, you

don't deserve this…'

The consultant glanced at Mark compassionately, but continued to address Jenny who had reached out for Mark's hand, the implications of what had just been said to her slowly starting to sink in.

'The next step is to look at what medication you need and we'll arrange a follow-on appointment with the specialist MS nurse. Although this diagnosis will be a shock to you both, please take some comfort from the fact that we have caught it early, and we are seeing some good outcomes from the new drugs we have access to now. You have Relapsing Remitting MS, Mrs Damerell, which means you'll probably experience times when you have hardly any symptoms at all, but there may be other times when you feel very poorly, with fatigue, muscle spasms, difficulty thinking logically, problems with your balance and memory, that sort of thing. The nurse will give you a leaflet about it when you leave, and your GP will be informed of your diagnosis so if you do have any intermittent problems, you can get the right medication. I'm going to put you on a steroid now, to give you a boost, and we'll see you again in six weeks' time. You can do a lot to help yourself, Mrs Damerell, by keeping as active as possible and reducing any stress you experience to an absolute minimum. Stress is one thing that has been shown to seriously impact MS so do try to reduce this where possible. Any questions?'

The news was momentous but Jenny felt curiously calm. At least the bone-crushing tiredness she'd been feeling now had an explanation. Jenny could feel Mark's palm leaving an imprint of sweat against hers and he was anything but calm.

'So, should Jenny stop work then?' Mark asked the consultant.

'Is your work stressful, Mrs Damerell?'

'It is rather,' Mark replied on her behalf.

Jenny roused herself. 'It's not my work that's stressful, Mark – being the mother of two young children takes it out of me more. Work seems like a walk in the park by comparison.'

'Perhaps you could get some help with the childcare, Mrs Damerell?' the consultant ventured. 'Is there a family member who could support you?' she enquired, looking pointedly at Mark.

'My mother already does quite a lot…'

Yes, yes – we can get some help for Jenny, but I think your design business will have to be put on the back-burner Jenny, for a while, at least,' Mark interrupted, though Jenny had only undertaken a couple of consultations since the children were born.

'Well you will both have a lot to think about,' said the consultant, standing up to usher them out, 'but my advice would be not to make any rash decisions. Just take your time, see if you feel better once you're on the medication and make any changes to your lifestyle in due course.'

As they walked to the car, Mark was deep in thought, his hand still clasping Jenny's.

'Don't worry darling,' Jenny whispered, trying to console him, 'people cope with MS all the time. Look at whatshisname… y'know, that chap you met last year at the rugby – doesn't he have MS and he still plays for the local club? People live their lives, make the best of it, and so will I. At least I know I'm not a terrible mother and there's a reason for my utter exhaustion.'

Mark's shoulders sagged and he began to weep. 'I'm sorry, Jen, I know I should be strong for you but it's just such a shock.' Tears ran down his flushed cheeks. 'I need you so much. You can't leave me now.'

Jenny handed him a tissue to blow his nose, touched by how the news had affected him – and there she was, not two days ago, thinking he didn't love her any more.

'Don't worry, honey, we'll get through this,' she soothed. 'Everything will be okay, you'll see.' She stroked his back, which was heaving with sobs. For once, she felt like the stronger one in their relationship, but how strange it was that her ill health had shook him to the core like this.

Mark was still in too much of a state to drive, so Jenny drove home. She firmly gripped the steering wheel and focused on the road ahead between the wiper blades dissecting the windscreen, clearing away the rain. When they got back, Mark headed straight for the office saying, 'I'm too upset to face your mother, right now Jen. You tell her, will you, and say I've got an urgent appointment. She'll understand.' He wandered towards the office, head bowed. The office lights were on. *Rachael must still be there*, Jenny realised.

'Mummmeeeee!' screamed the children, bounding into her arms.

'How did you get on?' asked Eleanor. 'The kids have been really good.'

'Not great,' Jenny answered, flicking her eyes towards Jessica and Marcus. 'Shall we make a cup of tea?' In the quiet of the kitchen Jenny explained her diagnosis to her mother, and this time, couldn't stop the tears coming.

'Oh, Jenny love, don't worry… It's so frightening now but you'll soon find ways of coping with it,' said her mum, wiping her own eyes, as Jenny wept on her shoulder, taking comfort in that same warm, woollen smell she'd always known. 'Remember when Marcus had that scare? You were such a rock. You can be again this time.'

When Marcus was two, he suddenly developed mysterious bruises and the GP ran blood tests, wondering if there was something sinister behind them. The word *leukaemia* hovered above the family like a dark cloud. Fortunately, he was given the all clear and they never really found out what was the cause of the bruising, but Jenny remembered the fear she and Mark felt during those few days. She also recalled the fierce, almost primal urge to protect her son from harm, to fight for him. She needed to summon up that same instinct now, for herself.

In bed that night, just as Jenny was drifting to sleep, Mark said: 'Hearing your news today reminded me of losing my dad when I was little… I'm not going to let anyone do that that to me ever again.'

'I'm not going to 'do' anything to you Mark, darling. We'll fight this together, eh? Tell me, what happened with your dad?'

Mark sighed, and was silent for some time. Then he spoke. 'It was my fourth birthday. He gave me a bike… and

65

then he just upped and left. I never saw him again. My mum couldn't stand the sight of the bike – it must've represented him in some way. She just chucked it away – she put it in the boot of the car, put me in the back seat and drove to the dump and threw it into one of the skips. She never said a word – isn't that hateful, Jen? She became really depressed after that and she never seemed to care about me at all. I really resented her for that. She was so weak. Not like you, Jenny, you're strong.'

'I'm so sorry, Mark, that must have been awful for you.' *And it explains how weird he was about Marcus' bike*, Jenny realised. *He really has had a hard time, I need to remember that.* 'That's sad, it really is. Why did your Dad leave, do you know?' Jenny said, snuggling up to him. Any little glimpses Mark revealed of his childhood – and they were sparing – were like a window into his soul.

'I don't want to talk about it, any more,' Mark snapped, and abruptly switched the bedside lamp off. He felt he'd already opened up too much to her.

Jenny understood. It was so hard for him to talk about his family. She couldn't imagine what would possess anyone to chuck a child's present away, but then she hadn't really known Mark's mum, Cynthia, or what she'd been through. Cynthia had died in the early years of their relationship, before they were married, and Jenny had learned very quickly not to mention Mark's father in front of either of them. It was an unspoken rule that he must never be discussed. She did notice that Mark and his mother were very cold with each other on the few times that they met, and that there was no love lost between them. Mark seemed positively embarrassed at

Cynthia's funeral, refusing to give the eulogy and blanking the few friends who had turned up. Jenny noticed that Cynthia had no other family apart from Mark, and this saddened her deeply. One thing Jenny did remember though, was Cynthia saying, 'You're a strong woman, Jenny. Stay strong. It's great that you have your own business, and that you're financially independent. Make sure you keep it that way.'

At the time, she felt galvanised by this – had seen it as some affirmation from one generation of women to another that independence was worth fighting for. Sometimes it was hard to be strong, because the tides of life were too powerful and the currents that tried to drag you under too persistent, but she was strong, despite her recent diagnosis, and she would be there for her family. For whatever reason, Mark's father had left his wife and son, and the repercussions of that were still haunting Mark. She wanted to help him heal from that trauma

The next morning over coffee, Liz was as pointed as usual. 'You what? Mark was blubbing and you were comforting *him*? I get so cross, Jenny. It should have been about you – you are the one having to cope with MS – but no, it ends up being all about him. He puts on those crocodile tears and cries like a little boy. He's just like Clifford – when the going gets tough, he falls apart.' Liz's own marriage had crumbled because her husband couldn't cope with their son Joe's medical and emotional needs. He'd left his wife and son and somewhat typically had taken up with a younger woman, and then failed to pay any child maintenance. Liz didn't have much time for men these days.

'Shush, Lizzie,' Jenny urged, knowing the kids were in the playroom and not wanting them to hear a bad word about their father. 'It wasn't like that. It was really helpful to find out about what happened between his mum and dad. It explains so much about him, don't you think? He loves me and I love him. I always will, he's my husband.'

'I know you love him, Jen, but it worries me that he can't see beyond the impact all this is having on him. It shouldn't be about him, it should be about you.'

'It's about US, Lizzie. It's a breakthrough. I understand him a little better now, and he *is* worried about me.'

'Yeah, worried who's going to iron his shirts, more like,' snorted Liz as she unloaded the dishwasher. Liz's dislike of Mark was palpable.

After Liz left, Jenny wandered over to the office, where Mark and Rachael were deep in conversation. They stopped immediately when they heard the door.

'Oh, don't mind me, carry on,' said Jenny.

'How are you, Jenny? You're looking a little peaky,' said Rachael. 'Sorry to hear about your illness.'

'I'm fine, all things considered,' replied Jenny looking around. The office seemed different. It had been a while since she'd been over, as she'd been so utterly wrung out and she didn't have any new contracts booked in, but something had changed. Her large abstract canvas had disappeared and been replaced by a set of monochrome architectural prints. The colourful cushions had gone too, even the mugs were now black.

'It's all very stark in here. What's happened to my stuff?'

'Oh, we decided the office should be more business-like and less homey. We wanted to keep the decor pared down a bit, simplify things,' answered Rachael, 'especially for when clients come over. Your stuff is in the back room.'

'We did, did we?' Jenny said, askance. Mark ignored her, engrossed by something on his computer screen. 'Mark? I'm not happy about this,' she continued. 'Why didn't you discuss this with me? I'm the interior designer around here, and the office looks awful now, all corporate and bland.'

'Oh, give it a rest, Jen,' Mark murmured. 'It's just business and you've not got a lot of that going on right now. Don't get stressed about it – you know that's not good for you.'

She let it go. Life is too short to get stressed over cushions and curtains, but nonetheless, it irked her that she had no say in even the little, insignificant things of her life.

'I'm off to that meeting now, Mark. See you later,' said Rachael, clipping out in her spike heels, a waft of citrus perfume billowing after her as she slammed the door behind her.

After she'd gone Mark looked up from his computer. 'Hey Birdy, I'm glad you popped over. I've been wanting to talk to you. We've been looking at the business and we think we need to fully integrate your interior design company within the family's portfolio. Dad's behind me.'

'Dad? Oh, you mean *my* dad,' replied Jenny, aware that he used the 'Birdy' nickname when he wanted to get into her good books, thinking she found it charming. Actually, she hated it, but at least it gave her a heads-up that she was about to be worked-on.

'Yes, your dad, *obviously*. Look, you'd still have a role in the business, but you can't do as much as you'd like to any more, can you? You've missed a few calls from clients recently and there have been appointments that I've had to cancel for you as you were in no fit state. I want to make sure that your portfolio of clients is fully looked after. We think it would be a great idea to merge the two businesses to offer a full package – property development and interior design: "From a pile of bricks to a home you'll be proud of".'

'Wow, you've put a lot of thought into this…' answered Jenny. She didn't know what to think. Her first instinct was to hold tight to her business, to ring-fence it from Mark and Rachael and even her dad, but what missed calls? What cancelled client appointments? It was the first she'd heard of it. But maybe it was true. She had been so muddled and overwrought recently that her mind felt like an overflowing waste-paper basket. Relinquishing control over Truscott Interiors might seem logical to Mark *et al*, but it really stung to let go of her baby. It was something she built up herself, and her reputation was now well-established. Or it used to be. Life had been very hard and it was a struggle to keep on top of everything: kids, housework, the business, all attempted under a fog of MS exhaustion. The confusion and memory problems didn't help either, and the MS nurse had explained that although sometimes she may feel perfectly lucid, at others she wouldn't and this was an unfortunate part of the condition. And then there's the whole stress factor…

'Look, Birdy, I'm doing everything I can to make your life easier,' Mark added. 'If I step-up in the business, it will also take the pressure off Dad. I think he's been struggling too.'

'What's all this with calling him Dad?' asked Jenny. He was *her* dad, not Mark's. Who said he was suddenly an honorary son? After this thought she checked herself – *it's only a word*. 'Never mind, carry on.'

'Yes, some of *George's* decisions have not been the wisest of late, shall we say… Some investments have not performed as well as he thought… He's an amazing businessman and I've learnt so much from him, but maybe now's the right time for him to relax and reap the benefits of his hard work.'

'Retire, you mean? I'm not sure what he'll say about that…' said Jenny. Her father had always been 100 per cent dedicated to his work and his identity revolved around it – well, that and having been in the Army.

'Can I think about this Mark?' Jenny suggested, playing for time. 'I can see where you're coming from, but I love my business, and I don't want to let it go.'

'I'm only thinking of you darling. We'll keep it running smoothly until you're ready to come back, assuming you're going to be well enough.'

That hurt, but the truth does hurt. Would she ever have the energy to run her business again, without help? Maybe this was the right thing to do – and yet, Mark's mother's words kept ringing in her ears.

When Jenny spoke on the phone to her father about Mark's suggestions, Mark had clearly been working his magic on George.

'Mark is the man for the job, Jenny,' he said. 'I've known for some time that he'll eventually run the family business. Definitely not your brother Paul – he's more interested in surfing and hanging out with eco-warriors than knuckling down and doing a bit of real work. No, Mark is more than capable of becoming CEO. You focus on being as well as you can be. You're a coper, you always were, and your little business will be the icing on the cake for us all.'

'I suppose you're right, Dad,' replied Jenny who still respected her father's opinions. 'I suppose I just have to accept that I don't have the capabilities that I used to have. While we're on the subject of restructuring, what do you think about Rachael? I wonder about her accounting skills. If business is booming why don't I seem to see any of the revenue?'

'Rachael knows what she's doing, Jenny, don't you worry. She's sharp as a pin, unlike you. It is just cash-flow: money needs to be moved around to make the most of interest rates, not left stagnating in one account. You have to make money work for you, you know. What is it with all these questions? Haven't Mark and I always provided for you and your Mother – little thanks we get for it though…'

'Oh, Dad! Please don't be like that. I'm only asking your advice.'

'Well, bloody well take it for once, Jenny, and do what's right for everyone, not just for you.'

Jenny put the phone down, stung by her father's words. She always seemed to irritate him, though she had no idea why. *Hmmm*, thought Jenny, *Rachael seems to be everyone's flavour of the month…*

Then she had an idea. She would state her terms. She would agree to the merger, as long as she was paid a generous monthly retainer into an account that only she had access to, and that she retained the name Truscott Interiors, just in case she ever had the strength to relaunch on her own.

When she told Mark her terms a few days later, he raised an eyebrow, but reluctantly agreed.

'I can set up the account for you, Birdy. Save you worrying about it.'

'No, need Mark,' she replied. 'I popped in to see my bank manager when I was in town yesterday, and he's recommended a thing called a PEP savings account. I've got the sort code and account number here. Just make the money payable into that please.' She darted off to tuck the children up and kiss them goodnight, before he had the chance to argue.

Jenny was due to go to an MS support group, but on the way there she felt the urge to pull over in a layby. It was right by the coastal path and had glorious views over the bay. On a clear day, you could see Lundy Island, but today it was overcast. The wind was whipping up white horses on the sea. As Jenny watched the spindrift fly up the cliffs and over on to the headland she tried to properly get her head around the diagnosis for the first time. What did it mean for her future? Would she ever be able to relaunch her business? What about Jessica and Marcus – would she be able to look after them like she always had done? And Mark too. She knew he always liked things just so, and she enjoyed making his life comfortable, but what about their love life? After the kids were born they had sex less and less often – she was too exhausted – and now, hardly ever at all. The sex-toys had been put away, but surely Mark's libido remained as strong as it once was? Would he start looking elsewhere? Had he already started…? She was so afraid that her life would begin to slide into oblivion and that Rachael would take her place in the business, the bedroom and even in the lives of her children. She would be trundled off in a wheelchair while Rachael would neatly slip into her place, smiling like the Cheshire cat. And now it sounded like her father was giving in or giving up too.

Jenny felt desperately alone and a tear slid down her cheek. She rested her head on the steering wheel as her mind swirled with thoughts. A gust buffeted the car as she turned the ignition back on. *Come on girl, enough with this doom and gloom*, she said to herself. *I won't always feel like this. The drugs will work and I'll bounce back, I will!* Ever the eternal optimist, Jenny pulled out onto the A39, noticing a twinge in her leg every time she had to put her foot on the clutch – yet another symptom. It was nearly time for the group.

Walking in to the community centre in nearby Bideford, Jenny immediately noticed a woman, who patted the chair beside her, a warm invitation to join her. She had beautiful almond-shaped eyes and long blonde hair.

'You're Jenny, aren't you? I'm Joy – welcome to the club no one wants to join!' she joked.

'Thanks, I think…' said Jenny, smiling.

'My husband Tony knows your husband Mark – what a coincidence, eh? Mark mentioned to Tony that I should keep an eye out for you.'

Jenny felt like Joy was a much-needed breath of fresh air in her life. They had a lot in common but since Joy had had MS for a few years, she had a reassuring perspective. She was also very spiritual, which was a new one for Jenny, and despite her illness, she still managed to help her husband Tony run one of the more up-market restaurants in town. Jenny mused on what Joy had said on the drive home: 'I'm a great believer in karma. If you open up to the universe, it will provide. The answers to your problems are out there.' She didn't really know what that meant, but meeting Joy certainly seemed like her pleas of desperation in the layby had been heard, but could the universe do the weekly shop?

The following week Jenny met up with Liz for a cream tea and invited Joy along, and just as she thought, Joy and Liz hit it off immediately. *Cut from the same cloth*, thought Jenny. As she poured them all tea from a rose-painted pot, Jenny mused, 'The steroids have definitely kicked in. I'm feeling a lot better than I have done for months, but the trouble is I could eat a horse. Have you found that, Joy?'

'Oh yes, clotted cream is my friend,' Joy replied with a smile.

Jenny took a deep breath and broached something that had been troubling her for a while. 'Okay, girls, crazy question here, but do you think Mark could be having an affair?'

Liz immediately replied, 'I wouldn't put it past him,' while Joy gazed at her for a moment.

'I haven't met Mark yet, so obviously, it's hard for me to say, but what makes you think he might be, can I ask?'

'Oh, I don't know. It's probably just post-baby paranoia, but he's just so cosy with Rachael. She's our Financial Manager, by the way. She's absolutely gorgeous, skinny as a rake, always immaculate and they're thick as thieves. When I come into the office, they stop talking and look vaguely guilty.'

'She's always immaculate because she hasn't had kids,' Liz chipped in. 'But thinking about it, if Mark's going to go for anyone it would be her. Fit body, a whizz with money, likes rugby…'

'Thanks, Liz, very helpful,' said Jenny. 'Actually, she tried to have children – she had four cycles of IVF with Rob and when it failed, she left him.'

'…And shallow as a duck-pond, I was going to add, Jen. She's got nothing on you – you're creative and compassionate and the mother of his children. I remember. Rob… now he was the cardboard cut-out, wasn't he?' Liz chuckled. 'The one-dimensional man. All talk and no trousers as my Dad used to say!'

'It sounds like it's been an emotional rollercoaster for this Rachael woman,' commented Joy. 'She had the heartbreak of infertility followed by the trauma of divorce. Maybe she's just thrown herself into her work, which is why she sees so much of Mark?' said Joy.

'Oh, I don't know, I'm probably imagining things. I seem to do that a lot these days.' She reached for a scone but remembered Rachael's lithe figure and thought better of it.

That night, despite feeling very far from alluring, Jenny invited Mark up to bed. He got down to business and she attempted to get into the spirit of things. She felt she must keep hold of him, do anything to stop him leaving her. Now she had MS, her life seemed so much more precarious than before and she felt reliant on Mark for so many things. He was her lynchpin.

Afterwards, Mark rolled off and turned away to sleep.

'I'm sorry I'm not at my best,' said Jenny.

'I love you, Birdy. It doesn't matter what size you are. You can't help your extra curves, it's just the medication. You're a fantastic mother and that's what's important,' he replied.

Jenny stared into the darkness as Mark's breathing lengthened into sleep. She hadn't been talking about her appearance.

The next evening the phone rang whilst Jenny was cooking tea. She gingerly picked up the receiver with oniony fingers. 'Hello?'

'Hi Jenny, it's Guy here. Marco told me things are not easy for you right now. How are you?'

'Oh Guy! Nice to hear from you. I'm fine now the drugs are kicking-in,' she said, making light of things. 'How's the waterworks?' Jenny could never resist teasing him about his job at the water company.

'Flowing smoothly thank you,' he replied.

Mark walked in and mouthed: 'Who is it?'

'Guy,' she mouthed back. Mark gestured for her to give him the phone but she ignored him and continued to chat, watching the wind buffet the trees out of the window. She knew this would annoy Mark but she was enjoying this rebellion just for a moment.

'So, you must come over for a meal sometime. It's been ages since we've seen you. Mark tells me you've got a lady friend.'

Jenny just heard the beginning of Guy's reply when Mark hissed, 'Give me the phone,' and snatched it off her.

'Sorry about that, Guy. I just can't find the help these days,' said Mark smoothly, giving Jenny the elbow.

After he finished the call, he went over to the office without a backwards glance, but Jenny followed him there.

'What's the problem with me chatting to Guy? I can't understand why you're so upset.'

'I'm not upset. I just don't want people phoning the landline with things to do with the Rugby Club. They should ring my mobile.'

'But it's Guy! I've known him for years!'

'No, I don't want people hassling you, Birdy,' he said firmly, ending the discussion. If truth be told, Jenny felt pleased that he cared so much. However, the next day, Jenny returned home from a physio appointment to discover that the home phone had been moved into the snug – the room where Mark liked to watch TV, whereas Jenny rarely went in there. She couldn't stand the programmes Mark watched and usually stayed in the kitchen trying to get on top of the ironing or went to bed in a state of utter exhaustion. And the extension upstairs was now in the spare room, which was Mark's domain too.

When she tackled him about it, he said, 'You need to rest, Birdy, you know that, and I don't want you to be disturbed.'

'But I like to be able to chat on the phone in bed.' Jenny could hear the whine in her voice.

'Jenny, you don't seem to realise that you're not the person you were. You need to rest and you shouldn't be disturbed all the time. I'm doing this for you. I'm trying to help and all you're doing is making life difficult for me.'

She was aware that her condition was making his life harder and he was bending over backwards to accommodate her different needs. He had even suggested getting in a mother's help although most of the time, she felt she was able to keep up with the children and housework. She felt ashamed of doubting him about Rachael. He'd been so good lately. And it was true that she needed to sleep more, and sometimes when she couldn't manage to get out of bed in the mornings she would listen to the sounds of the household as the children got themselves ready for school, and as Mark reminded them to take their packed lunches. It made her feel both guilty and lucky to have someone as capable as Mark taking care of the kids.

'Close the door quietly, Jess,' she'd hear him say. 'We don't want to wake Mummy, do we.'

One morning some months later, while Jenny was drowsing she heard the phone ring and the answerphone click in but when she went to check the message, it had been deleted.

'Who called earlier?' she asked Mark.

'No one's rung this morning, well, not the landline anyway. Why, are you expecting a call?'

'No. I could've sworn I heard it earlier, that's all.'

'You must have dreamt it,' he said.

As the weeks went by, Jenny got into the rhythm of her illness. Some days were better than others, and when she felt well enough, she'd go into town and catch up on errands. One day, at the post office, she saw Tina who worked behind the bar at the Rugby Club and went to say hello, but Tina turned away as if she hadn't seen her.

It happened again in the chemist as she was picking up her prescription. She usually had a chat with the pharmacist, whose husband was in the Rotary Club with Mark, but the pharmacist asked her assistant to deal with Jenny's prescription, declining to chat as usual. And then Carol, Jessie's friend's mother, seemed to cross over the street when she saw Jenny coming. *Am I just being paranoid about this?* Jenny asked herself.

She told Liz about it over coffee. 'What's going on? Why am I being sent to Coventry?' she asked her friend. 'You can tell me.'

'Maybe because you didn't make it to the charity auction

the other day? People can get awfully sniffy about that kind of thing.'

'What charity auction?'

'It was last week – don't you remember? I left a message about it on your answerphone.'

'It's the first I've heard about it,' said Jenny.

'No Jen… You promised a free interior design consultation – everyone was excited about it but then you weren't there to deliver on the promise…'

'I promised what?' Jenny was completely bamboozled. And worried too. She had no memory of making the pledge at all. 'Oh god, Liz. I must be losing my marbles. They told me to expect some confusion and memory loss but this is unreal! This fucking illness… it's the pits,' she said, just as her cup slipped out of her hand and smashed on the floor, splashing coffee everywhere.

'Oh babe, no use crying over spilt coffee,' said Liz, dabbing at the expanding stain with a napkin.

She didn't recall the message on the answerphone – or Mark telling her she must've dreamt it, either.

It happened again when she got home. A brand-new Range Rover was sitting on the drive and her first thought was that they must have unexpected visitors.

'Whose is the jeep?' Jenny asked when Mark came in.

He gave her a quizzical look. 'Yes, the car's arrived. Isn't she a beauty?'

'What?'

'Our new car's arrived.'

'I didn't know we were going to get a new car. And where's the money come from? It's always disappeared when I need some housekeeping money,' she exclaimed.

'Oh, stop moaning, Birdy, I give you plenty of housekeeping money. We talked about this, don't you remember?' he said, sighing. 'About a month ago… You agreed that a new car was a good way of clearing the overflow account before the end of the tax year. Rachael explained it all.'

'To me? She explained it to me? What overflow account?'

'You don't remember. We all sat in the office and discussed it. The "overflow account" is the contingency money we keep for a rainy day. You know how it's really built up over the years and now with tax rules tightening, we have to declare everything, so we decided on the Range Rover which we can offset against the business, but it's for us, for the family really. You must remember Birdy because it has heated seats, which we thought would be perfect for soothing your aches and pains. It was the night before you were going off with Liz for that spa weekend. You must have had too many glasses of bubbly and forgotten.'

Jenny remembered the spa break, but nothing about the car.

'But that money was partly from the profits of my business over the years, and the premium bonds that Mum cashed… I thought of it as the kids' college fund. I've never touched it, so how come you did?' Jenny had always seen it as her own money, even though in the heady early days of their relationship, she'd added Mark to the account.

'It was a joint account, so it's ours, not yours.' He looked thunderous at her accusation. 'It's got to be taken into consideration for tax purposes, even you know that, Birdy.'

'If you say so…' Jenny relinquished, racking her brains trying to recall the conversation, but she couldn't. This felt like a bolt out of the blue to her. She felt she was unravelling like a ball of wool.

She stopped Jessica later. 'Do you remember Daddy mentioning about getting a new car, darling?'

'Erm, what? Vaguely, Mum. I dunno, maybe. But those heated seats are something else! Have you tried them? You'll think you've died and gone to heaven.'

Jenny slumped down in despair. The short-term memory loss was one of the hardest things about MS. She could cope with the exhaustion, but that, combined with the weight-gain from the steroids made her feel like a fat, sloppy muddle.

'What's wrong now?' said Mark, discovering her weeping on the sofa.

'Oh, I'm just having a pity party,' she said.

'Well try to snap out of it Jenny. Try and look on the bright side, for a change. Things are going from strength to strength with the business, and the children are doing well at school. It's not all bad, you know,' said Mark.

'I'm so lucky to have you,' said Jenny and she really meant it. She felt so lost and alone and Mark was her one constant, but Mark didn't hear her. He was already heading off to his snug. He'd bought himself a laptop – another expensive luxury – and now shut himself off in the evenings doing whatever it was he did on it. Playing computer games, he said.

Jenny woke up the next morning determined to develop some coping strategies to help get control of her life again. The house was a mess, she was a mess, her memory was shot to ribbons and she'd had enough of it all. She brought it up at the next appointment with her MS nurse.

'Everything feels like a car crash in slow motion. I'm too tired to do any housework, the kids are just eating ready-meals and having sleepovers at their friends' houses. Apparently, I'm forgetting important conversations, and my social life has gone to pot because it's getting harder and harder for me to drive – especially in that great big bloody Range Rover. I can hardly get in the damn thing, let alone drive it. I'm sorry to moan on about this, but I'm at my wit's end. What can I do?'

The nurse looked at her sympathetically. 'Let's deal with one thing at a time, shall we? You're eligible for disability allowance, you know, so that could pay for a cleaner.'

'Really? But I thought we wouldn't qualify for benefits, what with the business and what Mark earns.'

'Mrs Damerell, you are entitled to the allowance, not your husband. It is not means tested. *You* are eligible, because *you* are suffering.'

Jenny's mood lifted instantly. 'Really? Oh, my god – a cleaner would be brilliant. I thought I was coping, but I'm not really.'

'And we could look into getting you a disability car too.'

'Really?' Jenny repeated herself.

'I think you'd get the full disability living allowance, so you could spend part of it on a little automatic car to help you get about. There's a scheme called Motability, especially to help people in your kind of circumstances. You wouldn't have to change gear or worry about the clutch.'

'That would be amazing!' said Jenny, relieved that there was such help available for her.

'And what about writing a diary? To help you remember important things. You can keep a daily journal of family life: who said what; who's going where; important events, etc., then you won't forget what's been said, or things you need to do.'

'Brilliant!' Jenny exclaimed. 'Why didn't I think of that?'

'It's what I'm here for,' the nurse replied, and Jenny could've kissed her.

Jenny left the surgery feeling uplifted. Maybe her illness was manageable after all? On the way home, Jenny remembered the mobile phone that Mark had bought her as a peace offering after he'd removed the phone from her bedroom – so that she could 'natter to her heart's content' with Liz and her mother. She didn't tell him it gave her a terrible headache when she used it. Instead, she texted Mark with the good news about the car and the cleaner on the bus journey home, thinking he'd be pleased that she'd finally got the hang of sending a text message. Instead, she got a terse reply.

Disability car? When I've just got the Range Rover especially for you! Well that was a waste of money.

Jenny knew that the Range Rover was Mark's toy, that he planned to take it to car rallies and show it off at rugby matches, and he must know deep down that it was difficult for her to drive, but she still dreaded the confrontation when she got home.

Instead of the usual icy calm that signalled Mark's bad mood, he was all smiles. 'We don't need a disability car, darling. I'll be your chauffeur and the allowance can go into the joint account. Where to, Madam?' he said, doffing his Harris tweed cap.

'We'll see how that goes,' she said, enigmatically, knowing that Mark would soon get bored of driving her to appointments. She also knew that the disability allowance was for her, and that once the dust had settled, she was going to get that car. After nearly a dozen years of marriage, she had learned that she had to let Mark feel like he'd won, before launching her own pincer movement.

And so it was that the years ticked by. Jenny had good weeks and bad weeks with her illness. When she was feeling good, she felt like their family life resembled normality, at least from the outside looking in. She was a stay-at-home mum now, and that seemed to be exactly where Mark wanted her, even though the kids were growing up and going their own ways. She disliked the way Mark expected them to be the best at everything: 'Remember, you're one of life's winners,' he would say to Marcus on a regular basis, but Jenny had a good relationship with both her children and they felt they could confide in her. For that, she was thankful.

Jenny had tried to show some interest in the Interiors department of Damerell & Truscott on several occasions, but Mark didn't want her to 'undermine' the new designer, Giles. 'He won't want the boss's wife poking her nose in Birdy – you've got to let him have his head,' Mark once said, and so she did, slightly relieved that she didn't have to summon up the energy to go back to work.

Her days were busy, but quite lonely. Mostly, she was up in time to see Mark off to work and the kids off to school and later, college, but once they were gone, the day stretched out in front of her. The cleaner came three times a week, so there was no housework to do, and Liz worked long hours now as a veterinary nurse. Her best friend's life had been turned upside down not long after Jenny's MS diagnosis: her son Joe caught pneumonia out of the blue, and passed away after a brief struggle with the illness. Liz was bereft and for a long time, she shut herself away from the world, even from Jenny. When she emerged from her grief she retrained to become a veterinary nurse. She'd already completed half her course before she got pregnant with Joe, and Plymouth Uni were very understanding and flexible. Liz made a brilliant veterinary nurse, spending all her time caring for animals rather than people. She said she liked animals better. Liz and Jenny's leisurely coffee mornings were now a thing of the past.

Jenny's other confidante, Joy, lived in Bideford which was 25 miles away, so they only saw each other at the MS

Support Groups these days, although their friendship had deepened over the years. Joy was always there for Jenny, but she had her own cross to bear, and quite often, she was incapacitated by the illness to such a degree that they didn't see each other for months on end.

Jenny did get her automatic car in the end. She didn't tell Mark, but just arranged it with the benefits advisor at the group after holding off for six months or so. One day it was delivered to their house, and sat on the drive waiting to greet Mark, like the Range Rover had greeted Jenny. He went incandescent with rage. She had never seen him so cross in all their years of marriage. He'd once said to her, 'I would never hit a woman,' but at that moment, she felt like he might just break that rule.

'What the fuck is that *fart-box* on the drive?' he spat at her.

'That is my car,' she replied calmly, anticipating this confrontation.

'I told you we don't need it, Jenny. Haven't I always ferried you about whenever you wanted to go anywhere?'

'You have Mark, but this is to give me some independence back.'

'Independence? What the fuck are you on about, woman? You have MS. You are dependent on me, and I know what's best for you. You'll go and kill yourself in that contraption. You'll be a laughing stock,' he said, kicking the wheel viciously.

'I don't care. It's mine and there's nothing you can do about it,' she said.

'Really? Don't tempt me,' he hissed. She knew that although he wouldn't raise a hand to her, he would find other ways of punishing her, because in Mark's world, Jenny getting a car paid for from her benefit entitlements might look to other people like he wasn't providing for her, and this was something he really couldn't cope with: that other people may think the less of *him*.

When she spoke to Liz about his outburst that night on the phone, Liz responded in her usual insightful way. 'Well, you've defied him, haven't you Jen? You've got yourself a car, and some freedom so he's lost a bit of control over you.'

'Do you think so, Liz? You never did have a good word to say about Mark. He cares about me you know, he really does.'

'He doesn't know the difference between care and control, in my opinion Jenny, but don't tell him I said that.'

Unfortunately, the car turned out to be quite unreliable, refusing to start on cold mornings, and suffering from an odd assortment of intermittent problems; so she exchanged it for a different model – and it too was equally prone to breaking down. The mechanic at Bassett & Sons in Holsworthy scratched his head, unable to work out why these usually reliable cars just weren't. Nonetheless, Jenny loved her car and the freedom it gave her.

One tip that Jenny took away from her meeting with the MS specialist nurse all those years ago was to write a journal, and on the way home that very day, before she caught the bus, she went into the stationery shop on Bideford Quay and bought a beautiful diary and a refillable ink pen. And so began her passion for writing. It started off as just a list of things to remember or events to attend, but as time passed, she realised that just like interior design, writing was a creative outlet for her. She described the weather and what flowers were in the garden, and how she felt on a particular day, and where the kids were going. But these jottings morphed into poems and longer pieces of prose, which she never showed anyone, but which she treasured for the sheer joy of knowing she could still marshal her thoughts into coherent, even interesting diary entries.

Mark filled much of his spare time in the evenings and weekends on his laptop, doing goodness knows what – he wouldn't say – but after filling several dozen journals, Jenny decided to buy her own laptop and transfer her journals onto the hard drive for safe-keeping. She had learned to touch type at college, and the skill came in useful for this task. And so she filled her days.

They did have fun too. Mark took the whole family on two or three overseas holidays a year, although Jenny found them more and more tiring, especially the last one to Australia. The never-ending journey and the heat on arrival seemed to pole-axe her more than ever before. She slept a lot while Mark and the kids lounged by the pool. She remembered Marcus coming up to see her one afternoon as she lay in the sunlight streaming through the open French doors of their massive suite.

'How're you doing Mum?' he asked, his sweet face poking around the door. 19 years old and barely a bristle on his upper lip. Oh, how she loved him.

'I'm fine, sweetheart – what're you guys up to?' and then when Marcus didn't reply, she enquired, 'What's up darling?'

'Oh, nothing really… it's just… oh, I don't know. Dad just keeps trying to make a man out of me, Mum! He keeps challenging me to beat him at two lengths of the pool, or who can drink a glass of lager the fastest, or who can cycle around the grounds the quickest. It's exhausting! Why is he so competitive all the time? I'd rather stay in here with you.'

'Oh darling – I don't know. I think it's his idea of fun! Shall we be really subversive and have a game of Travel Scrabble?' They both burst out laughing and set up the board, snuggling down for a quiet, thoughtful time together.

Jess on the other hand was her father's daughter all right. She idolised her father and was somewhat contemptuous of her mother. She would sting Jenny with her comments, which sounded as if they'd come straight out of Mark's mouth. But Jenny let them pass, knowing that Mark had a habit of insinuation that influenced their daughter's opinions.

The years seemed to pass by so quickly. Jenny's illness had, on the whole, stayed mostly in remission. As long as she didn't over-exert herself or become stressed or anxious, she remained fairly well, if constantly exhausted. But she paid a great price for her precarious health: she knew her relationship with Mark had suffered as a result; they never slept together these days, for a start. He barely spoke to her unless he had to and couldn't be less interested in what filled her days if he tried, nor did he share with her how he filled his days. He didn't discuss the businesses and he didn't seek her counsel, but he always made a great show of his love for her in public. They had grown so far apart that she often wondered why he stayed with her at all, and thought that if it wasn't for the sake of the children, that perhaps he would have left her many years ago.

It was the day after their 25th anniversary party, as Jenny was writing up her journal that Mark walked into the kitchen swigging from a pint glass of water.

'Feeling a bit delicate?' ventured Jenny, pushing her luck.

'No, just keeping hydrated. You should drink more water, Birdy. It improves your concentration and clarity of mind, and god knows you could do with some help in that respect. Eight glasses of water a day is what's recommended. It's great for your skin too – Rachael swears by it. Maybe you could give it a go.'

Ouch. And Rachael certainly looks good for her age…

'I already do that, Mark. Well, I try to.' *There's water in my cup of tea, anyway.*

'I know, Birdy, but I've got you a special ice-cube tray in the freezer, so you can have ice and lemon with your water. Try and make a habit out of it, a good one.'

Jenny felt so touched. 'Oh, thank you darling – what a kind thought.' Any warmth he showed towards her, no matter how small, was lapped up by Jenny, who missed his touch, missed being the most important person in the world to him. When she investigated the ice-cube tray, it was rubber with heart-shaped compartments so the hearts of ice popped out easily, which was ideal as Jenny had developed problems with her grip.

So sweet of him, Jenny thought.

These heart-shaped ice cubes became known as 'Mum's Ice,' and no one else in the family was allowed to have them, under strict orders from Mark who topped them up religiously. Water (sometimes sparkling if she was feeling adventurous) with ice and lemon became Jenny's signature drink, instead of her usual vats of tea. She'd look down at those little ice hearts in her glass and think that even though Mark could be a tricky bugger sometimes, he did still care for her.

One Sunday, her parents came over for roast dinner, which Jenny and Jessie had knocked-up between them, mother and daughter having a bit of a lark in the kitchen for a change, radio on with a bit of shimmying around the central island to boot. Mark had been at a car rally all morning with Marcus, and George and Eleanor arrived just as Mark was about to carve the joint.

'George, are you a breast or leg man?' he said with a wink. 'And Eleanor, I've saved your favourites – the oysters are supposed to be the most tender part of the chicken.'

Jenny was in the kitchen, finishing off the gravy and draining the vegetables, the steam billowing up, her face flushed from the heat of the kitchen.

'Glass of wine, Jenny?' asked Mark, as she placed the remaining food on the table. 'Oh no, it looks like you've had enough already. You'd be better off with your iced water.'

Everyone laughed as Jenny made light of it and tried to fluff up her matted fringe. 'Yep, that's my tipple,' she replied taking a big swig.

After her parents had left, Jenny put her feet up on the couch – *just for five minutes,* she told herself. Marcus and Jess had gone to the beach to watch a surfing competition, and she was exhausted from head to toe. She must have drifted off, because it was already getting dark when she awoke to Mark's raised voice.

'You've left the kitchen in one hell of a state, Birdy,' he huffed. 'I suppose I'll have to clear it up.'

'No, no – I'll do it now,' she muttered trying to gather her thoughts. 'I was just having a rest… I must've fallen into a deep sleep.'

'Your life is one long bloody holiday. I work hard all week, and I have to put up with this shit at home?' he shot back.

'Hey, hey!' she rallied, 'what's got into you? You were all sweetness and light at dinner.'

'Well someone has to put on a good show for your parents,' he retorted. 'I don't want them seeing what a dys-functional bunch we really are.'

'Are we?' She was shocked to hear him say this.

'I miss you Birdy. I miss us.'

'I do too ~~Mark~~. I wish it wasn't like this. I want to be your wife, in every way, but I just feel so awful. I hate that the MS has done this to us.'

'It's why I go away so much you know, on the car rallies and the shows. It fills the hole in my life that you've left and when your Dad joins me, or Marcus, things feel normal… Do you know what I mean?'

'I do. I'm sorry Mark. I want to beat this illness, but I just don't seem able to.'

In truth, his hobby took up a lot more time than he was making out, and she wondered if his 'missing her' routine was his way of appeasing her for his regular absences – but she'd realised long ago that she could no longer read what was really going on behind her husband's impassive façade. From the moment he got that first Range Rover he had become a complete 'petrol-head'. Now he changed cars like he changed his socks. He was obsessed, his new love being Audis. He was away most weekends and sometimes overnight during the week, going to some rally or race meeting up-country, or some show or exhibition – but Jenny knew better than to question his movements.

He would throw her the occasional bone like this, the occasional loving word or gesture, like the ice hearts, and she would pounce on it like a hungry dog. She got up and began to tidy the kitchen.

A few days later she heard Mark laughing and went into the snug to find him, as usual, on his laptop. He slammed it shut when he saw her.

'Who were you chatting with?' Jenny asked. 'Your girlfriend?'

'Very funny. What's that you've got?'

'I was going to ask you that,' replied Jenny, holding up a blonde wig. She had found it at the back of the wardrobe when she'd been having a clear-out earlier that day, sorting out what things she needed to take to the charity shop. After her initial weight-gain with the steroids and medication, her metabolism had settled down, and she'd lost quite a lot of weight since, so most of the clothes in her wardrobe no longer fitted her. She'd decided to have a purge.

'It was for that Rotary Club dinner – you know, The Belle of the Ball. And I went as Cinderella? You must remember? You did my make-up? Stuffed one of your bras? You didn't feel up to it so I took Sam.' Mark looked at Jenny questioningly. Sam was a new interior designer that they'd taken on recently, to help Giles. She was Rose Red to Rachael's Snow White – blonde, young and gorgeous. And hugely talented, much to Jenny's dismay. Of course she wanted the business to thrive, but Sam's appointment, more than Giles', had felt so symbolic. Jenny had been the beautiful, creative one, the one with all the flair, and now Sam had come along and usurped her.

'When was this Ball, exactly?' she asked.

'You don't believe me, do you? You think I'm making this up? It was about six week ago. Just after the Easter holidays.'

Jenny just shook her head and walked up to bed. This scenario played out all too often – Mark reminding her of something she had no recollection of. She looked back in her diary. There it was in black and white – the details of the Belle of the Ball make-up party. It seemed they'd had a bit of fun, as well.

As she cuddled her hot water bottle, the sound of the waves crashing on the beach beyond the wooded valley, failed to lull her as they usually did. What was happening to her life? She did a mental audit: she was totally pushed out of the business, her circle of friends had diminished to just two, the children were grown-up and didn't need her and Christ knows where she stood in her relationship – at times it felt like Mark loathed her.

She thought of what Liz had said, over and over again. 'Leave him! He's a control freak and he's vindictive, and he just treats you like shit.'

But how could she? It all seemed like a monumental effort to her. She felt so trapped. It wouldn't just be divorcing Mark, it would be letting her parents down too, and there would be a huge upheaval in the business. Who would take over the helm if Mark wasn't there? Her father was retired now, and Paul – he was just a sleeping partner; they didn't want him interfering. She certainly couldn't run it all on her own.

It did not occur to Jenny that Mark had wrapped the business up in layers of contracts and caveats, so that he couldn't be ousted. Jenny might own 33% of the business along with her parents' and Paul's third, but Mark had managed to negotiate with George when he was made CEO that he should have the casting vote. Mark held 34% of the business, something Jenny didn't know.

Jenny turned over and remembered what Joy had said. 'This too shall pass.'
She hoped she was right.

CHAPTER 4

Structural Damage

Force 9 on the Beaufort Scale

Jenny awoke to the sound of the hoover. *Never has there been a more welcome wake-up call*, she thought. It would be Ava, their new cleaner. Ava immediately understood the limitations of Jenny's condition and insisted that she suppress the compulsion to tidy-up beforehand. When she first agreed to have some help, many years ago now, Jenny was embarrassed at first to let someone else do her housework. Employing domestic help was very complicated, emotionally, for her. It was all tied up in feelings of duty and pride and guilt; she felt she was letting Mark down and not being a proper mum to Jessica and Marcus, but all her cleaners over the years had become her friends and confidants. They'd often have a coffee when work was finished, and Ava was no different, enjoying a bit of down-time in Jenny's sparkling kitchen.

'You want I get you some shopping?' said Ava. 'Is no problem, no charge.'

'Oh no, I can manage that, but thank you Ava. You're very kind.'

Jenny used to rely on Mark to take her to the supermarket. It had been Mark's suggestion to help her with the groceries, just as he had suggested becoming her chauffeur before she got her little car. Jenny appreciated the gesture but the reality was less 'help' more 'hindrance'. The routine was that Jenny perused the supermarket aisles as fast as she could manage, leaning on the trolley for support, whilst Mark waited in the car, drumming his fingers on the steering wheel. She would pack each bag only half-full, so that she could place them more easily back in the trolley to ferry them to the car, as she found them hard to lift. It was exhausting.

'You took your time,' he'd mutter when she came back and started loading the bags into the boot.

On one occasion, Jenny had been as quick as she could, and had forgone the opportunity to use the Ladies to save time, but as a consequence, she then felt desperate for a pee. Another unfortunate side-effect of the MS was the inability to hold on for long. Mark roared off towards home in silence and Jenny didn't feel she could ask him to pull over but as the urge grew, she had no choice.

'Sorry Mark, I'm bursting for the loo. Can you stop at the Esso garage?'

'We're nearly home now, surely you can wait? I've got an important meeting to go to.'

'No, I don't think I can.'

When he drove past the Esso Garage, Jenny looked at him in horror. 'Mark? I'm really desperate…'

'Don't you dare piss yourself in my car,' he replied curtly.

'Mark! You've got to stop, please,' Jenny implored as the hedgerows flashed past in a blur. They were going at nearly 60 miles an hour and their house was only a mile away, but she knew her pelvic floor was about to give way.

'Oh, for Christ's sake,' he said, swerving roughly into a layby. Jenny got out and hunkered down by the car, hanging her head to avoid being recognised. The relief was glorious but it was tempered by shame. She pulled up her trousers and got back into the car.

'That was ridiculous. *You* are ridiculous,' Mark barked. Back at home, he strode off to the office, leaving Jenny to unpack the heavy bags.

Once she had defied Mark and got her little car, Jenny would go shopping several times a week, pootling into town and getting a couple of days of groceries rather than a whole week's worth in one go. This helped immensely, and then the advent of internet shopping was like a godsend to Jenny. The Sainsbury's delivery man had become her friend too.

But whilst some things in life got easier, others got worse. The chronic exhaustion had now been joined by terrible headaches and nausea and Jenny was often on her knees with fatigue, feeling wretched. One afternoon she'd felt at death's door. She couldn't face getting out of bed and stayed there watching the shadows move around the room as the sun began to set. She felt too tired to cry. She was incredibly thirsty but the kitchen felt like a million miles away. When the thirst became too much she dragged herself to the en-suite and cupped a handful of water to her lips.

What sort of life is this? she thought. She yearned to be outside, pottering around the garden or going to the beach. She felt out of touch with the seasons, dislocated from the elements that normally kept her grounded. Back in bed she slipped into a doze and when she awoke, she found a roughly-made sandwich on her bedside cabinet, and a glass of water with the remnants of the ice cube hearts in it.

She was grateful for this because she hadn't eaten for hours and the constant nausea put her off eating anyway, but she knew she must as her energy levels were already at rock bottom. But it was something about Mark not waking her up that made her feel so alienated, like a prisoner in her own home. *Next he'll be installing a hatch in the door so he can just slide in a plate and slam it shut.* She chuckled mildly at this thought and chastised herself for not being grateful to Mark for bringing her a sandwich in the first place. But she was sick and tired, literally, of her MS and decided to ring her lovely nurse the following day for advice.

'Let me check what you're taking…'

Jenny could hear her tapping at a computer.

'Hmm – your new symptoms *could* be caused by the disease-modifying drugs. I'll speak with the consultant about it and ask her to prescribe you some anti-emetics and an antacid. That should help. In the meantime, rest when you can,' she advised.

Strangely enough, rest was one thing she wasn't short of. Her daily routine was a couple of hours of 'paperwork' as she called it in the morning – mostly writing her journal – before having an ice-cold frappe made by Mark. He generally brought it in to her at around 11. 'Decaffeinated, of course. Caffeine's a diuretic and we wouldn't want any more little accidents, now would we?' he'd commented.

If truth be told, she'd much prefer a cappuccino from the new coffee machine they had in the office, but she was so grateful for this little show of affection from Mark that she always said, 'Lovely, thank you darling,' when he left it on her desk.

After that, she found all her energy reserves were used up and she was too wrung out to do anything but sleep. One afternoon she woke up feeling very foggy-headed. She'd been out for the count for hours. She opened her eyes and the world was in double-vision. She tried blinking and rubbing her eyes, but it remained like that. Eye drops helped a little and after a few minutes the world started to clear. She walked over to the office, hanging on to the new metal railings that Mark had installed to help her keep her balance, but she felt so dizzy. She stopped at the French windows to catch her breath, and looked in.

She couldn't quite make out what was happening as her vision was still somewhat blurred, and at first it seemed like there was no one in the office. *Giles and Sam must be on a commission*, she thought, but then she saw Mark and Rachael behind the store-cupboard door. As she opened the office door, they emerged. Rachael looked flushed and she was barefoot. Mark was smirking.

'Where are your shoes, Rachael?' asked Jenny.

'Oh, it's so hot today I took them off.'

Jenny glanced over and saw her shoes by the sofa. She also noticed that the sofa cushions were awry. Rachael walked over and adjusted them whilst slipping her feet back into her heels.

'Are you okay, Jenny? Your eyes look a bit red,' Mark said, closing the store-cupboard, clutching an armful of folders.

Jenny told them about her double vision and they made sympathetic noises but Jenny wasn't really listening. Instead she was thinking: *What have I just stumbled upon? And why was I so deeply asleep? Is it so Mark can have his afternoon delight with Rachael?*

She rang Joy, but was hesitant to come right out with it because she didn't want to sound
paranoid.

'Joy, do you find that after you've taken your medication, you're completely dead to the world? It feels like I've been drugged rather than treated, the meds are so strong.'

'Sometimes, yeah. Everyone reacts to the drugs differently, just as everyone with MS presents with different symptoms, and I do think that eventually you adjust to the medication. Your tablets have been changed recently, haven't they? If that's what the consultant has prescribed, I'd just go with it for a while, hun – you'll probably settle down again. They're the experts. Try not to overthink it.'

'I'm wondering if it's just the medication though, Joy… Something doesn't feel right in my gut. I didn't think MS would have such a dramatic impact on me – the symptoms, the medication, the side-effects, I feel like I've been flattened.'

'Always trust your instincts, Jenny.'

Jenny continued hesitantly. 'It's just that, I think maybe Mark might be, I don't know… seeing someone else…'

'Really? Oh, no Jen. I know Liz has never got a good word to say about him, but he loves you, he really does. He always talks so highly of you when I see him, saying how strong and brave you are – and what about those gorgeous pearls he gave you for your 25th? That was a show of love if ever I saw one. No, I think it's just because you feel so low, you think you're not worthy of him, so you're reading things into situations that aren't there.'

However, mindful of Joy's words, 'always trust your instincts,' Jenny decided to start noting in her diary the daily ebb and flow of her side-effects. If she could try and work out what tablets were making her feel so ill, maybe she could try a different brand? She remembered reading on an online forum once that different brands of the same medication sometimes had less side-effects. She was holding on to normality with her fingertips, and was desperate to regain some semblance of control.

Unfortunately, life had a nasty habit of getting in the way.

One morning her mobile rang, its urgency waking her out of a deep sleep.

'Jenny, can you come over, it's your mother…'

'Errr, Dad? What is it? What's wrong?'

' She's breathing strangely. I've dialled 999.'

'I'm coming.' Jenny flung down the receiver and swore. Mark was away on business, so there was nothing for it – despite the double-vision, she was going to have to drive herself. She got dressed as quickly as she could, slipping a colourful jersey tunic and leggings on, and easing into her Velcro-strapped trainers. She twisted her hair into loose bun and hooked her keys off their peg in the hall. Something that would've taken Jess ten minutes to do, took her over 20.

As she slammed the door of her car, a white-hot wave of pain washed over her. She ignored it and started the engine. It turned over, but would not catch.

'What the fuck!! No, please car, just this once, please start!'

She turned it again and by some miracle, it started. The sensors detected the movement of her car and opened the garage doors, closing them neatly behind her.

She drove like Lewis Hamilton, fast and competently, but her mind was elsewhere: *I must get there, Dad needs me… And Mum… what if she's…* Jenny dried her eyes with her cuff so she could see the road. At her parents' house, Trethorne Manor, the beautiful honey-coloured stone place of her birth, she ran in through the front door to find her father knelt on the kitchen floor. Beside him was her mother, lying unconscious.

'You're too late! You idiot. You should've got here sooner!' her father roared. His eyes were locked on Eleanor's face, which was grey, apart from her lips which were blue.

'It's not my fault, Dad,' Jenny replied, stung by his words, but trying to forgive him, under the circumstances. She crouched down and rested her ear on her mother's chest. She tried to control her own gasping breaths enough to listen. Nothing. Then she heard footsteps in the hall: the paramedics had arrived. She sat back on her heels and watched as they took over, so calm and skilled beside her.

'When did she collapse?' they asked as they examined her mother.

Jenny's father just repeated, 'Collapse…?' He seemed to be in a trance. Jenny hurriedly guessed 25 minutes ago. The paramedics murmured to each other as they opened Eleanor's blouse to stick electrodes on to her chest. Jenny tried to decipher what they were saying.

After a few moments, they hurriedly packed their equipment up, saying to Jenny and her father: 'We need to get her to the hospital as quickly as possible.'

Jenny's father jolted out of his reverie. 'For god's sake, man, do something! I'm going to lose her.'

'We're doing everything we can sir. Just follow us in your car.'

George did not reply. His hands simply dropped to his sides and he watched helplessly as Eleanor was taken into the ambulance on a stretcher. Jenny was on autopilot as she listened to the paramedic's instructions. She didn't let her brain process the stark possibility. *My mother is gravely ill. She could be dying* remained waiting outside a mental portcullis.

'Dad? Dad, listen to me, we've got to go to the hospital. Are you okay to drive?' But George remained mute so Jenny steeled herself for the lengthy drive to hospital. 'Dad? We'll go in my car, alright? C'mon.' She gently tugged his sleeve, and he followed her on autopilot. His previous sense of panic had been replaced by resignation.

When they arrived, they were ushered into a private room. A consultant came to see them and turned to George: 'I'm so sorry Mr Truscott, but unfortunately your wife was pronounced dead on arrival. We suspect a massive heart attack.'

Both Jenny and George were stunned into silence, then began to sob uncontrollably, George turning to his daughter for comfort. 'What will I do without her?' George gasped. 'She was my life.'

Even in the depths of her despair and brain fug Jenny made a private, mental retort: *If only you'd been kinder to her then, Dad.*

After the formalities had been dealt with in the hospital, Jenny drove them both home, the journey slow and silent, Jenny blessing the fact that she'd insisted on this automatic car, that just eased through the traffic and bought them home safely. Once back at Trethorne Manor, they gravitated towards the kitchen, which still echoed with the shock of the earlier scene. Jenny stepped over some discarded medical packaging to make a cup of tea. She whirled round when she heard a flat, slapping sound. It was her father crouching on all-fours, smacking the floor with his hand where Eleanor had lain.

'Why weren't you here sooner, you stupid girl? You should've been here for her. It's your fault, Jennifer!' he shouted. 'Your fault.'

'Dad, I came as soon as I could. And it's nobody's fault – nobody is to blame here…' she answered, voice quavering.

'I know, I know, I know – sorry, Jenny. Sorry, old girl,' he sobbed, stroking the floor where his wife had lain. Jenny knew that it was just the grief talking; that her father lashing out like that was the only way he knew how to express his own emotions. He was of the 'stiff upper lip' generation, where blame and retaliation were his go-to emotional props. 'And as for your useless brother – gallivanting around the world when he should be here…' As he continued to rant, Jenny stood quietly, waves of sadness and exhaustion washing over her. With her mother now gone, the dynamic of her relationship with her father would inevitably change. Her mother had formed the cushion between them, helping her to see beyond her father's misogyny. But George was a difficult man, charming on the outside, vicious on the inside – that was the reluctant conclusion Jenny had come to over the years. She loved her father, but she didn't like him very much. Even now, in his grief, George had to lash-out, to blame, to deflect his own guilt for being a care-less husband onto someone else.

To say that George couldn't care less for his family may seem a bit harsh, considering he was a 'provider' and that they never lacked anything material, but he seemed unable to love his wife and children in a fatherly way; his love had been selfish, manipulative and narcissistic. He had been so absorbed in his business, his ex-Army mates and his colleagues that he had very little time for anything else. Jenny definitely wouldn't describe him as a family man, in fact, he was similar to Mark in many ways, something she'd never realised until this very moment. How blind she'd been. *Oh my god, I've married my father!* The realisation made Jenny's blood run cold.

Jenny had discovered in her teens that she was the result of a one-night stand. Her parents had to get married when Eleanor had become pregnant with her, and this revelation explained a lot. Previously he'd been enjoying the bachelor life in the Army; rowdy nights with friends from the barracks. After Jenny came along, he was forced to move into family quarters and that chapter of his life closed. Jenny had always believed that in adversity, people's true feelings come out, and she had always felt to blame whenever her father was unhappy. She was his emotional punch-bag, a role she had grown up with and eventually learned not to take to heart.

Jenny left her father in his study. He insisted that he just wanted to be on his own, and so she made her way home, vaguely aware that she'd had nothing to eat all day. She decided to cook up a batch of chilli for supper that evening – never had the hackneyed phrase 'life goes on' felt truer – when she heard the scrunch of gravel that signalled Mark's car finally returning. He'd been to visit a company in South Wales that he was doing business with, and although it was only around four hours away on the motorway, she didn't know what had taken him so long to get home. She'd left a message for him about Eleanor early that morning, when they were waiting around at the hospital.

'My darling Birdy, I am so, so sorry about Mum,' he said. Jenny appreciated his arms around her even though the 'Mum' stung, especially at a time like this. She felt her tears absorb into his shearling jacket.

'I can't believe she's gone. It was so sudden,' said Jenny. However complicated their relationship had become, it still felt good to be comforted by him. 'I'm dreading telling Paul and the kids…'

Mark was all set to start organising the funeral and contacting family friends but Jenny was adamant that she could do it herself. This was something she had to summon the energy for; it was something she wanted to do.

Although she still felt very raw, she realised that her mother's death signalled a new chapter in her own life. She was now the matriarch of the family but it also meant she would need to be there more for her father, a task she didn't relish. Jenny talked it over with Liz and Joy, who came around the following evening with a huge bouquet of beautiful lilies to express their sympathies.

'Life is a continual circle of endings and beginnings,' said Joy.

'I feel a song coming on,' remarked Liz, winking at Jenny and reaching to top up her wine glass.

'Obviously I'll support my dad any way I can, now he's on his own…' There was a catch in Jenny's voice as she said this. 'But I need to look after myself too. I feel like it's the dawning of the Age of Jenny.'

'Now I definitely feel like singing!' said Liz. 'Good for you, we're behind you all the way.'

'Maybe it's symbolic? You're now the matriarch of the family, you're coming into your power,' reflected Joy.

'I hope you're right,' said Jenny, blowing her nose. 'I could do with feeling powerful right now.'

Despite the terrible trauma of the previous day, Jenny had already begun to think practically; it was like she had been jolted into action. Her mother's death meant that she would inherit Trethorne, the family manor house. For generations it had been passed down the female line, a fact her brother Paul was absolutely fine with, but not her father. Mark also found this tradition absolutely infuriating when he first heard about it.

'That's very antiquated, isn't it? Must've been some old lesbian relative of yours who first set it up. Surely it can't be legal?' he'd said. 'What does your father think of this arrangement?'

'Oh, he thinks it's mad too,' Jenny had replied. 'It was the only time I've ever seen Mum stand up to him, actually. He wanted to re-write the deeds so that the spouse or male heir inherited, but Mum would have none of it. They didn't speak for weeks. Dad actually left her for a while, but then Mum found out he was sleeping in his car at the end of the lane and made him come home! It's all long forgotten now,' she'd said.

After investigating the deeds with the family solicitor during probate, Jenny was still relieved to discover that the covenant was still in place, and she felt strangely comforted that whatever happened to her, Jessica would inherit Trethorne after her. They would, of course, ensure that Marcus would also inherit the equivalent in monetary terms, but it was more than that for Jenny: it felt like one in the eye for all the male chauvinism she and her mother had experienced; it felt liberating to have this unassailable female power.

It was cathartic to have the funeral to organise. With a glass of iced-water by her side, she systematically worked through her lists. Speaking to hundreds of relatives and managing to track down her brother at a remote surfing spot in Indonesia reminded Jenny that she could be efficient and effective. She just wished that the double vision would stop plaguing her. It would come and go, never staying long enough for ophthalmologists to spot a problem.

The day before the funeral, when she was squinting at a document, trying to make out the words, she felt a strange sensation: an unnerving sense of déjà vu, her brain swimming and fuddled. Then she smelt a bitter, unmistakable scent. What was it? She knew she recognised it but couldn't put a name to it. Then tiny pinpricks of black crowded into the corners of her vision. Alone in the house – as usual Mark was away – Jenny picked up the phone and dialled 999.

'I'm not right, I mean something's wrong,' she slurred to the operator. She managed to get out her address and, 'backdoor's open,' before blackness descended on her. Jenny fell forwards on to the desk as all her muscles went rigid and then she started to jerk uncontrollably. An area of the paper she had been working on darkened under her chin as saliva seeped out of the corner of her mouth.

'Not dead yet, Birdy?' It was Mark, looming over her. The room seemed too bright and Jenny tried to shield her eyes, but found she could hardly raise her arms, they felt so weak and floppy. Adrenalin flooded her system as she panicked, desperately attempting to move. She looked around her to see a drip-stand and the regulation blue curtains of the hospital. Her head was pounding and she felt extremely sick. *I mustn't vomit* she told herself. She looked down to see she was wearing a hospital gown. *Oh god, did I wet myself?*

She tried to speak, but her tongue felt as thick as an in-sole. 'Wass happen?' she managed.

Mark was texting on his phone and didn't reply. *Mum's funeral,* Jenny remembered. *Have I missed it?* 'Wa' day is it?'

'Don't you worry about that,' he replied, slipping on his Harris tweed jacket and leaving the room.

Jenny was absolutely parched. She eyed the water jug on her bedside table and tried to reach for it, but her hands were ragdolls. She lay there, unable to do anything, her mind racing.

Eventually, a nurse came into the room, immediately guessed what Jenny wanted and gently fed a straw through her lips so she could sip some water from a beaker.

'Welcome back,' she said. 'Good to see you awake again. We were getting worried there.'

Jenny asked what day it was again, and this time received an answer – Thursday.

She'd missed the funeral. Tears seeped out and dripped into her ears.

'Oh dear, I never realised a day of the week could be so upsetting,' said the nurse as she took her blood pressure.

Jenny tried to smile, but her face felt numb. Mark came back into the room and clocked the nurse. He immediately rushed over to Jenny's side. 'You're awake, Birdy, you're awake. Oh, it's so wonderful.'

'Thursday,' she said.

'Are you thirsty, darling?' Mark said, raising the beaker to her lips. The straw had lifted out of the water, meaning Jenny couldn't suck any up, but Mark didn't notice.

The nurse finished writing on the clipboard at the end of her bed and left the room saying: 'I'll get the doctor to come and see you.'

'God, you look a sight,' said Mark after the squeak of the nurse's black Sketchers echoing down the hall had faded away.

Just then, her father and brother walked in and Mark made a show of tucking Jenny's hair behind her ears. 'There, that's better. You're a sight for sore eyes, my darling,' he said.

Paul was bronzed apart from two white circles around his eyes where his sunglasses had been.

''lo Panda,' said Jenny and Paul laughed.

'You haven't lost your sense of humour at least,' he said, bending down to kiss his sister.

Jenny's father stood awkwardly with a bunch of flowers. 'Good to see you're back in the land of the living,' he said gruffly. 'Good girl.'

The doctor explained that Jenny had had a seizure and they were trying to identify the reason. Over the next few days, Jenny had numerous tests and scans but nothing had shown up. Everyone was stumped as to the cause.

'Could it be my medication?' Jenny asked the consultant. Her speech had slowly returned and she managed to sit up in bed, but walking was still out of the question. And her grief at missing her mother's funeral overwhelmed her and left her listless.

The consultant examined her chart. 'No, but tests have shown that your adrenal glands are working overtime and your kidney function isn't what it should be. This is unrelated to the seizure, of course, but I don't understand why you're so overloaded. Is there any chance you could have overdosed on your medication?'

'No, I'm always very careful about that. I even have a pill-dispenser so I get it right,' replied Jenny.

'The CT scan shows your MS hasn't worsened since you were diagnosed… We'll keep on looking until we get to the bottom of it,' said the consultant.

As she left the room, Jenny saw Mark collar her and they walked off together.

At the next ward round, the doctor came over. 'I've spoken with your consultant, and she thinks that you must have had an NES – a non-epileptic seizure. This can have a psychogenic cause in that it can be brought on by stress. I understand that your mother has died recently – well this could certainly be attributable to that. Perhaps you should consider counselling to cope with your stress levels. You're well enough to go home,' he said briskly, handing her discharge papers to the waiting nurse.

Jenny felt a mixture of emotions: relieved that her seizure didn't have a sinister cause but also deflated. Surely being virtually paralysed and unconscious for two days can't have been just 'all in the mind'? She suspected that it was a convenient explanation for the medics, who dwell in a world that likes tidy conclusions. They'd been fed a convenient line – stress-related – and had seized on it as greedily as a fish being duped by an angler's maggot.

When she got home, mortified because she had to limp into the house with the aid of a Zimmer frame, she discovered that Mark had been busy. He'd installed an array of disability equipment – hand-rails in the shower, raised toilet seats and a wipe-clean easy chair that rose up with a remote control.

'I'm not that bad, Mark! The doctors say I'll recover full mobility,' exclaimed Jenny when she saw her room, which now looked bleakly clinical.

'Oh, you never know when you'll need it,' he said. 'I thought it would help.' But to Jenny, it felt like an ill omen. Jenny also discovered that Mark had arranged a carer to come in for 15 minutes twice a day to dispense her medication. 'We don't want any more mistakes do we?' he said.

'What do you mean, mistakes?'

'You missed taking your tablets, remember? The doctor said that was partly what triggered your seizure.'

That was precisely the opposite of what the doctor had said, thought Jenny, but she remained silent, too exhausted to talk. She felt infantilised, humiliated. *I'll be fucking spoon-fed next*, she thought. She was glad to be home though, after the noise and disruption of the hospital ward. It was lovely to get back into the rhythm of her life – and the chance to have a proper night's sleep in her own bed. She also realised that her headaches and nausea had ebbed away during the week in hospital, making her feel clearer than she had in weeks.

The next day, she was awoken by two wet noses nudging at her arm. She shot up in bed. 'What on earth…?'

'Ralph! Hugo! Down!' laughed Mark, as two chocolate Labradors sniffed her covers. 'Edgar was getting rid of them so I took them off his hands.'

Edgar was a local farmer that Mark had been palling-up with. He was practically landed gentry and owned acres for miles around them. Just the sort of friend Mark now cultivated. Mark had taken to carrying a shooting stick, for god's sake. 'I've got to look the part now that I'm Lord of the Manor, haven't I?'

'If you mean Trethorne, then no, actually, it's me who's the Lady,' observed Jenny.

Mark ignored her, muttering something about 'semantics,' then added brightly: 'Not bad for a lad from a council estate, eh?' Mark had only alluded to his childhood growing up in Ilfracombe a few times. It seemed like he was ashamed of being an estate kid, although Jenny couldn't give a damn about where he had lived, even if Ilfracombe did have a bit of a bad reputation for drugs and antisocial behaviour. 'Did you know that we're sitting on a multi-million-pound investment? I've been talking to Dad. The kitchen garden alone is two acres – enough land to build an executive housing development – exclusive, of course. I've talked to the chaps at the council about sustainable housing and that's where the money is. With eco-properties you get more grants, it's a win-win. It could be called Trethorne Gardens.'

Jenny flushed hot all over. 'Absolutely not, Mark! No. I forbid it. Trethorne is mine, and I won't have it desecrated like that,' said Jenny. 'It's not about the money, there's centuries of my family's history in that house. I absolutely forbid it.' She shuddered at the thought of the grounds of her ancestral home being carved up to make into wendy houses. 'Besides, the covenant means that you can't do anything to it; it's going to be inherited by Jessica when I'm gone.'

'Yes, Jessica will inherit the manor house, but the actual wording doesn't say anything about *development of the estate.* That leaves it wide open. You've got to move with the times, Birdy. Paul's in agreement,' replied Mark.

'What?'

'That darling brother of yours. He's sold me his shares of the family business, so basically with George retired and you out of the picture, I'm in charge now.'

'Wh…? You should have told me before, Mark. Why do you always drop these bombshells when I'm at my lowest ebb…?' sobbed Jenny, but Mark wasn't listening. He'd walked off, whistling to the dogs who raced after him, claws skittering across the parquet.

'What the fuck have you done, Paul?' she half-shrieked into the receiver as her brother picked up the phone.

'Jen, Jen… chill out, for god's sake. You'll give yourself another seizure. Look, I've signed my part of the business over to Mark,' Paul explained. 'No big deal. Mum dying and then your dice with death has really made me think: life's too short for all this wheeler-dealer crap, Jenny. I'm just not cut out for it. It doesn't float my boat.'

'But it is a big deal, Paul. Didn't you think about me and how I'd feel in all this?'

'Well – he's your husband, isn't he? He'll look after you, won't he?'

'I don't know about that.'

Silence. 'What do you mean, Jen?'

'Well, what does "looking after" actually mean? Does it mean building over our ancestral home, trampling my hopes and dreams just to make more money, or does it mean actually caring about what's important to me?'

'I don't know, you've got me there, Sis. Like I said, it's all above me, all this business and family stuff. You should see what it's like in Bali, Jen, it's paradise. I've decided, with my money from the shares, I'm going to move there permanently. It feels like my spiritual home. Yoga at dawn followed by a day's surfing.'

'But you're just running away, Paul. Running away from the family and your responsibilities.'

Silence again, but then when Paul spoke, his usual light-heartedness had evaporated. 'Look Jen, apart from you, I have no family now Mum's dead. I can't stand the old man. He's a manipulative, lying old bastard who doesn't give a shit about me, or you for that matter. The only thing that's important to him are his crony mates and how much money he's got in the bank. I just want to get as far away from him as possible. Trethorne will be perfectly safe. I trust Mark. He has given me his word that he'll look after it.'

'Do you trust him though, Paul? Do you really?'

'I… I… well, I don't think he would do anything to hurt you or the kids, Jen. And *I* didn't mean to hurt you by my actions. I realise now, I should've discussed it with you first, but to be honest, Mark, Dad… they're the kind of men who want power and prestige, and I just want a simple life. I don't fit in, so I'm gonna live somewhere I do fit in.'

Jenny began to sob. 'I feel like you're abandoning me,' she cried. 'You're about the only one who understands me.'

'I'll always love you Jen, but I have to get away. Please don't hate me for it.'

They said their goodbyes and Jenny hung up. She didn't hate him and she did understand that he had to live his own life, but nonetheless, she felt more alone than ever, now.

She massaged her temples – just a day at home and her headache had come crashing back. Maybe the doctor was right, maybe getting wound up did affect her physically. Her head was pounding so much she wished she could have a couple of paracetamol, but no, the medicine cabinet had been completely stripped bare. She had to wait until the carer came for any pain-relief.

She downed a glass of water Mark had left her, hoping this would help. As she gulped, she imagined how Mark had mesmerised Paul, stroking his ego during a 'man-to-man chat' with talk of 'doing the right thing', and 'no need to bother Jenny with it.'

But something Paul had said did hit home: *Life's too short.* She couldn't just watch as her world collapsed in on itself, leaving her sitting in a wipe-clean chair, powerless and alone. Jenny needed to rally the troops; she needed her own plan of action.

She persuaded Joy to join her on a week's spa break to Crete at the end of the month, which she paid for out of her savings. Sadly, Liz couldn't get the time off work, so was unable to join them, but Joy was used to travelling with a disability and she helped make it possible for Jenny, despite the fact she was still very weak. Jenny just hoped that some Mediterranean sun, sea and seafood would put her right and help her to see a way forward through all this mess.

What is it they say? 'If life gives you lemons, make lemonade,' thought Jenny, determined to do just that. She was damned if she was going to sit back and let Mark Damerell destroy her inheritance. Her female forebears would turn in their graves.

CHAPTER 5

Violence and Destruction

Force 12 on the Beaufort Scale

As Jenny lugged her case through the front door she heaved a sigh. It was good to be home. Crete had been amazing and Joy's serenity calmed her soul. It had been a real restorative, helping her to get some perspective on her life. She looked at herself in the hall mirror. Her strawberry-blonde curls had lightened in the Mediterranean sun and her cheekbones looked slightly more defined under a gentle tan. She sniffed her wrist and smiled. She'd treated herself to some new perfume in duty free – Jo Malone's lime, basil and mandarin, a real change from her usual Chanel No. 5. Mark had been buying it for her all these years and frankly she'd always found it too overpowering, but she'd used it every day nonetheless, just to please him. Well, no more.

After a cup of tea – proper tea, not that insipid Liptons stuff she'd had all week – she went over to the office, determined to put on a show of strength. Talking of strength, when she thought about it, she'd not had that awful nausea and dizziness all week whilst on holiday, and neither had she taken her usual afternoon siesta. *Yes*, she decided, *in the shit-storm that is my life, holidays are the way to go!*

'I'm back!' she said as she walked in through the office door, as both Mark and Rachael looked up from their computers. 'Anyone fancy some baklava?' She waved a fancy box of the delectable honey pastries.

'Hi Jenny, you look a lot less peaky than usual,' said Rachael, unable to bring herself to say that Jenny looked fabulous. 'Oh, baklava. It's so sickly-sweet, don't you think? Anyway, I couldn't, I've just eaten.'

Yeah right, yesterday, thought Jenny.

'You should have told me when your flight landed and I could have picked you up from the airport,' said Mark, scowling.

'No problem, I got a lift back with Joy, and then a taxi from Bideford,' replied Jenny. She was determined not to let either of them dampen her post-holiday high. 'So, what's been happening here? Have I missed anything fun?'

'Not much, unless you call being audited fun,' said Mark.

'Ouch, I don't like the sound of that,' said Jenny, clocking the furious look that Rachael threw Mark.

'No, it's not a barrel of laughs,' said Rachael and they both looked back at their screens. They were flushed and agitated and the air thrummed with nervous tension.

Jenny went over to the water cooler and was about to pour herself a cup when Mark said, 'Birdy – we're in the middle of some difficult accounting here. Can't you go and get yourself a drink from the kitchen? I'll see you later, okay?'

She stopped pouring and decided to leave them to it. They weren't exactly over the moon to see her. She'd go and visit her dad and have a cup of tea and some baklava with him instead. She didn't feel too concerned about the tax inspection – she'd had it drummed into her so many times that Mark and Rachael were the financial whizzes that she was sure they'd cope. She was a bit fuzzy about the details but couldn't your accounts be audited at any time? They'd definitely be prepared for that, she decided.

She drove over to Trethorne, and George didn't hesitate to get stuck into the baklava. Soon they both had pistachios and filo pastry everywhere.

'Ah the taxman cometh, eh?' said George, when she asked about the audit. 'Yes, they last visited a few years ago, if I remember rightly. You've got to doff your cap and shuffle a bit of extra paperwork for a few days, but it's soon over. So long as everything's shipshape and Bristol fashion we won't have anything to worry about. Mark will cope with it, he's up to anything. Glad it's them not me though…' He wiped the crumbs from his mouth with his handkerchief. 'One of the perks of retiring, I suppose.'

Jenny caught a hint of sadness in her father's voice. It must be hard for him not to be in the thick of it anymore. And with Eleanor no longer around, he seemed smaller, diminished somehow, and living in this big house all on his own only emphasised that. She decided to take the bull by the horns and broach a subject that she'd been mulling over on holiday.

'Dad, I've been thinking. Now that probate has been sorted, I want to move the family into Trethorne Manor. I want us to live here so that we can look after you. We could convert the billiard room and library into your own suite, so that you have some privacy, but you could come and eat with us if you wanted to, and be part of the family. How does that sound?'

George's face darkened. 'Have you talked this over with Mark?'

'I don't need to Dad. It's my house and I want to live here, and we finished the renovations on The Rectory ages ago. No, it'll give Mark a new challenge, and anyway, he's always fancied himself as lord of the manor, so I doubt he'll have any objections.' *Plus, I need to keep an eye on you and Mark to ensure neither of you does anything underhand to my estate*, she thought to herself.

'Well, it would be nice to have a bit of company and some life in the old place again,' George mused, tugging at his left ear, a habit he had when he was thinking something through. 'I do like the library too. Eleanor always used to sit there every morning, in the window seat, and do her crossword...' he drifted off in fond remembrance of a woman who in life he chastised and scorned more than he loved.

'I can design the refurb Dad, so that it'll be a really nice, self-contained space for you, and once that's done, we'll think about moving in.'

'Well, that'll be something to look forward to, I suppose,' George said, and for once, it didn't sound grudging.

Jenny was pleased to be able to kill two birds with one stone: to move back to Trethorne to keep an eye on things, and return to her true love – interior design. She didn't exactly relish the thought of spending more time with her father, but at least she would be able to keep tabs on him.

Feeling dynamic and capable for the first time in a long time, she spent an enjoyable afternoon sketching a new layout for George's apartment, looking at paint charts and fabric swatches, and deciding on the perfect colour scheme in honour of her mother's favourite room. Then she got out her old contacts book and rang a contractor she used to work with. He was surprised and delighted to hear from her – and she soon had the work booked in, with the builder due to start by the end of the month.

In fact, once she'd got her eye in, she felt ready to tackle other areas of the crumbling manor house, which would need work before the family moved in. The kitchen and scullery were in dire need of renovation – of course, she would respect the integrity of Trethorne and keep the original butler's sinks and antique dressers – but there were easy ways to make it brighter and more comfortable. And then there was the drawing room, where those beautiful big windows were crying out for proper attention… Luckily the monthly payment she'd negotiated with Mark all those years ago when he took over her design business had been accruing in her bank account. With the odd freelance job she'd done over the years, and the interest she'd gained, she had a tidy sum to work with; money she didn't have to beg Mark for. At least he had honoured that agreement.

Away from the headache of Mark's moods Jenny felt much happier, although inside her, dread and tension were already building about telling Mark of her plans to move. Would he really be pleased, or would he try to thwart her? Whatever his response, Jenny had decided that she was going to protect her inheritance. She saw it as part of reclaiming her sense of wellbeing, something she'd talked at length about with Joy on holiday.

As things turned out, she hardly saw Mark over the next few weeks. He came home late muttering about, 'the damn audit,' and it was all he could do to retrieve his dinner from the Aga and wolf it down before retiring to bed. For the first time in their marriage, Mark looked tired and worried. He looked his age. Wisely, Jenny decided to bide her time and keep the details of her Trethorne plans to herself, but that nagging sensation of dread in her stomach stayed with her. She knew that taking her life into her own hands would not go down well with her husband. She knew she had it coming, but precisely what 'it' was, remained to be seen.

Nonetheless, it was wonderful to spend time at her family home and finally feel like she belonged there. She had great fondness for this ancient old lady who was in need of much TLC. George and Eleanor had moved their family around many times during her childhood due to her father's military career, so Jenny and Paul rarely got to spend time at Trethorne, only visiting their grandparents there at Christmas and on special occasions. When Jenny's grandmother died, her mother, Eleanor, inherited Trethorne and the family moved in. Jenny and Paul spent their teenage years there. Now the manor house belonged to her. She was its guardian; it was hers to look after and she felt a wonderful sense of peace and contentment.

Jenny also began to notice a subtle change in the dynamic with her father. The power balance was shifting, albeit with glacial slowness, but she no longer viewed George as the all-powerful patriarch. She saw him for what he was: an old man, growing dependent on his family. And perhaps his willingness to defer to her regarding the house renovations signalled that he too was finally allowing her to grow up.

Almost a month had gone by since her return from holiday before Mark noticed Jenny's absence. During that time, work had started on George's apartment and Jenny spent most of her days project-managing the build. She felt better than she had done for ages, drinking tea and having a laugh with the men during their breaks and overseeing the quality of the work that was being undertaken. She was back in her element.

Jenny had decided to go to Trethorne one Saturday morning to inspect how the plastering was going-off, and whether it would be dry enough for the first coat of paint on

Monday. She was searching high and low for her Jo Malone perfume, wanting a quick spray before she left because she associated it with her new-found confidence, when Mark walked into her bedroom.

'Going somewhere?' he asked. He was holding a glass of iced water for her. 'Here, you've not been drinking your eight glasses a day lately.'

'No, I read online that there's absolutely no basis for the eight glasses regime. Anyway, I'm not thirsty, thanks. Have you seen my new perfume anywhere?'

He placed the glass beside her bed. 'New perfume? What's wrong with the Chanel I buy you?'

'I don't know… it smells a bit weird to me these days. A bit like bitter almonds.'

He shrugged. 'Well? Where are you going?'

Jenny's legs went to jelly, as she realised this was her moment to appraise him of her plans. 'I'm off to Trethorne. I'm doing some renovation work there.'

'Really? That's the first I've heard of it,' he said, bristling instantly.

'Well, I would've told you before, but you've been so busy with the audit…'

'Yes. Keeping the family business going to pay the bills – someone has to. So, tell me now then. What's going on?'

And so she told him of her plans; of how she'd designed George's apartment, and put in a new Aga in the kitchen, and repainted the scullery. As she did so, Mark's face became set, his jaw clenched, his eyes piercing into hers. She felt his anger like a punch in the stomach, but she refused to be cowed by him. 'I think it would be good if we moved in as a family,' she finished. 'We can sell The Rectory now that it's finished, and you can have the east wing for your offices, if you want. I might even re-launch Truscott Interiors…' she added.

'Oh, for god's sake, Birdy! You do a bit of painting and decorating, and think you're well enough to go into business again. Don't be absurd. And as for moving into Trethorne, you can forget it. I like it at The Rectory – I've spent thousands renovating it for fuck's sake. Why would I want to move out?'

'Well stay then,' she replied, calmly, whilst a sea of anxiety roiled within. 'But I thought you'd love to "lord it up" at Trethorne. Isn't it always what you've wanted? To be lord and master of all you survey? You can stay at The Rectory if you want to, but I'm moving to Trethorne and I'll ask the kids if they want to come with me. I want to be there to look after my dad and my inheritance. To me, it makes sense.'

Mark looked at his wife, perhaps properly for the first time in years. Something had changed. She had a new determination about her that he didn't like one bit. She was getting above her station. 'Have you asked the kids what they want to do? I think you'll find that they'd rather stay with me at The Rectory, if they had to choose.'

That hurt. 'Well, why do we have to make them choose? If we move as a family, they move with us or find a place of their own. Can't you see this is best all round Mark? It'll be a new chapter in our lives. Plenty of garden for the dogs;

you can impress your work colleagues by bringing them to the manor for meetings, you can even install Rachael in if you really must...' she trailed of, unsure as to why she was trying to persuade him to come with her. For some time now, she'd felt her marriage was over, and in all honesty, she'd rather have Trethorne to herself. Perhaps it was a last-ditch attempt to rekindle some of the affection they'd once shared, but she knew it was falling on deaf ears.

Her parting shot, was the one that floored him. 'By the way, I've spoken with Dad about your idea to develop the grounds and he's in agreement with me that we are absolutely not in favour of any housing development within the estate. We're both adamant about that.' George had taken some persuading, but her insistence that Eleanor would be appalled had finally swung it.

'You fucking interfering bitch!' he hissed, raising his hand as if to hit her. 'Been whispering in his ear, have you? Been poisoning him against me?'

'Actually, no. It's just that, like me, Dad respects the heritage of the place, and wants to keep it as it is.'

'Well that's a turn up for the books because when I last spoke to him about it, he was all for the idea.'

'Well he's not now, Mark. He's grieving, can't you see? He wasn't thinking straight. And I'm grieving too. My mother loved Trethorne with all her heart and it would have devastated Eleanor to know that you would willingly destroy our family's ancestral home just to make money. It's so vulgar.' She knew this would be like a slap in the face for him, the council estate kid being called vulgar. He'd been so careful to hide what he considered to be his lowly roots, but now they were being laid bare.

'How *dare* you call me vulgar. You bitch.'

But Jenny was on a roll. She knew what would hurt him and this was a fight. 'You know Mark, Cynthia once told me that I should hang on to my business and my independence at all costs. I now know why your mother said that: because you're like a parasite. You get your teeth into someone's life, their business, their inheritance and you won't let go. Well, let me tell you this, you won't bleed me dry. I am not going to just lay down and take this. I am going to fight for Trethorne and Jess's right to live in it unadulterated. You can either work with me or against me.'

Mark looked like he would literally blow his top. His face was puce with rage and his fingers ached to throttle her. And whilst Jenny wanted to collapse, her heart racing in her throat and her eyes pricking with tears, she would not give him the satisfaction. She turned her back on him and walked downstairs. It dawned on her that he'd probably smashed her bottle of perfume like he'd done once before.

Jenny still returned to The Rectory in the evenings after her day working on the Trethorne renovations, but unfortunately there was no sign of a thaw in relations between her and Mark. He was distracted, haunted almost, like a wounded animal. She knew better than to ask why, as she'd just be rounded upon, chastised for her audacity to make a decision for herself. He had stopped confiding in her long ago, and had now stopped speaking to her altogether – all bar the necessities in life, that is: *where's my grey shirt* or *have you put the bins out*? The intensity of their early years had faded. Now they led separate lives, in separate bedrooms, and it was looking like it was soon to be separate houses. Mark had made no further mention of her plans for Trethorne. He was uncommunicative, monosyllabic when pushed, and to Jenny, it seemed divorce was inevitable. That made her sad but her sadness was tinged with relief that she would no longer have to second-guess him all the time.

As soon as George's apartment was ready, he moved in and proudly asked Jenny round for a cup of coffee. 'Look at this,' he exclaimed with pride. 'Boiling water out of the tap, but instantly ice cold if I need it. What a miracle.' Jenny laughed. He'd forgotten that she'd installed these gadgets especially for him, to make life easier. 'When are you lot moving in then?'

'Oh Dad, I don't know. Mark's not keen on the idea, and I don't want the kids to have to choose between The Rectory and Trethorne. Maybe I'll just keep some rooms here for my business and stay at The Rectory for now. It'd perhaps be easier all round.'

'Nonsense!' barked George. 'The whole idea of me moving in to this apartment was so that the family could have the manor. Leave it with me. I'll speak to Mark.'

'Oh, no Dad,' Jenny gasped. 'Please don't – it'll only make things worse. Mark's hardly speaking to me as it is.'

'Time to put that right then, my girl.' He stalked over to his phone and dialled Mark, then went into his study and shut the door on Jenny.

Three days later when Jenny got home from Trethorne, which was now looking fantastic after its refurbishment, she saw a 'For Sale' sign at the gate to The Rectory. *Dad has managed to move mountains, then,* Jenny thought. She went into the kitchen and switched the kettle on. Since she'd been working at Trethorne she'd gotten out of the habit of drinking her iced water, and her iced frappes from Mark were a thing of the past too. These days a cup of Earl Grey quenched her thirst. As she spooned the loose leaf into her favourite teapot, the Japanese one with the bamboo handle, she was aware of Mark coming into the kitchen.

'Selling up, are we?' she ventured.

'I've got no choice, have I?' he muttered. 'I can't have you *and* your bloody father breathing down my neck all the time about Tre-bloody-thorne. If it was down to me, I'd turn the place into flats, build a complex of apartments in the walled gardens, sell the whole damn thing and make a fortune and go and live in the south of France. Somewhere the sun actually shines from time to time.'

'Well, fortunately, it's not up to you Mark, but I'm glad you've decided to come with us rather than split the family apart. Was it something my Dad said?'

Mark popped the lid off a bottle of lager and took a long swig. 'George just reminded me about the importance of families sticking together, that's all. He said he wanted me at Trethorne, and so I'm going. Now can we drop the subject please.'

Jenny didn't know whether to be pleased or concerned that this human maelstrom would be moving in to her ancestral home.

That night she woke in the dark, absolutely parched and felt around on her bedside table for her glass of water, but it was empty. She went downstairs to the kitchen and poured herself a glass from the filtered water jug and out of habit went to the freezer for some ice. When she took a sip, she smelt a familiar almondy smell and the water tasted bitter. She spat it out and made a mental note to ask Mark to change the filter, now that he was reluctantly speaking to her again. Those kinds of jobs were tricky for Jenny as her coordination was sometimes quite poor. She took a bottle of sparkling water from the fridge, but as she turned to go back up to bed, the hairs on the back of her neck stood on end. Out of the window towards the office she saw a dim light throwing shadows on the wall, as if made by a torch. It was 2am. Who on earth could be there at that time? First the tax man, now burglars – their business was being targeted from all quarters.

Jenny crept to unlock the back door and found it open. She walked as quietly as she could across the gravelled courtyard and pressed herself against the wall to the side of the window. Slowly, slowly, she slid her face across so just one eye could glimpse inside. There was a figure sat at a desk, faintly lit by the computer screen. As her eyes adjusted to the dim glow she realised it was Mark. *For god's sake!* She'd been all-but ready to rugby tackle an intruder, despite her frailty! She went to turn the office door handle and discovered it was locked. She rapped on the glass and Mark looked up at her, face pale and startled. 'Let me in,' she mouthed.

He clicked on the mouse and his screen went blank, then came over to the door. As he walked, she noticed the bottom of his silk dressing gown flapped open, revealing bare legs. A triangle of hairy chest showed at the collar. He was naked underneath the paisley robe.

'What are you doing? It's the middle of the night!' said Jenny.

'I could ask you the same question,' he replied.

'I just came down for a drink of water.'

'Let me guess, iced water, a Birdy special,' smirked Mark.

'Actually, no – the filtered water tastes disgusting. Can you put a new filter in tomorrow? So, what *are* you doing then?'

'I couldn't sleep so I came to check out some vintage car parts on Ebay.' This was his latest hobby – at the car rallies he'd got pally with the vintage crew and now had started collecting them himself. He had two old bangers in the garage already.

'Why's the door locked?'

'Oh, it's always good to be careful.'

'But you left the back door open, that's hardly careful – anyone could've come in!' said Jenny.

'There's far more important things in the office than the house,' he said and walked back to his desk.

Thanks! I'm obviously not important to you then, she thought. As Jenny returned to bed she couldn't quite fathom why he couldn't look at his laptop in his bedroom.

She mulled it over with Joy and Liz the next day over chai lattes. 'So, what do you reckon he was up to on his computer? It could be chat rooms or internet dating, I suppose. To be honest, I would understand if it was,' said Jenny.

'Why's that?' asked Joy.

'Because our love life ground to a halt years ago. He has his needs, I know that.'

'Ugh Jeeze, I hate it when men bang on about their "needs". Like their balls are going to explode if they aren't regularly emptied,' snorted Liz. The women laughed.

'That doesn't justify infidelity though,' said Joy. 'There's always self-celebration if you feel sexually pent up.'

'Self-celebration? Oh, you mean wanking! I've heard it all now, Joy,' said Liz. 'I love the way you put things, it cracks me up. Trouble with wanking is that it doesn't stroke your ego. Online dating, Tinder and the like do. I would think that's right up Mark's street. Physical excitement with no emotional attachment – typical male behaviour. I did see him in Bristol the other day, did I tell you? Maybe that was part of his naughty business?'

'Bristol?' said Jenny. 'He didn't say he was going there. Are you sure it wasn't Plymouth? I know he went there last Thursday.'

'Ugh no, definitely not Plymouth, you would never catch *me* going there. It's all concrete high-rise car parks and pound shops. No, it was Bristol. Broadmead.'

'I don't think it's fair to stereotype all men like that Liz,' Joy interjected. 'From what I can gather, Mark may be moody and secretive, but he's a good family man. None of us is perfect.'

'Oh, Joy! Wake up and smell the roses, won't you? He's cruel and manipulative and childish to boot,' Liz replied, rolling her eyes and huffing with indignation.

Jenny sat listening to her two friends take issue over her husband. He was such a complex man that after all these years, not one of them could work out his motivations.

The next day a large manila envelope arrived with a Bristol postmark. Jenny examined it and decided to ask Mark about where he'd been last week.

'Last Thursday?' He looked up, scanning his mental diary. 'That would be Bristol,' he replied.

'I thought that was when you went to Plymouth?' Jenny frowned.

'Nope, Bristol. Definitely Bristol. I remember the M5 was chocka.'

'Why did you say Plymouth then?'

'You're getting confused again, old girl. I told you I was going to Bristol, remember?'

'No,' said Jenny flatly. 'I must be mistaken. Well anyway, Liz saw you there, so what were you doing?'

'Liz *saw* me? What is this, some crappy detective show? Is she following me like a second-rate Miss Marple? She'd be disappointed. I was only going to see the solicitor.'

'What solicitor? Morgan & Morgan are based in Holsworthy, not Bristol.'

'Not those old fogies. THP Legal is cutting edge. They've got branches in London and Birmingham too.'

'But, we've always used Morgan & Morgan. Michael Morgan was my dad's best man,' said Jenny.

'Exactly! He's ancient. We need better advice than that dinosaur can give us. He's past it. He probably still thinks in pounds, shillings and pence. He's totally out of his depth with the audit.'

'Oh, right,' said Jenny. She felt sad about losing their old solicitor. He may be nearing retirement but she trusted him, she always had.

'Jamie at THP is looking into a new business model for us. Far more profitable. The accounts will be set up differently, but the tax man will be none the wiser and you'll have more personal cash as it won't be tied up in the business. See, I'm only thinking of you,' said Mark.

'But is it legal?' she asked. 'Anyway, how's the audit going? I thought it would be finished by now.'

'They're still investigating, but they've turned their beady eyes onto Rachael's personal accounts now. Turns out she's been fiddling the books for the Rugby Club and the Rotary Club – not declared certain investments and so on…'

Jenny just looked at him, gobsmacked. *Little Miss Perfect? Rachael, who never put a foot wrong, being investigated for fraud?* Jenny smelt a rat. A Mark-shaped rat. Rachael must have done something really bad for her to suddenly end up in the shit, but what?

Mark carried on, oblivious to Jenny's shock. 'This means she can't operate as an accountant for us. I've demoted her to company secretary. Lucky the golden boy can come on board eh?'

Their son Marcus had just graduated with a degree in business studies and was due to join the family firm. The timing seemed too good to be true. Perhaps Mark had engineered Rachael's downfall so that Marcus could take over her role and 'keep it in the family', thereby avoiding having to pay Rachael any severance pay?

As Jessica was also coming home after volunteering in Kenya for three months, Jenny decided to throw a party to celebrate one of the few positives in her life: her children. It would also be a perfect opportunity to show off her work at Trethorne. The drawing room was perfect for entertaining.

On the afternoon of the party Jenny stood back and tilted her head to one side to admire her hard work. Floor-length linen curtains emphasised the perfect proportions of the room and complemented the dark wooden floorboards. Large vases of lilies flanked the fireplace, filling the air with intoxicating scent. She may be falling apart but she'd still got it. *A little like Trethorne*, she thought archly.

She could hear Marcus and Jessica good-naturedly joshing as they came into the room. They'd met at Exeter train station and Mark had picked them up and driven them straight to Trethorne. 'I think you'll find that the return of the prodigal daughter beats a crappy old degree any day,' said Jessica, 'so I'm the guest of honour.'

'Not when it's a First-Class Honours, it doesn't,' replied Marcus, nudging his sister.

'First, schmirst. I only got a third and I've done all right for myself,' said Mark, coming in behind them.

Jenny saw Marcus' shoulders sag as they always did. Mark never failed to find a way to deflate his son. 'You sound like Alan Sugar, Mark,' said Jenny lightly, making Marcus smile.

'Mum, it looks gorgeous in here, like an interiors magazine, *Elle Deco* or something!' exclaimed Jessica.

'Thanks, darling.' Marcus and Jessica drifted off to pick at the buffet. 'Kids! Leave it!' called Jenny. They may be in their 20s but old habits die hard.

'Not bad when it's scrubbed up,' commented Mark. 'This could be my snug when we move in.'

'Move in?' said Marcus and Jessica in unison.

'Yep, our house is on the market. I'm keeping the office for the business,' replied Mark, pouring himself a large scotch, 'but we're all moving in here.'

'When were you planning on telling us?' asked Jess.

'We've only just decided ourselves that this is the right thing to do,' interjected Jenny, taking a swig of her iced water. She didn't show her trepidation at Mark's decision to join her at Trethorne and she certainly didn't want her kids to know that she was covertly keeping tabs on both her father and her husband in case they tried to do anything dodgy with her ancestral home. Then the familiar smell of almonds assailed her senses. 'Here, Jess, take a sip of this water would you. It tastes funny to me.'

'No, no,' Mark snapped, swiping the water from Jenny's hand. 'Leave it Jess. It's my fault – I forgot to change the filter. I'll do it now.'

'We've made an apartment for Granddad in the library. Come and see before everyone gets here,' said Jenny, taking her daughter's hand, not twigging that the water filter problem was at The Rectory, not at Trethorne.

'Which one's my room, Mum?' asked Jess, easily swayed by a bit of glamour.

Just the thought of packing up all their possessions from over 25 years of marriage was exhausting but Jenny had to make a start. Jess had offered to help, but it seemed that today she simply had to go into town to meet her bestie, Charlie. As Jenny was labelling a cardboard box in the old house, ready for the removal men, she smelt a familiar aroma. Before she could identify it, black dots crowded her vision. *Oh no, not again*, she had time to think before the world went black. It was another seizure.

This time, the doctors spent far less time deliberating over the cause. The consultant took one look at her history and immediately decided it was psychosomatic again. 'Stressful time recently? Feeling overloaded?' she said, her sympathy thinly disguising impatience.

'Well, we have to move house,' Jenny answered blurrily, 'but I thought I was on top of everything.'

'Ah, one of the most stressful life events, after the death of a spouse and divorce,' said the consultant, looking at her watch. 'You've got to take it easy, Jennifer. You've got to look after yourself.'

'But, I've been feeling so well recently,' Jenny persisted.

'The seizures are signs that you're still doing too much; pushing yourself beyond your physical capabilities,' the consultant replied. 'I want you to bear in mind that your MS is an underlying health issue that limits what you can do. Don't forget that.'

I'm never likely to, said Jenny to herself as she got up to leave. She was utterly devastated that her health had stopped her in her tracks once again, just as she was really getting her life on track.

'You've got to take it easy and look after yourself,' said Mark, when she returned home after just a few hours in hospital. Luckily her symptoms were much less severe this time.

'Have you been talking to the consultant?' answered Jenny. 'That's exactly what she said.'

'It's common sense. You run yourself ragged then collapse. It's like a dot-to-dot puzzle. You're your own worst enemy,' he said, leaving the room, taking his laptop with him.

At the next MS Support Group in Bideford, Joy made a bee-line for Jenny, giving her a big hug.

'How are you darling? How are things in the new place?' she asked.

'Oh, you know, we're like strangers living in the same house,' Jenny replied.

'How do you feel about that? It might be the natural ebb and flow of a relationship but if it saddens you then maybe you should consider going to Relate?'

'Oh god, I can just imagine Mark's reaction if I suggested that,' laughed Jenny.

And sure enough, when she broached the subject, he was appalled. 'I'm not talking to a random about my marriage.'

'But they're not going to judge, they'll just listen and feed back to us so we can reflect on our relationship and improve things. Oh please, Mark.'

'Not a chance,' he said with a finality Jenny recognised. But then a few days later he came into the kitchen and said: 'Go on then, I'll give the head-shrinker a go. I suppose it will benefit all the other relationships around me. And I can learn from our mistakes.'

'What do you mean by that? What other relationships?' asked Jenny, confused.

'Friends, colleagues, contacts, you know.'

This didn't sit right with Jenny. Why the U-turn? And he sounded so arrogant, his ego was even more inflated than usual. Where was he getting this grandiose attitude from?

At the Relate session, the counsellor clasped her hands and leant towards them. 'So, what brought you here?'

Jenny started to sum up their situation when Mark suddenly let out a sob. 'I feel like she's leaving me,' he said. 'First the MS, then the seizures and now she's so distant and chilly. I'm going to be all alone,' he sniffed.

'Is that how you feel, Jenny? Do you feel distant towards him?'

'Er, well… I have been very busy recently…' Jenny was thrown. She had a strong feeling of déjà vu, and couldn't place it for a moment, but then it dawned on her: Mark's reaction was the same as when she was diagnosed with MS. And then Liz's words came back to her: *crocodile tears…*

'And she's stopped wearing my perfume. She's constantly rejecting me and everything I try to do for her,' he continued.

Jenny was amazed. *What's going on here? Am I rejecting him…?* She had to admit that changing her perfume was an act of defiance, but to think that he saw it as rejection… She started to question her motives. 'Look Mark, I didn't know it was so important to you. I just fancied a change, that's all. I'll start wearing it again if that's what you want.'

Mark nodded and for a moment she saw a glimpse of him as a little boy, sad and abandoned. Then she remembered a more recent Mark and rallied herself.

'It's hard to be affectionate when Mark spends all his time on his laptop. It feels like the third party in our relationship. A virtual betrayal.'

The counsellor nodded. 'Mark may be using his computer as a way of distracting himself from his fears of the future if your disability worsens. Are you expecting to rely on him more if that happens?'

'Oh no, I'm sure I'll manage,' Jenny answered quickly. Somehow the session had become skewed towards Mark, and his needs. She didn't know how he'd done it.

The counsellor lent her a book called *After the Affair*. 'I'm not suggesting Mark has been unfaithful, but it has some useful strategies to rebuild trust after it has been jeopardised.'

When they walked out of the session, Mark gave her a hug and kiss. 'I do love you, Birdy. I want to get our marriage back on track, really, I do. I promise you, I'm not seeing anyone else, and if you want me to, I'll stop the late-night gaming sessions on the laptop. Let's go on holiday shall we, go all-inclusive, get some winter sun.'

'But we've only just moved house. There's so much to do.'

'Why do you always push me away, Jen? I suggest something nice, and you shove it back in my face. I don't think you're committed to this Relate business at all.'

Jenny felt a brief burst of optimism. Perhaps a holiday would give them the chance to reconnect; putting all the negativity to one side, as Joy would say.

'Sorry. Okay, Mark – let's do it. Maybe we could even share a bedroom?'

He looked at her, one eyebrow raised, but didn't say anything.

When she saw the online booking for the holiday, she realised he'd taken her at her word: a master suite with one Emperor bed. *Christ! I'll have to shave my legs and nether regions*, she thought, having let them go *au naturel* of late.

But she needn't have bothered. Mark's burst of affection after the counselling session was short-lived. He spent the holiday propped up at the bar, drinking heavily.

'Mark, can we talk?' asked Jenny one morning before he'd got a chance to get stuck into the G&Ts.

'I've done enough talking to last me a lifetime, Jen' he replied, popping two paracetamol out of the packet.

Not with me, Jenny thought. She supposed he was using this break as a chance to totally unwind after all the stress of the audit, and, it has to be said, her decision to move to Trethorne. It had been very stressful recently – what was that quote about death and taxes? That pretty much summed up their year.

At least the holiday gave Jenny a chance to read the counsellor's book. It was eye-opening, especially the chapter entitled: 'Internet dating'. It was practically a tick-list of Mark's behaviour. *Secretive, change in habits, protective of phone and computer.* But then there were a few red flags that didn't fit too, such as Mark's new Ralph Lauren shirt and Tag Heuer watch. Was he simply enjoying his 'Lord of the Manor' look or was there another woman in real life too?

When they landed back in England, it felt strange to go straight to Trethorne rather than their old house, but she was glad to be home and back in her own bed, no longer fearful of what mood Mark would be in after a night of drinking and brooding.

Jenny decided to consult Google as the book had made her think. Never mind *After the Affair*, what about during it? 'How husbands cover up affairs,' she typed. Hundreds of pages popped up, all repeating the same thing. *Does he take long walks?* Yes – with Ralph and Hugo, the two labs. *Does he regularly go away?* Yes, at those car rallies, supposedly, but they were often with her father too, so that allayed her concerns somewhat. *Has his appearance changed?* Yes, he was dressing far more carefully and he'd bought a halogen air-fryer, saying, 'I'll be a lean, mean sex machine.' She'd wondered at the time why he'd said that – their sex life was about as healthy as a deep-fat fryer.

'Mark, are you having an affair?' she asked him, fed up of googling.

'Oh, for fuck's sake! I told you before. You're just paranoid, delusional. That book has put ideas into your head.'

Jenny listed the evidence and Mark smiled. 'There's a simple explanation for all your concerns; it's just your vivid imagination. I like to keep myself in good shape, I like to go out and enjoy life with the lads, I love my dogs. What's wrong with that? It's a shame you don't have more hobbies, or more friends other than those two nosey lesbians you hang out with.'

She chose to ignore his jibe about her friends. 'It's just that I could understand it if you were. I know we've drifted apart, we don't have sex any more…'

Mark chuckled and she felt embarrassed, but plunged on.

'I don't mind if you want a divorce – we could split everything 50/50, except Trethorne, of course.'

Mark's laughter increased. '50/50! You're joking, aren't you? Get real Birdy. You're not getting your mitts on my money. I'm the one who's worked my bollocks off all these years, whilst you've just lain in your bed feeling sorry for yourself.'

'But, in law, we're equal partners,' she stumbled on.

'There are ways and means, my dear. There are ways and means,' he said. 'Oh, little Birdy, last to cotton on, as always.'

Jenny felt foolish. Maybe she needed to go and see Michael Morgan and get some legal advice about her situation. Maybe he had stitched her up like a kipper.

The next morning Jenny was browsing the bookshelf, marvelling at how Mark had organised the books alphabetically when he came in with a glass of orange juice tinkling with heart-shaped ice.

'See? Would a cheating swine do this?' he said, handing it to her. 'And I've got a new sim card for your phone. I've updated your mobile data so you don't have to worry about how long you're online. Give it here and I'll replace it for you. You know you're hopeless at that.' He grabbed her phone and immediately started tapping away on the screen.

'Hey, that's my phone… I don't want anything changed.'

'Why not? What are you hiding? And there's me being accused of having affairs.'

'Oh, don't be daft Mark. I haven't got the energy for subterfuge. What are you doing here, anyway? I thought you'd gone to the office,' replied Jenny. She was utterly confused by him blowing hot and cold; declaring his love for her and helping with her phone, and yet inferring that he'd secreted money away in case of divorce. He was such an enigma this man; there were so many layers to him.

'Oh, I had a couple of bits to do here,' he answered.

Just then, the doorbell rang and Jenny went to answer it, to find two smiling people on the doorstep.

'Jenny Damerell? We're from the local AMHS – the adult mental health service. You should have had a letter about our appointment,' the man said.

Jenny's heart sank. What was all this about? She hadn't had a letter, but then maybe it had been delivered to the old house. 'Oh… okay, you'd better come in.' She ushered them into her office to find Mark ensconced in one of the chairs.

'I'm Hannah and this is Jason.'

'Er, hi,' replied Jenny as they shook hands. 'This is my husband Mark. Cup of tea? Or maybe an iced water?'

'Tea. I'll make them tea,' said Mark.

'What's this about?' asked Jenny as he left the room.

'We're concerned about your welfare, Mrs Damerell' said Hannah in a singsong voice.

'I'm fine thanks, just a bit tired and nauseous, but what else is new?' Jenny said, looking from one to the other of them.

'I see. It's just that it's been flagged up by several service providers that you need a little bit more support, emotionally. You've had a lot to cope with recently.'

'I can assure you that I feel fine,' replied Jenny, but her intuition was telling her something was up. 'The death of my mother was traumatic but it gave me clarity about other things in my life in a positive way. I'm actually better than I've been in ages.'

'I see,' Hannah repeated, but it was as if Jenny hadn't said anything. 'Ummm, there are a few things we'd like to discuss with you. For example, we're given to understand that you feel your perfume is poisoning you.'

'My perfume? Where did you get that from? I changed it, but not because I think it's poisoning me. I'm not psychotic or anything!' said Jenny instantly regretting saying that.

'Well, it's best to let the professionals decide,' said Jason smoothly as Mark came back in with a tea tray. 'Would you be willing to see a psychiatrist?'

'…?'

'Birdy, we're all just concerned about you,' Mark said, head tilted to one side. 'Jessica, Marcus, your father, everyone. We're all concerned. You've not been yourself lately, since your last seizure especially…'

'But, I'm fine. Honestly I am. Mark, what have you been telling people?'

'I just mentioned to the consultant at the hospital about your propensity to accuse me of things: I'm having an affair; I'm trying to split the family up; I'm poisoning you with Chanel No. 5, I'm a parasite trying to bleed you dry… Need I go on? The counsellor suggested I could seek help from AMHS and that's what I've done. I can't go on with you twisting everything I do with your paranoia.'

'But Jess, Marcus… why are they worried?'

'Mrs Damerell,' interjected Jason. 'This is not about apportioning blame. It's about working with you to ascertain your levels of anxiety and to try and help control them. It may be that you need some medication that can help you manage your condition.'

'Manage my condition…? What condition? This is crazy…'

'We think there are grounds for concern here, Mrs Damerell, and so do your family. Now will you consent to seeing a psychiatrist?'

'I don't need to see a psychiatrist! I'm telling you, there's nothing wrong with me.'

'Well, that may mean we have to go down the legal route.'

'You mean *section* me? Oh my god… Mark?' But Mark remained silent, refusing to look at her. 'Okay, okay I'll see the psychiatrist, but only to get you out of my house' replied Jenny more aggressively than she intended.

He really had – he'd stitched her up like a kipper, but just not in the way she anticipated. The bastard, twisting everything she said so that he was some kind of victim. So, this was what he had in store for her – she knew he was plotting something.

She felt utterly manipulated and betrayed. A wave of nausea washed over her and she took a swig of her juice. Her whole family, her closest loved ones had been discussing her behind her back and coming to all sorts of conclusions. She resolved to speak to Liz, as she was always straight with her. Just as she picked up her mobile phone, it rang, and Jessica's name flashed up on the screen.

'Hi Mum, how did the appointment go? Hannah's just rung – you're booked to see a Dr Trewin at 3 o'clock next Friday at the Hatton Unit. She's asked if I can accompany you and ensure you get there on time.'

'Has she now?' said Jenny. She was tempted to give Jessica a piece of her mind but something told her that this would work against her. 'Don't worry. I'll be there,' she said briskly and hung up. She was shaking all over as she finally managed to get through to Liz and unloaded the whole sorry tale.

'Wow, it hasn't taken Mark long to twist your daughter around his little finger. Jessica's only been home a few weeks!' her best friend exclaimed.

'What do you mean?' asked Jenny.

'He's working her,' said Liz. 'Like he does everyone. He's even tried it on me, you know. Smarming up to me, trying to get me to say things about you that he can use against you.'

'Really? Christ,' replied Jenny. 'They'll have me locked up before long.'

'Not if you stay strong and focussed, babe,' replied Liz, firmly. 'Think about it, didn't Mark have a cosy chat with the consultant after your second seizure? And maybe with the counsellor too. He's gone and planted lots of false information in their minds. Your kids aren't against you darling, they're just being manipulated by that bastard.'

'But why would he do that?'

'That, my darling Jen, is the million-dollar question,' Liz replied. 'Be strong. Don't let them bamboozle you. Are you still keeping a diary? That will help keep the facts straight.' When Jenny hung up, she heard a faint click on the line. *Shit*, she thought. *Always use my mobile, not the house phone – in case he's bugged it...* Then she felt stupid for even having that thought.

When Marcus popped in, she asked him if he knew what the clicking could be. He had a quick listen, smiled meekly and said: 'I can't hear anything, Mum.'

It felt surreal to go to the next Relate session whilst her family obviously doubted her mental health, but Jenny reasoned that at least it was a neutral space to discuss things. This time, there were no histrionics from Mark. He remained completely silent, apart from one sentence: 'I won't leave Jenny because of her MS.'

Jenny felt that somehow this was a veiled threat, not a declaration of support. What was happening to her? She was distrustful of everyone and now felt she couldn't open up in front of Mark in case he wilfully misconstrued anything she said. The counsellor suggested that their next sessions could be on a one-to-one basis.

'I have nothing more to say,' said Mark.

And then it struck Jenny. He'd only agreed to come to Relate so that it would look like he'd done everything in his power to save the marriage, but he had no intention of committing to the process at all.

'Well I'd like to, thank you,' said Jenny gratefully.

When they got home, Jenny ran herself a bath and went to bed, even though it was still light outside. She had a pounding headache and just wanted to switch off. Mark took himself off to his snug. She saw him settle into his favourite armchair with a bottle of whisky.

Jenny woke later and felt hungry, so she ventured downstairs for something to eat. She saw that the light was still on in Mark's snug.

'Birdy, is that you?' he called.

She stuck her head round the door. 'What do you want?'

'Come in would you. I've got something to tell you.' said Mark.

'Is this why you've been drinking? For Dutch courage?'

'It's about Dad. He's given me approval for my development ideas here at Trethorne. Eventually, the manor is going to be split up into luxury flats – we might even keep one – but first, we're going to develop a small estate in the walled garden.'

'What? You can't! Trethorne's in my name! The covenant…' said Jenny.

'Only applies if the owner is of sound mind…' answered Mark.

The penny dropped. So, this was what it was all about. This was why he'd been to see a new out of town solicitor; this was why he'd tried to get her sectioned; this was why he'd decided to move in – so he could work on George and make a killing by selling out on his own family, his own wife and his children's inheritance. Finally, she saw the light.

'You utter bastard! Get out! You evil fucking bastard!' Jenny grabbed him by his shirt collar, which ripped. 'Get out of my house!' she screamed, 'and leave your keys as you go. Take yourself to the fucking Torridge Bridge and fling yourself off – save me the paperwork!'

'Birdy, calm down. It's for the best. We'll be rich. You'll never want for anything in your life again.' Mark gripped her by the top of her arms so she couldn't move.

'Get off me, you LOUSE. I was right, you are a parasite. I'll see you in court, you evil, calculating bastard! Go back to the council flat you crawled out of!'

She wrenched herself out of his grasp, surprising herself with her strength, and ran out into the garden. She lifted her head to the sky and screamed. It was a scream of desperation, despair and utter sorrow.

CHAPTER 6

Slates Blown From Roofs

Force 9 on the Beaufort Scale

When Jenny finally came in from the garden, eyes stinging and throat sore from her torrent of grief, the house was quiet. Strangely quiet. She didn't need to look around to know that Mark had gone, and taken the dogs too – where to, she couldn't care less. Her father was still at his bridge club and Marcus and Jess were at a festival in Cornwall, so she was alone.

She blew her nose and put the kettle on. As it was boiling she noticed Mark's house keys on the table. He hadn't put up a fight then? *I wonder why not?* He'd just accepted it and left, but she knew it was all part of his scheming. She checked in his bedroom and sure enough, his overnight bag was missing, and even his shaving gear from the en-suite had gone. *He had no intention of living here… He's got somewhere to stay lined-up already,* she realised.

Despite the late hour, she dialled Liz, knowing that she would bring her usual blend of common sense and indignation to the table.

'You're the sanest person I know,' Liz said. 'I'll come over first thing in the morning and I'll bring Joy.'

It was so comforting to see her two best friends the following day. Her only friends, in reality. They always knew what to say to make her feel better.

'Well, I say this can only be a good thing, Jenny,' said Liz. 'Ever since I first met him all those years ago at your birthday party I've never been sure about Mark. And what you've put up with. He's been abominable. It's brilliant that you've finally chucked him out, that is definitely the action of a woman with all her marbles.'

'But how are you feeling about it? That's what's important,' asked Joy.

Jenny looked at Joy and took a sip of her coffee before replying. 'I'm raging, Joy. I can't believe that the two men in my life who are supposed to love me have sold me out like this, and turned my kids against me.' She began to sob. 'But the good thing is, that when Mark was being kind, you know, taking me on holiday and going to Relate, I started to question myself, thinking that maybe I *was* just paranoid; that maybe the MS *was* messing with my brain. At least now I know he really is a conniving bastard.'

'You're still in shock, probably. You're such a sweet, compassionate soul and it must have been so hard to stand up to him – that's bound to shake you up,' replied Joy.

'That's true. One thing that's keeping me buoyed up during all this is that his little plan didn't quite work.' Jenny looked at her friends, eyes glistening from her tears. 'I've done some research online and the fact that I volunteered to see the psychiatrist, and wasn't sectioned is very much in my favour. I know I'm not insane and by going to see the psychiatrist, I will have that confirmed, I'm sure – especially when I explain the reasons why he's tried to certify me.'

'So, then he can't sell off Trethorne?' asked Liz.

'No. I need to tie-up that loophole very quickly, and I'm going to see my solicitor to look at how I can secure my inheritance properly, once and for all. Mark tried very hard to bring me down, but he didn't quite make it. And there's another piece of good news. I have cancelled the Relate sessions.' They all laughed.

It felt good to finally admit her marriage was over and that she no longer had to try and understand Mark's behaviour, his moods and secrets. Maybe this would be the beginning of a new chapter in her life? One in which she was the lead character, not just the victim.

After they'd gone, Jenny dried her eyes and rang her solicitor, Michael Morgan.

'Ah, Jenny, nice to hear from you. I'm glad the whole family hasn't abandoned us. I've been trying to ring you on the number Mark gave me, but I just get unobtainable. How can I help you?'

Surprise, surprise, she thought. *The new sim card Mark put in must've had more functionality than just updating my mobile data allowance – the bastard! I'll get a new phone, today.*

'Can I come in and see you? I need to discuss something very urgently.'

The solicitor squeezed her in that afternoon and she explained the whole sorry situation to him. 'So, you see, Mark is trying to get Trethorne on the grounds of my mental incapacity but he can't, can he? Not if I can prove my sanity with the psychiatrist.'

'But, Jenny my dear, you've already given him Power of Attorney,' said Michael, looking over the top of his glasses at her.

'I certainly have not!' replied Jenny.

'That was what I was wanting to discuss with you. It seemed so at odds with your previous wishes. Wait a moment… ah, yes, here it is.' Michael showed her a document.

'That's my signature!' said Jenny. 'But I didn't sign it, I promise I didn't! He must have forged it…'

'That's quite a grave accusation, Jennifer. I believe you were unwell at the time? In hospital? Perhaps you just don't remember signing it. See here, it's been witnessed by one of the doctors.'

'Oh my god… who else is in on it?' said Jenny. All those cosy chats with the doctor that Mark had now made sense.

'In on what, my dear?'

'Oh, never mind,' said Jenny. 'I need to get that Power of Attorney overturned at once.'

'Revoked? Certainly. You just need a Deed of Revocation form, it's relatively straightforward.'

'Is it? Thank god…'

'Jenny, if there's anything else I can do to help, don't hesitate to come to me. I may be old, and not quite up to Mark's standards, but I have years of experience, and I'm on your side. Remember that.' He got up and shook Jenny's hand with real warmth and she felt a surge of relief. Someone believed in her. 'Once we've got the Deed of Revocation in place, we'll look at other ways of keeping Trethorne safe,' he said as she opened the door to leave. 'I love that old place. It would be a travesty to desecrate it.'

As Jenny returned to Trethorne in the taxi she felt like she was on a fire-fighting mission. There had been metaphorical smoke rising for months but she'd been only vaguely aware of it. Now the fire was finally ablaze, she had no choice but to tackle it head on.

The next item on her list was a visit to Women's Aid. Joy had suggested it and Jenny didn't quite understand why, but when she spoke to them, it was as if the clouds of confusion and self-doubt began to clear, revealing a clear blue sky of insight. Marie, the Women's Aid worker not only understood what Jenny was describing, but she believed her. Jenny was so used to being dismissed, patronised and undermined that this felt incredible.

Marie said that Mark's behaviour all pointed to one thing: domestic abuse. Jenny couldn't take it in. She had never thought that term applied to her. In her head, domestic abuse meant battered wives in council flats with black eyes and broken windows. It meant runny-nosed kids and families on benefits. Now she realised how elitist her attitude was. She, Jennifer Damerell, was a woman suffering from domestic abuse. Mark didn't hit her, he never had. But when she looked at the evidence, she couldn't deny it: one of the key behaviour traits of an abuser is being controlling, and that summed up Mark completely. Ever since she had known him, he controlled their finances, their business affairs, even their sex life. And once the penny dropped, she began to think of more and more examples of his controlling behaviour – even the iced drinks were to get her to do something he thought was right: eight glasses a day, for god's sake! He ticked every box in the domestic abuse checklist. A total dominator in every sense.

Hindsight is a wonderful thing, she thought. Right back when she first met him he was up to the same tricks. *That can of spilt paint we cleared up together, I bet he did it deliberately.* And her poor old cat Smudge – he went missing but was it really Mark who was to blame? *I wouldn't put it past him.* In the cold light of day, it felt like she had never really known him, just the image he projected. Every element of her life was tainted by Mark's malicious manipulation. *Even the fucking disability car,* she raged to herself. *I bet he was tampering with it…* Frustratingly, even though she was now free of Mark, the seizures meant that she wasn't allowed to drive for a year.

'Men like your husband exert what we call 'coercive control' over their loved ones. They bully and intimidate their family into doing what they want or what they think is right. It's perhaps helpful to consider that your husband may himself be the victim of domestic abuse, and coercive control may be his own coping mechanism, although that of course does not excuse his behaviour.'

As Jenny returned home on the bus, she thought back to all the times she'd tried to understand Mark's behaviour and his family background, and how he'd shut her out. She'd even considered that he may be the victim of abuse, but right now, she wasn't so interested in what made Mark tick, she was focused on survival. Mark could hang for all she cared.

Back home, in the kitchen making herself lunch, she heard the front door slam and jumped out of her skin. Had Mark come back? What was he going to do? She felt a wave of fear. She peered into the hall, and saw her father disappear into his apartment. She decided to bite the bullet and confront him.

She knocked on his door, and a rather quavery voice answered for her to come in. She felt a spark of compassion, but reminded herself that this man, her father, had betrayed her too. Now was the time for straight-talking.

'Hello, Dad. How are you?'

'Fair to middling. And before you start giving me a lecture Jennifer, I just want to say that Mark's only been thinking about what's best for all of us. Trethorne's so big and so expensive to run. And it's Grade II listed you know, so it's not going to be easy to adapt to your disability. Mark's only thinking of you.'

'Where have I heard that before?' she retorted. 'Don't you dare use my disability as an excuse for what you have done. You always blame me for everything.'

'Mind your lip, young lady. Mark can decide what's best for this family. I think that Women's Aid has given you ideas above your station. Damn bunch of lesbians – you'll be having a crew-cut and wearing polo-shirts next.'

'Dad, don't give me that, it's so bigotted. We are in the 21st century now. I am in my 40s and perfectly capable of making my own decisions. And talking of decisions, this house is *mine* – it is not yours or his. It's mine. It was my mother's, and my grandmother's and one day it will be Jessica's.'

'Calm down, Jennifer, you're working yourself up over nothing,' George answered. 'The decision is final.'

'Well, that is where you are wrong, Dad. The decision has been revoked.' She said this with her fingers firmly crossed, knowing that she had yet to see the psychiatrist and finalise the legal issues, but she knew that even if Mark challenged her in court, she was in a strong position to contest him.

'What do you mean, revoked?' He swung around to face her, worry etched on his face.

'Has he promised you a small fortune, Dad? Were you planning on living *La Dolce Vita* with your ex-Army cronies somewhere hot and sunny? Well you can forget that, because it's not happening. Do you hear me? Oh, and whilst we're on the subject, I want you out of my house. I'm giving you a month's notice to quit, and don't think I won't force you out if I have to. You betrayed me Dad, and you betrayed Mum.'

George looked utterly crest-fallen. 'I thought it was the right thing to do, Jennifer. Mark said the house was a money pit, and that the sale of it would set us all up for life. Mark can be very persuasive you know… He…'

'Didn't you think to discuss it with me? Do I not have any rights in this? I am not a mere plaything for you men to control at your whim,' she sobbed. 'One month, Dad. I mean it.'

She left his apartment, so sad that it had come to this – that she was evicting her own flesh and blood from her home. But what could she do? George was a snake in the grass, and whilst she was thinking in metaphors, she realised that the scales were falling off her own eyes and that she was starting to see things clearly, perhaps for the first time in her entire life.

She sat on the lichen-covered bench overlooking the sea and breathed slowly, letting her heart rate return to normal. The wind ruffled her hair and cooled her skin. She felt the familiar shame and self-doubt begin to creep in. She shouldn't have shouted at her father like that. But then he shouldn't have belittled her. She was sickened to realise that her father was just like Mark – dominating and selfish. So that was why she had fallen under Mark's spell so easily, gravitating towards him like a moth to a flame: she'd had years of training. A whole life's worth.

But George's cutting remarks about Women's Aid kept going around in her head. She remembered a conversation with her children about why she needed to go to Women's Aid only the week before, with Jessica saying, "You're not a battered wife, Mum. Dad's never hit you, so why do you need to go there?" and Marcus adding, "And where's Men's

Aid for Dad? All he's ever done is provide for us…" Jenny felt frustrated that even her children couldn't see the depths of abuse she'd been subjected to, but she knew this was because they were still being manipulated by their father and grandfather.

The following Friday's appointment with the psychiatrist was relatively straightforward. She left Jessica in the waiting room, and determined to do whatever it took to prove that she was of sound mind. He asked her a lot of questions about her health and her current family situation and listened to her answers without comment, making notes. She was careful not to blame anyone, just explaining things from her perspective. When it came to Mark, she mentioned what he was proposing to do, and why she felt it was wrong. She didn't get angry or bad-mouth Mark, but presented it as a fundamental difference of opinion. He asked her to do some cognitive tests – even whether she knew who the Prime Minister was – and then explained why the health professionals were worried about her. She'd dressed in her most expensive trouser suit, tried to answer clearly and concisely, smiled constantly, looked him in the eye, and used the longest, most appropriate words she could think of. At the end of the process, she couldn't tell whether he thought she was mad or not, but he said he'd send a report to her GP within the next three weeks. It was another thing ticked off her 'To Do' list, at least.

At her next appointment with Marie from Women's Aid, she began the Freedom Programme – a course to help women break free from domestic abuse. During the session, Jenny continued to have her eyes opened to what she'd been living through for years. One valuable lesson was about 'gaslighting'. It was a term she'd never heard of before but when she learnt what it was, it was a massive revelation. 'Gaslighting is a form of manipulation that makes the victim doubt their own memory, perception and sanity,' explained Marie. Bingo! Mark had even managed to get inside her head and control her thoughts. She had genuinely believed that her confusion and bad memory was due to the MS, but now she could see it was Mark manipulating her. Even small details like saying he was in Plymouth when he was in Bristol. Why lie, if not to confuse her? It was yet another way to make her feel like a fuzzy-headed idiot, to grind her down, reduce her to nothing. He was a cruel, sadistic, calculating bastard.

'But why is it called 'gaslighting'?' asked Jenny.

'It comes from a stage play, believe it or not,' said Marie. 'In the play, the husband would systematically turn down the gas lights, but when the wife questioned it, he would say the lights were as bright as normal and that she was imagining it. In the end, she began to doubt her own sanity. It's often the way that fiction can shine a light on fact.'

That night Jenny couldn't sleep. She spent most of the night searching for a cool spot on the pillow. When finally she drifted off, she jolted awake again after an hour, in a hot sweat. She thought she'd heard a door closing.

'Mark…?' she called.

Nothing. She sat up in bed, switched on the light and took a sip of water, trying to moisten her dry mouth. *What has my life become? I've been manipulated and controlled for decades. Mark, my father, even Paul in his cool, passive-aggressive way. My kids think I'm mentally unstable, I don't know if I can rely on my friends… How has it come to this? What did I do to deserve this?*

But what had she done? Was this revenge for something that happened years ago? There must be something behind it all, rather than just sheer cruelty, but she couldn't put her finger on what it could be. She knew instinctively that he still had a hold over her, but how? What was the weapon, and why?

In the small hours, she felt very weak and powerless. She was up against someone with far more guile, more malice than she would ever have. He wouldn't just accept her throwing him out, she knew that. Her stomach churned with apprehension. It was like a game of chess and she was waiting for his next move.

Jenny waited until a reasonable hour and then phoned Liz.

'What's his motive, Lizzy? Why has he done this?'

'Oh, the usual: money, power, status – he wants it all. Taking your house is the ultimate goal to totally dominate you, but obviously you'll never get him to admit it. He'll always find a way to explain why it makes financial or practical sense.'

She phoned Joy, wanting the emotional angle.

'Joy, now I've taken my rose-coloured spectacles off, I want to see Mark for who he really is. Can you help me? I feel so confused, like I can't see the woods for the trees.'

'I can try. Let's start with the most important thing: how you are.'

'Well, these last few months, since we came back from Crete, I have felt pretty good on the whole, but then I'll get the nausea, headaches, confusion and exhaustion and I feel like I'm back at square one. Saying that, I have felt better since Mark left. No, actually, since we left The Rectory – I was under a constant cloud there, but here, it's intermittent. And my memory doesn't seem to be as bad as it was – but perhaps it's always been okay and it was his gaslighting that made me think I was losing it…? Oh, I don't know what to think any more. Are my symptoms MS or psychological torture? Jenny laughed drily.

'Go deeper, Jenny. The answer lies in your subconscious.'

'Does it? And how can I access that then?'

'It will come to you. Let your mind rest, stop actively looking and it will just present itself to you, I'm sure. Hang on, there's something in a book I was reading about supporting your spiritual recovery….' There was a clunk as Joy put down the receiver then ruffling noises as pages were turned. 'Yes, here it is. *You can help clear your channels by detoxing. Surround yourself with positive ions* – ooh, the beach, go to the beach.' Joy continued to read: '*Regular meditation will aid clarity of mind. An organic diet is vital, and drink plenty of water, preferably filtered. This will help cleanse body and mind.*'

It all sounded very ineffectual but what else could she do? As she hung up, the house phone made its strange clicks as usual, and Jenny kicked herself for not using her new mobile phone. *Come on girl! Beat him at his own game! If he's bugging the phone, don't use the damn phone!* She felt vulnerable, like she had said too much to Joy. She knew Joy was her friend, a true ally, but she was bound to confide in her husband from time to time, and her husband was a mate of Mark's. She still felt as if talking about Mark was putting herself in danger.

She decided to be proactive and install some CCTV cameras outside the house. She rang a firm they'd used for years for some of their commercial properties. After they'd been fitted she felt a bit less anxious – less like prey just waiting to be attacked.

One morning Jenny was in the kitchen and went to unlock the back door to put the recycling out. Her hand went to turn the key, as she had done a million times before, but found nothing there. The key was missing. *Have I been locked in? Am I trapped?* She turned the handle in a panic but to her relief the door opened. She knew it had been locked when she went to bed and her dad rarely used her kitchen, preferring the one in his own apartment. She stood stock still, trying to breathe, to make sense of it. The CCTV – she could check it on the CCTV. It was linked to her phone but when she went to look at the previous night's footage, she couldn't make sense of it – it was just a blank screen, as if the camera had gone wrong. She cursed herself for not being more technically savvy and rang the company. They checked the cameras remotely and confirmed that they were all working.

'If there's nothing to see, there's nothing to see, Mrs Damerell.'

'But someone must have been at the back door. Could the camera have been tampered with? The film wiped?'

'It's connected to the internet, so it's digitally filed. It would be hard to tamper with the recording. The only thing I can suggest is that someone may have covered up the camera for a brief while, but not to be filmed on approach to the camera would take some doing. Someone would have to know the property really well.'

That figures. She hung up and went to look round, to see if she could spot something amiss. *This was more of Mark's gaslighting, wasn't it? He'd probably had keys cut for all the doors and windows, he could no doubt get in at any time.* She went into the morning room and let her eyes drift over the contents. One thing immediately stuck out – the wooden block calendar: the date had been changed – it was now set to two months ago. She laughed out loud.

'Is this the best you can do, Mark Damerell?'

She refused to be intimidated by him any longer. Knowledge is power. She knew his game. She looked for her bank book in its usual place. It had gone. She rummaged around, checking in the drawers below even though she never kept it there. Still no sign. Instead she found a photograph of herself and Mark at their engagement party. A photo she'd never seen before.

She immediately rang her bank to notify them of the missing bank book and then rang a locksmith to arrange for all the locks in the entire house to be changed. Finally, she rang her keyworker at Women's Aid.

'Jenny, if he's been in the house, then it's time to call the police. It's called hard-targeting. He knows you're trying to protect yourself with the CCTV but he's still trying to dominate and control you. The photograph and date change are just messing with your head. He's trying to manipulate you. Don't buckle, Jenny, remember what he's done to you.'

Jenny felt a mixture of relief that Marie was there for her, advising her, giving her strength, but also fear. Mark had really ramped-up his campaign. She rang the local police station but they said with no evidence of a forced entry and no CCTV footage there was little they could do. Mark's fingerprints would be all over the house anyway, so they couldn't be used either.

Jenny slumped down on the sofa, mouth dry and heart racing. She just wanted to run far, far away but knew she couldn't because of Trethorne – he would have won. It was all such a battle and nothing was simple. She wasn't devious like him so it was hard to outwit him in this game of psychological chess. Her whole world had been overturned, her comfort zone invaded. What she had believed to be the truth was in fact a lie.

Over the next few days she fought hard not to be overcome by fear. She found herself being suspicious of everything and everyone, every little noise, every item out of place. It all became a clue, a piece of evidence in her mind. It was exhausting and her nerves were shot to pieces.

She looked through her booklet from the Freedom Programme to try to calm down and discovered that this state had a name: 'hypervigilance'. *Constantly scanning the environment for threats.* Yes, that was her. *A symptom of post-traumatic stress disorder.* She wasn't surprised. Marie had mentioned that PTSD was a common consequence of domestic abuse. *Add that to my list of ailments.*

Jenny tried her hardest not to freak out and keep focused on looking after herself, as Joy suggested, but it was difficult when she felt she was being attacked on all fronts. The landline started ringing in the middle of the night and going dead when she answered. Wrong numbers that insisted there was an 'Maxine Smithson' at her address. Trying to get a credit card and being refused due to her credit rating. (When she had it checked, it appeared that she hadn't been registered at her previous home address for the last three years. Thanks Mark.) Even her new phone seemed to be conspiring against her. When she turned it on, there was an app that she didn't install with a message that popped up, *Hello Jenny!* How did it know her name? Was she paranoid or being monitored? Or both? For every move she made, there was a counter-attack. Always anonymous, always untraceable. She knew who was behind it all, of course she did, but could she prove it? No.

Even Joy, someone she thought was untouchable, was getting dragged into Mark's net. Jenny saw her at the local supermarket and was about to say hello when she registered who she was chatting with: Sam, one of the interior designers who worked for Mark. Young, blonde, beautiful and doing Jenny's job. Sam was a woman who was definitely in the enemy camp. So, what was Joy doing chatting with her? Her heart slumped to her boots. Another betrayal?

When Jenny quizzed Joy about it later she said, 'Oh Sam? She's a lovely person, very holistic, you know.'

'But she's Mark's employee – she's on his side,' exclaimed Jenny.

'I sensed only positivity from her, Jen. And don't forget about karma. Karma is all about cause and effect so Mark will get his come-uppance.'

Oh yeah? When? For once, Joy's spirituality grated. Jenny's hypervigilance had been triggered. Who could she trust? No one, she decided. Not even her own father, nor her children who were being manipulated unknowingly. No, she was on her own. She had to look out for herself. She had no doubt that Mark would continue to try to crush her any way he could, and she was determined not to let him. The divorce would obviously be messy – he'd got all the paperwork tied up anyway – so she decided to make a clean sweep of it. Mark could have the business, the properties, everything. She would just keep Trethorne and somehow make it work for her.

Oh yes, and time was nearly up for George. She'd not seen him make any move to leave. She could not have him under the same roof any more. She couldn't trust him. She knocked on the door of his apartment. When he opened it, she had a shock.

'Dad! What's the matter?' George looked ashen and dishevelled.

'Oh, Jenny dear… Come in.'

She followed him into his apartment which was a mess of packing boxes, books, clothes – stuff everywhere.

'I'm getting in a pickle. Had some bad news… Feeling a bit sorry for myself.'

She'd rarely seen her father quite so distraught. Even at Eleanor's funeral he managed to keep the stiff upper lip.

'What's happened?'

'Can't talk about it old girl, but could you give me a couple more weeks to find somewhere to stay? I was going to rent a cottage on the outskirts of town, but it was so pokey and it had mice, can you believe, for 700 quid a month!'

'Dad… I've given you plenty of notice. You betrayed me, remember? You were ready to leave this house for Mark's money, and now all of a sudden you want to stay because of some mice?'

'Jennifer dear, I am your father. Have some consideration.'

'One more month Dad. But that's all.'

She shut the door on him, despite an overwhelming desire to forgive him and help tidy his room. Some filial sense of duty or obedience always kicked-in around her dad, even though he'd been ready to sell her down the river.

And then, two things happened that lifted her spirits. The first was the psychiatric report, copied to her GP, which declared that Jenny was suffering from post-traumatic stress disorder – echoing what she'd been told at Women's Aid, only for differing reasons. The psychiatrist pinned the reasons onto losing her mother, and the long-term shock of the MS diagnosis and the seizures. He recommended six counselling sessions that could be linked to her MS-support group visits, and a follow-up consultation in six months' time. So, she was not going crazy, and her timely action would thwart Mark's take-over bid of Trethorne, once and for all. She was elated.

Then, the same afternoon, she decided to take a look around Trethorne's numerous outbuildings where she found that although the stables and boot rooms were all very neglected, they still seemed structurally sound. They could be used for something. She went into one of the stalls and lifted an ancient old tarpaulin, intending to check whether the flooring was earth or concrete. It was an earthen floor and well compacted over the years, but something caught her eye. A very slightly raised area that looked different to the rest of the flooring, over in the far corner. She poked around with a stick, which promptly broke, so she went and fetched a mattock. As gently as she could, she scraped the earth away and revealed a small wooden door. Prising it open with the tip of the mattock, she peered inside. It was a shallow hole. It looked empty, just full of cobwebs and long-rotted straw. But right at the back was a hessian bag. She reached in and pulled it out. The uppermost layers of fabric had almost completely deteriorated and fell apart in her hands, but the inner layers remained intact. As she carefully unwrapped the package, she saw the gleam of a gilt-frame. It was a painting, quite small, of a woman. Beautifully done, in oils she suspected. What had she found? It had obviously been there for quite some time, undisturbed. She fetched a clean tea-towel and wrapped it up carefully. This needed checking out.

At the local antiques shop, the art valuer peered at the painting with his eyeglass for quite some time, rubbing his chin and looking closer. 'Flemish I would say, 17th century, possibly earlier. I can't make out the signature. You'd need to consult a specialist. But I'd say it could be valuable, certainly worth taking further.'

'How much, do you think? Just a guess…'

'Well, it's hard to say. I can't be sure – thousands, possibly tens of thousands.'

'You don't say…?'

Jenny carefully folded it back in the tea-towel and took it straight to her bank for safekeeping, the one she still used in town, the only bank left in fact. She felt elated – at last, a bit of good luck. Apart from her monthly allowance which had now stopped, Mark had controlled every penny of their income, but the old manor house had been guarding a secret that would help keep the wolf from the door. She chose to believe that it was a gift to her from her female ancestors.

As she travelled home on the bus, she had a brainwave. She would use the money from the painting to renovate the stables, turn them into holiday cottages. She knew Trethorne was a force for good. Was it ridiculous to think that the old manor house protected the women who lived there? Maybe, but she felt it was true. Finally, something was going her way.

She had to share the news with someone but who to call? The only person left who she felt she could trust was Liz. So, she rang Liz and explained her plan: 'I'm going to do summer lets.' She decided not to mention the painting, it felt like knowledge was power at the moment, and it was safer to play her cards close to her chest for once in her life.

'But isn't that what Mark was going to do?' replied Liz. 'I thought you were dead against it.'

'Mark wanted to sell off Trethorne and build a housing estate in the grounds. What I want to do is very different! I'll still own the cottages, I'll design the interiors, do all the letting and just rent them out during the summer. I'm going to do an Elizabethan knot garden too, with box hedges and formal planting. It can only enhance the property. There's so much potential.'

'Well, good for you, Jen,' said Liz. 'It's a great way of generating income whilst still respecting the integrity of the house. Sam suggested much the same.'

'…? What? You've been talking to Sam, about me?' Jenny felt the mist of rage descend, her hypervigilance instantly triggered.

'Ummm, well we didn't start off talking about you Jen, but you came into conversation that's all. She asked after you and I said you were at Trethorne, and she said that it was a wonderful place with loads of potential. I bumped into her and Joy last week in The Copper Kettle. We had a coffee.'

'You two are *fucking unbelievable*,' shouted Jenny. 'Can't you see she's in the enemy camp? I wish I'd never said anything to you now, in case you tell Sam what my plans are – and then it'll instantly get back to Mark and he'll move heaven and earth to try and stop me. Jesus Christ, can I trust nobody, these days?'

'Hey, hey, hey. Jenny! You're over-reacting – I only had coffee with the woman, I'm not her new best friend. I'm not betraying you.'

'Well it bloody well feels like it.' Jenny put the phone down before Liz had a chance to respond. She was too tired to slam it. At the moment, life was like going up a down escalator. As fast as she climbed up, she got nowhere. She couldn't believe Liz could be so thoughtless as to fraternise with the enemy. Jenny had never felt so utterly alone in her entire life. Even her kids were hardly ever home these days.

Keep on truckin', she thought grimly and picked up her address book to start planning the renovations. She knew the builder who'd renovated George's apartment was away in the Scilly Isles working on a private estate, so who else could she contract? *Brian Jones, he's always been reliable*. But mid-dial she stopped. He was Mark's friend now. In fact, all the contractors she'd originally worked with were now basically on Mark's payroll. She wanted nothing to do with them, or have them anywhere near Trethorne. God knows how Mark had them wrapped around his little finger.

She wondered if she would ever rid herself of Mark's insidious control over her when she heard the hoover upstairs. Ava! Over a cup of tea, she asked her cleaner if she knew any builders.

'Of course, Mrs D. Poland is proud of builders, you will find no better in world! Same with painters, carpenters, plumbers. We build fine houses.'

With Ava's help, Jenny had the job booked in for three months' hence, giving her time to get the planning sorted, and most importantly, to value and sell the painting at an upcoming auction in London. She then spent a lovely couple of hours browsing the internet looking for ideas for the Elizabethan knot garden, before the computer crashed and she couldn't reboot it. Could any area in her life be without problems?

The front door slammed, shattering her peace. It was Jessica and Marcus.

'We've come to talk to you, Mum,' said Jessica.

'Oh, have you?' replied Jenny airily. *Look at them, just like their father, talking to me like a minion.*

'Yes, Dad's really heartbroken about all this. He's living out of a suitcase, sleeping on Sam's floor. You've got to take him back. He was only doing what he thought was best for all of us,' said Jess, Marcus refusing to make eye contact with her.

'Sorry. Not possible.' Jenny wasn't sorry at all but she didn't want to drag her children into her and Mark's break up, even if they were adults. Sleeping on Sam's floor indeed! What about Guy's floor, or using some of his flash cash and staying in a hotel? Did they think she was stupid!

'Mum…' said Marcus. 'Dad does seem to be truly sorry. He really is worried about you. He thinks you might do something… y'know, hurt yourself…'

'Look my lovelies,' Jenny sighed, 'sometimes a relationship breaks down and it's nobody's fault, it's just something that happens. I'm not about to do anything stupid, but your father and I have, shall we say, irreconcilable differences.' It bloody well was Mark's fault but she couldn't tell them that.

'Mum, see sense, for god's sake. Dad looks after you. How will you cope with… everything?' Jessica gestured towards Jenny's walking stick, which was resting on the desk. Jenny could practically hear Mark coaching their daughter.

'I'm coping just fine, thank you,' said Jenny. 'You can always come and stay at home a bit more often, if you're that worried about me.' She tried not to bristle, even though the whole world liked to use her disability as a way of infantilising her. To Jenny's amazement, she managed to stay strong, not to buckle, despite those old motherly feelings of trying to make everything okay for her kids; to sacrifice herself for other's happiness. Her children left without achieving their goal, but hopefully comforted that she was all right.

This new resolve was tested again when her father broached the subject too, the following day.

'Jenny, I know you feel that I have let you down, but I was only doing what I thought was best. I know I should have talked to you first, I admit that. I made a mistake. But have you thought this through properly? You're giving up a lot, you know. Divorce shatters families.'

'It's not a choice, Dad, I have to do this. My life depends upon it.' This came out of her mouth before she even knew she was going to say it. But it felt right, felt true.

'Don't be so melodramatic. As far as I can see you're breaking up a perfectly good marriage for no reason.'

'You know nothing about it, Dad, nothing about how Mark has treated me over the years.'

'He's been a perfectly good husband and father. He's provided for you all, built up the business…'

Jenny felt the urge to rage at him again but she looked into his eyes and saw no malice, just an old man with traditional values. He didn't know what had gone on and couldn't see why Mark was so toxic – because he was created out of the same mould. There was no point trying to persuade him. She might as well ask a waterfall to flow backwards.

'Sorry Dad, it's not going to happen.'

'Well Jenny, I hope you understand that your destructive behaviour will bring about exactly what you deserve. You reap what you sow, you know.'

'Right. Well, you're on thin ice there Dad, because you've still got to find yourself somewhere else to live, and that's a consequence of your actions. So, I'd focus on that if I were you, and stop interfering with my decisions.'

Jenny flounced out of the room. Deserve? That was a bit Old Testament. She wanted to crumble, to beg for forgiveness, to retire to her bed forever. That would be so much easier, but she remembered what Marie had said. *Dominators will stop at nothing to win.* And in a strange way, hearing her father's judgment gave her strength. Look at what she'd been brought up believing. It was no wonder she had chosen the submissive path all her life. But no more. The worm had turned.

She went to the kitchen and opened the freezer. Out of habit, she reached inside for the heart-shaped ice tray. A pang of sadness washed through her – that was the one gesture Mark had made that seemed truly loving. As she clunked out the last two cubes into a glass and went to fill it with water, she stopped in her tracks. *Mark was never truly loving*, she knew this now. There was always a motive behind it. She looked down into her glass, the two hearts slowly melting. Mark had always been insistent that they were her own special ice cubes, and that no one else in the family could touch them. At the time, it made her feel special, but now she wondered what the real reason was. He had always encouraged her to make iced water her 'signature drink' – what a stupid phrase, what did it even mean? – and every morning for years he'd made her a frappe, with tons of crushed ice in it. And afterwards, she realised now, like clockwork, she slept so heavily she felt like the undead. She always woke up afterwards feeling sick and dizzy, with a pounding headache.

Tentatively, she raised the glass and sniffed the ice. There it was – the unmistakable smell of bitter almonds. There was something in the ice, there had to be. It came to her like a wave crashing on to the shore. Mark was trying to poison her. She reeled, needing to hold on to the table to steady herself. She was about to pour the ice down the sink, but then thought better of it. She'd ask Guy to have it tested. No, she wouldn't – she'll send it to an independent lab without telling a soul, and have it tested. *Remember Jen, you're on your own here.*

CHAPTER 7

The Uprooting of Trees

Force 10 on the Beaufort Scale

The rain was pattering against the darkened windows of Jenny's room when she finally opened her eyes. At first she lay there dozing, wondering what time it was, but then a jolt of adrenalin kicked in as she remembered that her husband had been systematically poisoning her for years. She switched on the bedside lamp, flung back the covers and sat bolt upright. Her first instinct was to ring Mark, to scream at him down the phone but she checked herself. That would be pointless. He would deny it, like he did everything. Then he'd find a way to use the accusation against her. In fact, it would tickle him that little old Birdy had her feathers ruffled. Now she thought about it, that nickname was all part of the mission to conquer and diminish her. It sickened her to realise how thorough his campaign was.

Instead of accusing Mark, she knew it was better to keep her powder dry, to form a plan to fight back. It was no good wallowing, she needed to be proactive and get help; this was too big to cope with on her own. But who should she call? Her second instinct was to call her best friend, but she'd been giving Liz the cold shoulder after the Sam debacle. At last count, there were eight missed calls and three text messages from Liz on Jenny's phone. All unanswered.

Marie! Marie from Woman's Aid. She'd know what to do. But the office would be closed at this late hour – 7.30pm. Marie had given Jenny her mobile number in case of emergencies – but was this an emergency? Jenny hesitated, her finger over the *Call* button. She was fine. A bit woozy, but okay in herself. Was it really worth bothering Marie about all this? Jenny's familiar demons of self-doubt and lack of self-worth crept in. *Don't minimise this,* she told herself. *He's been trying to kill you, so yes, it is an emergency.* She forced herself to make the call and was once again heartened by Marie's belief in her.

'Time for the police again, Jenny,' she advised.

'But they dismissed me before, so surely they will again?' Jenny replied.

'You have evidence now, hard evidence. You still have that ice, don't you?'

'Yes, I stopped myself as I was about to pour it down the drain.'

'You need to get it out of the house as soon as possible, and store the residue somewhere safe until the police can get it tested, somewhere he can't get at it. As soon as he suspects you're on to him, he'll try to cover his tracks.'

After Jenny put down the phone, she went downstairs to check the glass. It still contained the remnants of the ice, but there were no more ice hearts in the tray. Perhaps they could test the tray itself, too? Now to get it all out of the house, unnoticed. She cursed the fact that she couldn't drive – once again she was foiled by Mark as soon as she tried to do anything for herself. She called up to Jessica, who was at home, watching TV in her room.

'Could you run me round to Liz's please, love? I just need to give her something.'

Jessica leaned over the bannister and rolled her eyes. 'Really Mum? I'm watching *Strictly*.'

'Yes, really,' said Jenny, sharper than normal. She put clingfilm over the glass and shoved it and the ice tray in a plastic bag to avoid any questions from her daughter.

At Liz's, when her friend opened the door the two women just stood there and smiled. Then they threw their arms around each other in the warmest hug imaginable, tears in their eyes, forgiveness in their words.

'I'm so sorry Jen. It was utterly thoughtless of me to have coffee with Sam. I didn't think…'

'Oh, forget it Liz. I'm just super-sensitive right now; seeing threats and set-ups everywhere. But I know you'd never betray me. In my heart, I do know that.'

'I never would. Come in.'

Jenny motioned to an impatient Jessica that she would be five minutes, and followed Liz indoors. She came straight to the point: 'Strange request, but could you possibly look after this for me until tomorrow morning? I know you leave early for work, but I'll come around and pick it up before you go. Is that okay?' she asked, placing the bag on the worktop.

'Yes, of course. What is it?'

Her hypervigilance kicking in, Jenny suddenly became evasive. 'I'm sorry Lizzie, I can't explain why, but I do need you to keep this safe for me. And for god's sake, don't touch it. I'll explain all another time, okay?'

Liz's eyebrows shot up even further but she accepted the items. 'Time for a cuppa?'

'No, sorry, I've got to get back. I'll see you in the morning. Oh, and Liz, I do love you.' With that Jenny walked back to the car where Jessica was waiting.

With the only 'evidence' she had out of the house, Jenny felt slightly more at ease, but she knew it was still an uphill struggle. She now had a goal – to get justice – but the police were less than helpful last time, and even if the ice residue tested positive for something, she couldn't prove that it was Mark who had laced it. They could even point the finger at her, saying she was trying to frame him. She wasn't going to fall for any more mind games or gaslighting, and she really wanted to expose Mark for the cold-blooded bastard that he was, but he was clever, really clever, and she just didn't have the mind of a criminal. She was a blue-sky thinker, an eternal optimist and trusting too: but now she had to get into the mind of a narcissist and discover what made him tick. She'd have to sharpen-up, and quickly. She didn't want to give him any chance to build up an alibi or turn her story around so she was the one who ended up looking the fool, like he usually did. With this in mind, she vowed that first thing the next morning she would go to the police.

Unfortunately, when Jenny entered the police station after picking up the ice residue from Liz, it was the same desk sergeant that she'd spoken to before about the break-in. He was distinctly sceptical. 'So, now you're saying that your ice cubes are contaminated in some way?'

'Yes, they've been making me ill, really ill,' answered Jenny.

'And who do you think has done this?'

'My husband, well, ex-husband, Mark Damerell. Let me spell that for you…'

'No, that's okay, I know how to spell Mark's surname.'

Typical! The desk sergeant knows him, thought Jenny as she watched him fill out a form. *Probably from the Rotary Club, or even the Masons – some horrible, cronyish group that closes ranks and protects each other regardless of what they've done.*

'Well, the ice residue needs to be tested to confirm if there's any contamination, but you realise this doesn't implicate your husband, don't you?' continued the sergeant with an almost imperceptible tilt of the head that said: *nutjob*. 'Whatever the results are, unless you can *prove* that Ma… Mr Damerell was the perpetrator, then this alone would not stand up in court.'

'I realise that, officer, but for my own peace of mind, I need to know what's in that ice,'

Jenny, said, refusing to be cowed. She handed over the plastic bag containing the sealed glass and the ice tray and watched as the policeman put it in a specimen bag, labelled it and completed the paperwork. Then she turned on her heels and walked out, kicking herself that she didn't take a phial of the residue to be independently tested, as she'd first planned to do. It was a waste of time.

Back at home, she sat down and tried to work out what to do next. The police may not be bothered but she still needed to protect herself. Was there anything else Mark might have tampered with as well as the ice cubes? She looked around her kitchen. Nothing sprang to mind. She wandered around the house, arriving at the bathroom cabinet. Could Mark have interfered with her medication? She decided to collect a repeat prescription herself, just in case. In her bedroom, her eyes rested on her dressing table. Where was the bottle of Chanel No. 5? The perfume that Mark had always insisted she wore, right back from his first birthday present to her. He even wept about it to the Relate counsellor. Crocodile tears, she now knew; he just wanted her to keep spraying herself with something that he tampered with and made toxic.

There was a faint circle in the dust where the bottle had stood. Why had it disappeared and more importantly, when? She couldn't recall when she'd last used it. Certainly not since she'd thrown her husband out of the house. Had Mark retrieved it whilst she'd been out? Did this mean he knew she was on to him? Jenny felt a prickle of fear. Was she being paranoid, or would he really sink so low? No matter how hard she tried to escape him, she felt Mark's constant presence, monitoring her, second-guessing her, outwitting her. It was terrifying, it ground her down until she just wanted to give up, to lie face down on the floor and submit herself to whatever he wanted to do with her.

Jenny shook her head violently. Then a thought surfaced in her mind. *Perhaps I don't even have MS…? Perhaps the symptoms all along have been from the toxins in my perfume and drinks?* This thought was like a small ray of light at the end of a very long tunnel. *Maybe I will recover from this? I refuse to be a victim any more,* she said to herself. She reached for her mobile phone, deciding to phone Marie again; she always helped. When the Women's Aid answerphone clicked in, Jenny's heart sank. She texted her mobile and moments later Marie's answer pinged back: *Sorry, Jenny, I'm at a conference. Will ring when I can.*

Jenny tried to imagine what Marie would say. She was always very straightforward and practical – Jenny tried to channel this. Marie had advised going to the police, but the local sergeant was in the enemy camp. She could almost hear Marie say: 'So go to another police station, somewhere outside the influence of Mark.' The next town was Barnstaple – still too close. Exeter. Yes, she decided to try there. The next bus left in half an hour, just time to catch it.

When Jenny repeated her story for a second time, the reception was far more promising. The WPC took her seriously and didn't flicker when she mentioned Mark's name. But once again, her hopes for justice seemed to slip away from her. 'There are a number of people who could have contaminated the ice – anyone who lived in or visited your house regularly. Your ex-husband cannot be considered a suspect until he is directly linked to a crime,' explained the police officer.

'But I'm sure it's him. He's the only one who would do this. Can't you interview him?'

'There are not enough grounds to. It's your word against his, I'm afraid. If you get hard evidence, such as CCTV footage of him entering your home with malicious intent, then we'll be knocking at his door.'

'Oh,' said Jenny, her shoulders sagging. She couldn't face going into the debacle she'd had with her CCTV.

'But the ice is being tested which may confirm your suspicions, and have you considered a blood test too? If there's evidence of toxins in your system then that would provide extra weight to your case,' suggested the WPC.

Of course! It was obvious but Jenny hadn't even thought of it. 'And can you do this?' she asked excitedly.

'Not until it's officially police business. It's all about funding…' replied the officer. 'Bit of a catch 22, I know. If I were you, I'd get it done privately at a registered clinic. There are several places in Exeter.'

She thanked the policewoman and went straight to a café to Google where she could get a blood test done. And then, as if her brain was clearing and thinking straight for the first time in a long time, she remembered the little fridge/freezer in Mark's office in the grounds of The Rectory, the one he used for the ice in her frappacinos. Maybe there were still some left-over ice hearts in that? But how could she get them without drawing attention to herself?

As she contemplated the thought, she realised how sinister her situation really was. Instead of always second-guessing her husband, she now had to be one-step in front of him. And she was scared of him; scared of what he could do to her. She had to protect herself and her children, grown-up though they were; she had to keep eagle-eyed and sharp-witted with only herself to rely on. She began to think of all the other women in a similar situation to her, women who didn't have her financial independence or the benefit of an inherited home, women who weren't lucky enough to have had a decent education or even access to the internet – and her heart went out to them. She felt a kindred spirit to all of womankind and that gave her strength.

Later that evening, she was having dinner with Marcus and Jess, who both frequented Trethorne more than their friends' houses these days.

'How's things at work, Marcus?' she asked nonchalantly.

Marcus looked up from his pasta. 'Alright. Busy. Dad's never there. He's off with Sam looking at a residential development in Falmouth tomorrow – then it'll be all systems go to work out if the business should invest or not. That's my job.'

'Oh?' said Jenny seizing the moment. 'Would you do me a favour, love? There are some old bits and pieces of mine in the office, an old canvas print and some cushions and stuff. Could you ring Dad and ask him if I could pop in tomorrow and pick them up? It'll be a good time to do it if he's not around.' She was hoping that there would be an opportunity for her to rifle in the fridge for the old ice tray without Marcus seeing her, although quite how that would pan-out she didn't know.

'Alright… I suppose I better ask Dad, but you can just call round anyway because I'll be there all on my lonesome, so I can let you in.' Marcus returned his focus to his food – a picky eater at the best of times, he was separating the spinach and olives from the pasta sauce and leaving them on one side.

Later that evening, Marcus popped his head around her bedroom door. 'Dad said it's okay to pick up your stuff. He says it's in the store cupboard in a box. Come around about eleven, and we can have coffee, okay?'

The next morning, as she approached The Rectory, she was struck by an overwhelming sense of grief. She had loved the place and put so much of her heart and soul into the house and gardens over the years – and now it was someone else's. Just like that – gone. *How life twists and turns*, she pondered. She drove beyond The Rectory's gravel drive and turned left about 500m further down the lane, where Mark had put in a new entrance to the office, which he'd had separated from the grounds of The Rectory by high wooden fencing.

Marcus was waiting for her at the door and let her in to the place she knew by heart; all of it was so familiar to her.

'Coffee, mother?'

'Ooh, yes please, if I'm not stopping you from work?'

'No, that's fine. I'll put the kettle on. You know where the store room is,' he said, banging cupboard doors in a search for mugs.

She went over to the store cupboard to retrieve her things. She didn't really want them, but they were a means to an end.

'Just nipping for a pee, Mum,' Marcus shouted.

'Okay, I'll get the milk from the fridge and make the coffee,' she replied, and dashed over to the kitchen area. *Now!* was all she could think.

She opened the fridge and felt inside the tiny freezer compartment. Nothing. Her disappointment was palpable, her legs felt like they would give way under her. But then, right at the back, behind a bottle of something – probably vodka – she felt rubber. It was iced into the compartment and she had to scratch around it with her nails to loosen it, but then it released, and there it was – a full tray of ice hearts. She stuffed it into a plastic freezer box she'd put in her shoulderbag and hurriedly found the milk and began to make the coffee. Would this 'evidence' be admissible in court? Was she breaking any laws by taking something from a place that in theory she still partly-owned, seeing as they weren't yet divorced? She didn't know, but she was trying to cover all bases.

The next morning Jenny woke up feeling better than she had in ages. She didn't know if it was psychosomatic or whether now she wasn't regularly topping up the toxins with ice and perfume, they really were leaving her system, but it felt as if her body was rejuvenating. Buoyed up by the fact that she could now get her blood tests and the ice tests done, she booked in to the Exeter clinic for the following morning, knowing that she would get the results of both tests by the end of the week.

Reinvigorated and full of energy, she decided to sweep out the outbuildings ready for the renovations. After she finished, she lent on the broom, admiring the ancient old brickwork. An alcove high up in the eaves caught her eye. She got a ladder to investigate and found a dusty suitcase at the back. Inside was musty cricket stuff, clearly Mark's, but when she dug down, underneath were thigh-high PVC boots, a silk negligée and a variety of wigs and make-up. When she examined the boots, she discovered that they were Mark's size – 10. They reminded her of that film she'd watched once, *Kinky Boots*. At the time, Mark had reacted violently to it, calling it a load of rubbish. No wonder! It was obviously too near the knuckle for him. *A cross-dresser too – is there no end to your secrets?* she thought.

She replaced the boots and heard a jangle. Delving deeper, she found some handcuffs and whips, and shuddered. Once upon a time they'd been used on her.

Jenny slid her hand into the front pocket of the case and unearthed a crumpled porn magazine – *Dirty Boyz*. One look told her it was gay porn – but nothing about her husband could shock her now. Throwing it to one side, she continued to dig and found a diary from five years ago. She flicked through it. There were names and dates in it – *Bruce, Bristol, garages, Premier Inn*, said one entry. Bruce? So, was Mark gay as well as a transvestite? Jenny's mind boggled. Along with the diary was an envelope. Opening it, she discovered photographs inside. They were of her brother Paul, but much younger, bare-chested and sitting on a black leather sofa. And who was that next to him? A young man with a peroxide-blond quiff, pouting at the camera. He looked familiar but she couldn't put her finger on who. Then it clicked – Guy. It seemed incredible that they knew each other then; they never referred to the fact now. And in the photo, they both looked very cosy. What on earth had gone on? *Christ, Mark, you're getting very slack in your old age – leaving all this for me to find at Trethorne*, she thought.

Jenny immediately rang Paul, not bothering to check what time it was in Bali. She had to speak to him urgently.

'I've found the strangest photo of you at Uni,' began Jenny when he answered.

'Oh really?' Paul replied. 'You're waking me at three in the morning to reminisce?'

'It's you with Guy. You never told me you knew him…'

'Oh, didn't I?' Jenny could hear him sitting up in bed and then the click of a light switch. 'Yes, well, we were just acquaintances really, met at parties, you know the sort of thing that goes on at university.'

'Not from this picture you weren't. A bit more than friends I'd say,' Jenny shot back.

'Oh, for god's sake… what's the point? Okay, I admit it – yes, me and Guy were lovers,' said Paul.

'So… you're gay? Oh, Paul, why didn't you tell me?'

'You know exactly why – because Dad is the biggest bigot out, a total old-school "a load of limp-wristed pansies" type. He would have a heart attack if he knew I'm queer.'

Jenny could see his point though, as their father had always been completely against any sign of homosexuality. When she was little, she was forbidden from watching Larry Grayson because he was: 'an abomination', and John Inman's character in *Are You Being Served?* Her father turned the television off with such force he almost broke it. She'd always figured it was due to his military background where being gay was a court marshalling offence in those days.

'But I'm not homophobic, Paul, you know I'm not. You could have confided in me,' said Jenny.

'Yes, well, sorry sis…' he yawned.

'Can I ask you something?' said Jenny. 'Why did Mark have this photo? Is Mark gay too?'

'Oh Jenny, I don't know if I can go there… It's all in the past now and it's better to let sleeping dogs lie and all that. Talking of sleep…'

'For god's sake! Don't take Mark's side again, it's me, your sister! Have some loyalty to *me*. Stop protecting him and tell me, Paul. I need to know. I'm going through a difficult time at the moment, and it would really help clarify things.'

'All right, calm down. I suppose it can't hurt now. Look, I know I've always said I only knew Mark from the university Rugby Club but it was much more than that. We were both into the same scene… I don't know about now, Jenny, I really don't, but at Uni Mark was bisexual – "greedy" we used to call him. Actually, probably more gay than bisexual – he mostly had male lovers. There was just the one girlfriend but it didn't last long.'

'And then when he met me, you didn't think to mention this?' said Jenny bitterly. 'Didn't you think I might find it interesting?'

'Of course, Jenny. The first time I realised you were together, a couple of days before your birthday party I think it was, I'd just come back from travelling and I saw you driving off together, and Mark clocked me. Afterwards, he tracked me down to the Kings Arms, and pretty much warned me that if I ever revealed our past to you, Dad would be sure to find out about my sexuality and cut me out of his Will.'

'So, he was blackmailing you?' said Jenny.

'Yes, I suppose it was blackmail when you think about it. Somehow the way he phrased it didn't seem like that at all. More like friendly advice at the time.'

I bet it did. Jenny was now all too familiar with the way Mark operated. Charming people, manipulating them and then spitting them out. Just then her mobile rang – it was Marie. She quickly wrapped up the conversation with her brother and then answered Marie's call. After explaining her recent police encounters – neglecting to mention her night-time cat-burglary – Jenny moved on to the latest revelation: Mark blackmailing Paul. 'It's like he has zero thought or concern for anyone else's feelings. No guilt, no self-doubt, no compassion – none whatsoever,' she mused.

'I think you've hit the nail on the head there, Jenny,' replied Marie. 'Now this is a very strong word, and it might come as a bit of a shock to you, but everything you've told me about Mark is pointing to one thing: I think he could have psychopathic tendencies.'

'What? What do you mean? Surely psychopaths are violent, insane serial killer-types? Charles Manson and the like... Mark has always been calm and controlled. He's never raised a hand to me.'

'Well, that's the stereotypical view of them, yes. But if you look at the personality traits describing a psychopath I think you'll recognise Mark. Psychopaths are more common than you think – 1 in 150 people. They live amongst us and are often completely undetected, ruining people's lives without any consequences. I don't want to frighten you, Jenny, I just think knowing this could help you cope.'

As soon as they'd hung up, Jenny rushed to the computer. Every website she visited said the same thing repeatedly: *lack of empathy, lack of guilt and remorse, superficial charm, grandiose sense of self-worth, pathological lying, restlessness, risk-taking, manipulative behaviour...* The profile fitted Mark exactly. The traits even included sexual promiscuity – and the contents of the box confirmed that.

It was as if she had discovered an online tick-list for Mark's personality. Jenny felt elated but also horrified that she had been married to a psychopath for over 25 years. Even saying it to herself sounded unreal, over the top, like some sensationalist headline. But it was true. Going back to when they first met, she thought about the lager ring-pull he'd given her as an engagement ring. *He never truly loved me,* she realised with a jolt. *He was putting on a show to get what he wanted – my family money; my inheritance...*

Every memory she had of their relationship had to be reframed with this diagnosis in mind. How he treated her when he learnt she had MS: outwardly sympathetic, privately using it to further control her. Edging her out of the business, making her drink poisoned water, belittling her in front of the kids, trying to sell off Trethorne... all for his own ends. *I'm an idiot for not spotting it before*, she berated herself. Jenny continued to search the internet, she couldn't tear herself away. She drank it all in. Finally, she was learning who her ex-husband really was. She listened to a podcast by someone who had worked with a psychopath and it was chilling yet fascinating. It turned out that there were two types – stereotypical psychopaths and successful psychopaths. The former are the ones who end up in prison because of their impulsiveness but the latter are more controlled and operate below the radar. They often become very successful in business because of their ruthlessness. *Mark! Mark to a tee!*

She could hardly see the screen through her tears when she read the impact psychopaths have on the people around them: *there can be huge emotional and physical effects on the victim's health.* How true, how very true… The sadness turned to anger when she read on: *if you encounter one, back away slowly. Do not attempt to confront them, you will never win.*

It was deep into the night when Jenny turned off the computer. That last detail appalled her. Was she expected to sit back and take what Mark had been trying to do to her? Never! She couldn't accept that as soon as she'd woken up to what was really happening to her, she had to fight on. She wasn't thinking about revenge, she wanted justice. Public acknowledgement of the private torture she had been subjected to. He had been trying to poison her after all – no one should get away with that.

For the next few days, she mulled it over. She was still waiting for the water and blood test results. When she had them, surely the police would want to do something?

One afternoon she was just making herself a sandwich in the kitchen when there was a tap at the back door. It was Mark. A wave of fear swept through her but she told herself to be calm and act normally. She mustn't reveal what she had discovered about him, for her own safety.

'Oh, hello Mark. How are you?' she asked, trying to prevent a tremor from entering her voice.

'Hello Jenny. I was just passing… can I come in?'

She hesitated then opened the door reluctantly.

'I was thinking that even though we've split up, there's no reason why we couldn't still be friends, is there?' he continued.

What does he want? She didn't reply.

'I heard that Steve from the Rotary Club is going on holiday with Nicole to Portugal, even though they're divorced. Very civilised, very mature, don't you think? Something we could do.'

'I don't think so Mark.' said Jenny, 'I'm very busy.'

'But if Jessica and Marcus wanted to come too – it'd be like the old days. Separate bedrooms of course,' he laughed.

With the full beam of Mark's charm and confidence focused on her, Jenny found her mind going momentarily blank. Portugal did sound nice and she could do with some sunshine… But fore-warned is fore-armed and she knew his game. 'No,' she said. 'That is not something I would consider. Now, is there anything else?'

Mark's face darkened. 'Well, that's hardly a friendly attitude.'

'We're not friends, Mark. And we never will be. Now if there's nothing else, I do need to get on.' She opened the door and nodded for him to leave.

Mark gave her a long stare, obviously furious that he'd lost this particular spat. When he finally left, she felt utterly drained and shaky. It took all her energy to take herself to the chaise for a rest.

Waking up after an hour, her senses returned to her. *How dare he? The arrogance of the man. Such a fucking ego.* And the frightening thing was, she had started to be drawn in again. It really was incredible how she felt powerless with Mark, like he had programmed her to obey. The thought of going on holiday with the man was ridiculous but it just showed how skewed her thinking was when she was around him, because she had actually considered it – after everything he'd done to her. He could argue black was white and she'd find herself agreeing.

Two days later the test results arrived from the Exeter clinic. Jenny opened the envelope with trembling hands. It felt like her future was dependent on this piece of paper. In the cool, unemotional words of a laboratory was her salvation. Skimming through the chart with complicated chemical compounds she focused on five words at the end: *abnormally high levels of lead.* She had abnormally high levels of lead in her blood, but the ice-tray from Mark's office tested negative for toxins. Right. So, maybe it was too risky to keep the laced ice in the office fridge, in case Rachael or Sam, or god-forbid, Marcus used it. But the police specimen of ice residue would surely also confirm the presence of lead in the ice?

Lead poisoning, so that was what she had been suffering from. It was barbaric, almost medieval in its cruelty. As she returned to Google to check it out she found herself sobbing. *Fatigue, irritability, nausea, impaired concentration.* She knew those symptoms so well. And when the dose was raised? *Seizures and eventual coma.* So that was what she had coming for her, if she hadn't cottoned on to his plan.

Why did he pick lead, though, rather than rat-poison, for example? A little more googling and it didn't take long for the penny to drop. Mark had obviously thought it through very carefully. From a brilliantly evil man comes a brilliantly evil plan. He could poison her without taking the blame, because she'd been surrounded by lead for years, decades. Where else do you get lead poisoning from but old plumbing? That explained Mark's insistence on buying period properties. And what's another source? Lead paint. Banned now of course but splashed about with abandon until the 1960s. Each time she'd scraped it off umpteen of their renovations it left her swirling in dust, and despite wearing dust-masks, she often felt it clogging her nose and settling on her chest. And Mark never helped with the repainting: 'You're the interior designer,' he'd said. 'Your call.'

She despaired of it at the time, imploring Mark to buy a nice, modern house next time with no flaking paintwork and no rickety plumbing – despite her own love of old ruins – but of course he refused. 'They're goldmines, Birdy. A bit of TLC and the value goes through the roof,' he'd said at the time. Now she knew the truth. Now the rose-tinted spectacles had come off, her vision was 20/20. With a thudding heart, she saw the whole picture in high definition. She had been his puppet for their whole marriage, under his control. She had been his brood mare, giving him children. She'd also been his beard, providing the cover of a wife and children, preventing people from knowing his homosexuality and the sordid details of his past. It even explained the brutal, distant sex... And now he didn't need her any more he wanted to get rid of her. Drip by drip, until she eventually disappeared.

She phoned Liz, but when Jenny explained why she'd asked her to store the ice, Liz's reaction was not quite what she'd expected.

'Hang on a minute, Jenny, you're saying that Mark has been spiking your iced drinks to try to poison you?'

'Yes,' said Jenny.

'But the ice-tray tested negative, didn't it?'

'Yes… but I'm sure the one I sent to the police, the one you looked after for me, I'm sure that one will show traces of lead. It has to.'

'I'm sorry babe, but it all sounds a bit far-fetched, like something out of a Ruth Rendell novel. I don't think even Mark would do something like that. Don't you think it's possible that the lead is from the old plumbing and paint?'

'And the seizures, remember? I went into hospital.'

'I thought they were brought on by stress…?'

Jenny felt the exasperation rise in her. 'I had hoped you would understand, Liz…'

'Oh, I do, I do. I'm just trying to be rational, that's all.'

'Are you saying I'm being irrational? The evidence is there.'

'Well, you have abnormally high levels of lead in your blood, but… you live in an ancient house probably with lead plumbing, Jen… I'm just trying not to jump to conclusions.'

'Okay. Well thanks for your support, Liz.' Jenny hung up abruptly. That was not what she'd wanted to hear.

She decided to give Joy a ring – sweet, compassionate Joy. Maybe her friendship with Sam hadn't tainted her ability to Jenny's predicament clearly?

'You poor darling, that sounds awful,' said her friend.

Finally, some sympathy. Jenny felt like cheering.

'You are obviously craving some care, some attention,

to do that – we've been neglecting you, haven't we?' Joy continued.

'Do what? I haven't done anything.'

'Well, to go to those lengths. And what has it proved? That you have high levels of lead in your blood doesn't mean that you've been poisoned, not really. I mean, Trethorne and The Rectory are both riddled with lead I should think…'

'But nobody else has got lead poisoning, Joy! Nobody else suffers from seizures.'

'Well, perhaps your family should all get tested too? That would perhaps confirm that it's environmental, not anything sinister. I understand, I really do. He's hurt you and you're lashing out. It's a cry for help. I'm listening. My heart is open to you.'

Jenny put the phone down once again.

One thing she was discovering was that apart from Marie, who had unshakable belief in her, everyone around her found it easier to doubt her mental capacity than accept the truth of the situation. She knew it was hard to swallow, but it was the reality. She was beginning to see a different side to the people who she had thought were her loved ones. The ugly side of humanity. When the facts get too hot to handle, people prefer to create their own fiction to make sense of it.

CHAPTER 8

White Foam Crests

Force Six on the Beaufort Scale

The staff sergeant at the police station phoned Jenny a few days later. The results from the ice residue specimen were inconclusive. They showed raised levels of lead, but it was felt these were consistent with the levels that could be expected in water taken from old houses. Clever Mark.

When Jessica came home that evening, Jenny wondered whether to suggest that she might consider getting a blood test, but thought better of it. Her friends' scepticism was playing on her mind and she was now thinking that perhaps the lead really was down to the water pipes. At some point, she would broach the subject with her children and ask them to get tested. If they also had raised levels of lead, then she would get the whole plumbing replaced and hang the expense. She knew in her heart that Mark had covered his steps so well that she may never be able to prove his culpability.

'Hi Mum. Good day?' Jess asked, not waiting for a reply. 'Guess what? Sam's taking me for a spa weekend for my birthday next week. Isn't that great? I can't wait. We're going to get Himalayan salt massages. They're supposed to cleanse and detox at the same time.'

'Sounds lovely, Jess. Lucky you,' replied Jenny. She had thought spa days were their thing – not any more, obviously.

'You'd really like her, Mum, why don't you join us? I know she works with Dad, but she's a lovely person.'

'Oh no, you go and have fun,' answered Jenny. She took a deep breath and said brightly: 'Shall I do a birthday meal for you? You could invite Ben…'

Ben was Jessica's new boyfriend. He'd only been around for a few weeks and Jenny hadn't properly got to know him. She had done a double-take when she first saw him though – he was the spitting image of a younger Mark. Brown eyes, chestnut hair, he even dressed in a similar way. He was a mini-Mark… Once upon a time that would have made Jenny smile but now the thought of history repeating itself was horrific. She tried to push that dark thought to one side, to let Jessica be happy and enjoy the first flush of her relationship unclouded by Jenny's own emotional mess.

'Okay, great. I'll have a ring round and Marcus can bring his mates and make it a party,' said Jessica. That wasn't what Jenny had meant but she went along with it anyway. It seemed like any special time with her daughter was a thing of the past. But what was she hoping for? Jessica was in her twenties, an independent woman. It was wrong to rely on her daughter to combat her own loneliness.

Jenny's heart gave a thud when she realised that was what she was feeling. Recently, she'd been so busy processing the fact that Mark had been systematically dismantling her life that she hadn't had a moment to reflect. The reality of her current situation was bleak: an abusive ex, contrary friends, even acquaintances in the village believed the lies they'd been fed about her. She was completely alone. He may not have managed to kill her, but Mark had still done a fine job at squashing her down to nothing. Jenny had to rebuild herself, day by day, and make the foundations extra strong this time.

She booked a train to London for an appointment with the auction house that was putting her painting up for sale. It was a bit of excitement in her otherwise stressful life and she was looking forward to a change of scene.

As the train whizzed through Somerset, Wiltshire and Berkshire, she felt her spirits lift. Just as there was life outside Devon, so there was life beyond Mark. In central London, the appointment at the auction house went smoothly. The painting was by a fairly obscure Flemish painter from the mid-17th century, but it was nonetheless highly collectable. They put a reserve price of £50,000 on it, but they felt it could go for more. Jenny was delighted. Even at the reserve price, she would be able to renovate the barns and put her holiday letting plan into action, and if the painting fetched more, then she would be able to employ and landscape designer to create the knot garden. She blessed whichever of her forebears left that painting for her to find. For the first time since her marriage, a future free from Mark's control appeared before her.

Jenny found herself free by late afternoon and so she decided to wander down to Drury Lane and see if she could queue for a standby seat for a show. *42ⁿᵈ Street* looked light and fun, and as Jenny was waiting in line, a woman came over to her.

'Jenny Truscott, isn't it?' the woman asked, smiling. She had a warm, open face, framed by a shiny black bob and she was wearing a gorgeous teal wool coat. A crimson scarf was pinned with a jet brooch.

'Yes, well I used to be...' said Jenny cautiously, making a mental note to change her name by deed poll back to her maiden name after the divorce. The woman looked familiar but she couldn't place from where.

'I knew it was you! It's Cassandra, we went to Camberwell together.'

'Cassandra! Bloody hell, how long has it been?'

'Too long!'

They hugged and Jenny felt a rush of memories come back to her. 'You were studying textiles, weren't you? And going out with Ned... Ned Johnson? He was doing photography, if I remember rightly. Tall, dark and handsome.'

'And he still is! Well, the tall and handsome bit anyway, more grey than dark now!' Cassandra laughed. 'We've been married 30 years this year, believe it or not!'

Jenny looked round expectantly for him. 'Oh, he's not here right now, he's in Australia, on a photo-shoot for National Geographic,' she explained. 'I work as a textile restorer at the V&A. And what about you? What have you been up to?'

Jenny paused for a second, thinking how to sum up her life. 'I'm an interior designer, well I was… I'm not working so much now. I have two children and live in North Devon. Divorced…' She stopped, not wanting to get into recent events.

'What are you doing here? Up to see a show?'

'Not really – I just found myself free after an appointment,' replied Jenny aware she was being a bit cagey.

'In that case…' Cassandra looked up to see what was playing at the Theatre Royal, '…ditch *42nd Street* and come with me. I'm meeting two friends for a meal and I'm sure they won't mind you joining us.'

'Oh no, I don't want to intrude,' said Jenny.

'You wouldn't be, honestly!' Cassandra linked arms with her. 'Come on, it'll be so much fun catching up.'

Later that night, as Jenny lay in the hotel bath sipping a G&T, she realised that Cassandra was right, it had been fun. She could just chat and have a laugh with no agenda, no judgment. It felt like a breath of fresh air. The old Jenny Truscott could return, light-hearted and carefree… She hadn't realised she'd missed her so much. The Jenny Damerell she'd become was defensive, anxious, suspicious, on red alert. Her self-esteem had been chipped away during years of being in a toxic relationship.

On the train home, Jenny was determined not to slip back into the funk she'd been in. Seeing Cassandra had been a real tonic. The next day, she popped a card in the post to her, thanking her for the impromptu reunion and to her surprise, Cassandra rang the moment she received it.

'Seeing you really perked up my spirits – I'd forgotten what a great laugh you are,' she said.

Hearing Cassandra echo her own feelings gave Jenny another surge of positivity. She still had something to offer, she wasn't just a victim. She decided to broach what Mark had done, to see how Cassandra would react. After she'd finished explaining, to her relief, Cassandra was nothing but sympathetic. She was horrified with what she had been through and what's more, she came up with a plan.

'Look, Ned's brother is a retired policeman. He's now become a private investigator. He's based in Surrey and I won't lie, he's not cheap, but he may be worth a try? He might unearth something helpful for you.'

'Thanks so much, Cass. You're a genius!'

Before ringing the private investigator, Jenny had to get the bus into Bideford to have the last of her counselling sessions for the PTSD. She'd found them extremely helpful, offering her coping mechanisms for stress and anxiety that had really been beneficial. She also needed a few last-minute supplies for Jess's birthday party. Whilst out, she saw Joy at the chemist and thought she'd try a little experiment.

'Hi Joy,' she said breezily, walking over to the make-up counter. 'Nice to see you. I need to get some new make-up. I've got a hot date!'

'Oh? That's marvellous. See, didn't I tell you the universe would provide?' replied Joy, coming over.

Jenny drew lines of scarlet on her hand with the lipstick testers. 'It certainly has. A delicious man called Alasdair,' she said, smiling.

'I have to hear more – have you got time for a bite to eat?' suggested Joy. So, the pair went off to the local health-food cafe for buckwheat pancakes and salad.

'It's going to be a Highland fling,' said Jenny, mischievously as she sipped her green tea. Joy raised her eyebrow over her own steaming mug and Jenny continued. 'We're meeting in Fort George. I met him on the internet. He's 55, grey-haired, a beard. The most vivid blue eyes you've ever seen.'

'A photo! I must see a photo!' said Joy.

'Ah, I'm afraid not. My phone's playing up.' Jenny flashed Joy a look, but her friend just gazed back at her levelly, her green eyes unreadable. 'Anyway, trust me, he's gorgeous. A Scottish George Clooney. He was in finance in Edinburgh for decades but when his mother died a few years ago he returned to Skye to become a farmer – no sorry, what did he call it? A crofter.' Jenny was enjoying herself enormously. 'I've got a hotel booked for a few days. I'm quite excited. Mark's history – Alasdair's the main event now.'

'I'm so pleased for you. Make sure you meet in a public place though. I'm sure he's who he says he is, but you never can tell these days.'

'I will. Oh, and Joy? Don't breathe a word about this – I haven't told anyone yet. I want to see how things develop first. To be honest, it could all just be a flash in the pan.'

'I won't, your secret's safe with me.'

How long will it take for the secret to be vouchsafed?
Jenny wondered, incredulous at her own ability to lie
through her teeth. Again, she felt a twinge of guilt at such
double-standards, but she just had to find out if her friend
was as loyal to her as she'd once believed.

When she got home she rang Andy, the private detective. As they chatted, Jenny found herself being attracted
to his warm, mellifluous voice. Maybe it was all that talk of
the fictional Alasdair sending her hormones into overdrive?
Andy was confident and reassuring.

'Your case sounds like it has lots of potential for leads.
Don't say too much over the landline. I'll come to yours for
a meeting,' he said.

'Oh, better not. I still don't feel safe here – I think he
keeps watch on me. Let's meet halfway,' replied Jenny. A
meeting was arranged and they rang off.

The following Tuesday, the day before her assignation
with Andy PI (as she liked to think of him) Marcus came
home from work looking stressed and upset.

'Dad was in a right mood today.'

'Oh darling, I'm sorry, what about?'

'I dunno really. It started with him shouting at Rachael
about something. He was steaming and they had a massive
row – they don't really seem to get on any more. Then,
do you know what he said to me, Mum? I hardly dare tell
you...'

'What? You can tell me,' Jenny replied.

'He said, "I hear that whore of a mother of yours is

seeing someone," 'Sorry, Mum – sometimes he's so horrible about you.'

'Don't worry about that darling. We'll be divorced soon, and then he can say what he likes and it can't hurt me.'

'But are you?'

'No, I'm not even seeing anyone.'

'Weird… Not what Dad thinks,' said her handsome son, forking his dinner around his plate. 'He was ranting on: "What does she think she's playing at? How could your mother betray me when we're not even divorced yet?" Things like that. I hate it when he starts bad-mouthing you, Mum.'

Jenny could hear Mark saying this so clearly. 'I'm so sorry you had to hear this, Marcus. He shouldn't have taken it out on you. And none of it's true anyway. You can tell him from me that his sources must have gotten the wrong end of the stick.'

'Sources? He said you'd been seeing a man in Scotland for months before you split up, some financial wizard, or something. And that you're nothing but a gold-digger That you've got him all lined up for after the divorce.'

'Darling,' said Jenny going over to where her son was sitting at the kitchen table. She stroked his hair and kissed the top of his head, inhaling the scent she'd always loved. 'There's been some mistake, it's all rubbish. Me and Dad are getting divorced because we… we stopped getting along. But there's no one else involved, not on my part at least. Please believe that.'

Jenny felt mortified. She hadn't considered that her son would get caught in the crossfire when she'd tried her little experiment with Joy. Dabbling in Mark's brand of mind-games was illuminating but she hated the fact that people got hurt, and that made her feel tainted. Treating people like pawns with no thought for their feelings had given her a glimpse of what it must be like to think like a psychopath. But it was clear that the bush telegraph worked only too well, as she'd suspected. Say something to Joy and it gets reported back to Mark, via Sam or Tony, within days. Despite Joy's new-age mysticism and healing bullshit, she had hugely let Jenny down. She felt her eyes sting with tears. In her heart, she knew Joy's betrayal wasn't deliberate – Joy was just too trusting of others and too open with her own thoughts and feelings. But one thing was for sure, that was a friendship she could no longer rely on. Jenny knew it was no good ruminating about her grievances. She'd spent too long doing that already. No, she needed to forge a path ahead, to a future where she felt in control.

At least one thing had fallen into place though: George had finally moved out of Trethorne and fortunately, he was making a big thing of reclaiming his independence and rebuilding his life after his wife's death. He'd bought a share in a local country club, which was being rebranded with a big new golf course and luxury holiday chalets. He'd bought one of the chalets so that he could live on-site and help with running the place, and, it has to be said, have a golf course on his doorstep, golf being one of his passions in life. He left Trethorne without a backward glance, taking very few of his possession with him.

'Starting again Jennifer,' he'd said. 'I know when I'm not welcome. I would say I'd keep in touch, but I'm going to be so busy. Come and see my new place some time, if you like.'

And that was that. Her father had gone to seek his fortune elsewhere. She felt strangely sad to see him go. Even though he was a hard, selfish man, he was a link to her mother, and she felt that somehow, her once strong family was diminishing around her.

A few days after her father left, her *Decree Absolute* arrived in the post. Mark had not contested the *Decree Nisi* – how could he, when she had to all intents and purposes agreed that he should have all their jointly-owned assets apart from Trethorne. Neither had he contested the no-blame 'irreconcilable differences' declaration, which meant that in just over six months from their separation, they had been able to divorce. Both the negative influences in her life – her father and her husband – no longer lived under the same roof and could no longer exert undue influence on her. *Good riddance to them*, she thought.

Two weeks after her divorce, she once again found herself on a train, this time to Reading to meet Andy, and then on to the auction in London. She'd taken extra care with her outfit and was wearing her new lipstick. He may not be George McClooney but Jenny realised that it was the first time in years that she'd felt attracted to anyone. But when they met at the hotel by the station, seeing him in the flesh was a disappointment. Andy was on the short side, had a shaved head and was wearing a leather jacket. The spark she'd felt on the phone fizzled out instantly. *Oh well, no romance but he's still on my side*, she thought.

When they'd sat down with a coffee, Andy began to ask her questions. He wanted to know every single detail, from the ice-cube trays to the cross-dressing. It felt almost flattering, the amount of attention he was paying her. There was no glazing over or checking his watch, just listening carefully and taking notes on his laptop. Everything about Mark was covered, past and present, including his businesses, employees, family and friends. After Jenny had ransacked her brain for information, Andy sat back and gazed at her reflectively.

'It's much too early to say, but my hunch is that Mark's primary driver is revenge. He might have a lot to hide.'

'Revenge? But what for? Is it something I've done, then?'

'Possibly he holds you accountable for something, but he may be using you to get at someone else. You don't know who has ruffled his feathers in the past.' He covers everything up in so many layers that his motivations are obscure, but let me see what I can uncover.'

'Thank you, Andy. I'm losing count of the things I'm discovering about that man,' commented Jenny. This came as a shock to her. She had never even considered that other people may be in Mark's firing line. She had been so wrapped up in her own problems that the idea that Mark could have issues unconnected to her hadn't crossed her mind. In a strange way, it felt refreshing. Unearthing a whole new seam of Mark's murky past would be a curiously satisfying way to get even.

'Do you think my kids are safe?' Jenny asked Andy, suddenly remembering Marcus' words about Mark's anger.

'He may stop at nothing,' Andy mused. 'Keep an eye on them, but don't alarm them. In my experience, it is rare that children – flesh and blood – are in mortal danger, but he may use them as pawns in his games.'

This gave Jenny pause for thought. How could she lure them away from Mark's influence? After all, Marcus was working for him, and Jessica was friends with his employee, Sam. At some point in the not too distant future, they would have to know her concerns about their father – once Andy had done his job, and she knew what he was playing at.

After a couple of hours, they wrapped up their meeting and left the hotel. As they made their way out of the brass revolving door onto the street thronging with commuters, a man bumped into Jenny.

'Whoops, watch your step,' said a passer-by, grabbing her elbow to steady her. 'Jenny! What are you doing here?' It was Guy, and behind him stood Mark, his face thunderous. They must have followed her all the way up from Devon. Mark ignored Jenny and turned to Andy.

'You can't trust that fucking woman an inch' he raged. 'She's already got herself a man in Scotland, has she told you that? Don't touch her with a bargepole, she's nothing but trouble.' Mark's face was puce.

'Well, Mr Damerell, this little outburst tells me much more about you than it does about your ex-wife,' replied Andy, calmly.

'She's two-timing you! She's a whore!' Mark shouted, so that passers-by turned to stare.

'Marco, steady on, mate,' said Guy, moving him down the street.

Jenny and Andy went back into the hotel and Jenny sank down on one of the banquettes in the lobby. She was trembling all over and her body was covered with a film of sweat. Seeing Mark produced a primal reaction in her, so physical: the predator and the prey.

'Do you see what I'm up against?' she sobbed.

Andy nodded gravely. 'Having heard what he's like, it doesn't surprise me,' he said.

'But how did he know I was here?' said Jenny, fanning herself with a menu to cool down. 'I rang you from my mobile…'

'Oh, there are ways, believe you me. He's been a controller for 30 years, so he's not about to stop now, just because you're divorced,' said Andy. 'But think about it Jenny. He thinks we're having an affair, so he's got no idea who I really am. We're still one step ahead of him.'

That was reassuring and Andy now had a perfect example of how Mark operated.

'Another thing is that this kind of behaviour would be considered as stalking, a criminal offence, and I'm a witness. My advice would be to log it with the National Stalking Hotline. They'll also help you to monitor anything in the future to build up a case.'

'I will, thank you,' Jenny said, blotting her smudged mascara with a tissue. *Another helpline I never thought I would need,* she thought bleakly.

'It's all about power and control for these sorts of men. His ego doesn't allow you to have other partners, or a functioning life without him. You have to be careful,' added Andy. 'Change all your passwords – phones, bank accounts, emails, and speak to me in a few days. Now, let's get you to your platform.'

Andy saw Jenny onto her train to London and as the doors slid shut, she tried to blot out a wave of nausea. She was sickened by how much seeing Mark had affected her. He was still in her life and she hated it. She wanted to never think about him ever again. She rested her head against the carriage window and as the outskirts of Reading rumbled by, she remembered her diary. Her mind was still filled with the recent encounter so she started to write an account of the day's events. It may not be great literature but she found it therapeutic.

It wasn't such a great start to her trip, but the ending was fantastic. She went to the auction house the following day, jittery with nerves, worried that somehow, Mark had followed her there too. She looked around, but couldn't see him or Guy anywhere, and so she took a seat at the back to see how the bidding would go on her painting. She was disappointed that so few people were present, and thought that perhaps the painting would not make the reserve, but she needn't have worried. There was worldwide interest online.

The bidding started at £50,000 then went up by increments of £5,000 until it reached £75,000, then increments of £2,000 increased it to £77, £79, £81, £83, £85, £87, £89 – she couldn't believe it – £91, £93, "Any more bids… at ninety-three-thousand-pounds… SOLD to the internet bidder from New York."

Jenny just sat in her chair, unable to take it all in. Some stroke of luck, some good karma, had just made her a wealthy woman. She could renovate the barns and gardens, start her holiday business and even dabble in interior design again. For the first time in many years, she felt excited about the future. Her MS was in remission, and she was a free woman.

When she got back home Jessica greeted her at the door, full of her spa weekend with Sam.

'It was like something out of a magazine, Mum – fluffy robes and slippers, the works. And the treatments! OMG – to die for! Feel my skin, it's been pummelled to within an inch of its life,' she laughed, angling her cheek towards her mum.

'Soft as a baby's proverbial,' said Jenny, giving it a stroke. 'Although I seem to remember yours was less fragrant.'

'Muuum!' Jessica rolled her eyes. She may be nearly 23 but Jenny still caught glimpses of the child she once was.

'Sam was telling me that her dad had been in the Army, like Granddad was. What bit of it… what regiment or whatever was he in?'

'It's funny, I should know but I don't. You could ask him yourself. It would give you the chance to go and see him in his new place,' replied Jenny. She decided to keep her recent good fortune to herself. Walls have ears, and all that.

'I'm glad you had a good time, darling,' said Jenny to her daughter, privately awarding herself 100 parenting points.

'Oh, it was lush, Mum,' Jessica replied, her eyes shining. 'And Sam's asked me to help her with a local design commission she's working on. She says I have a natural sense of style. I suppose I must take after you!'

'Oh really?' 50 more points for not saying something derogatory about Sam.

'Yes, she's doing up some holiday lets nearby,'

That was it, forget the parenting points, Jenny couldn't help but be drawn in. 'Holiday lets? I thought they only developed residential projects?'

'Yes, it's a new venture.'

Nice, thought Jenny, *and it just happens to be stepping right on my toes.* But then, seeing sense, Jenny realised that Sam couldn't possibly know about her plans for Trethorne, and anyway, everyone who had an old barn around these parts was doing it up for holiday lets. Instead, Jenny took another tack.

'So, did she mention her love life, at all? Are Dad and her an item?'

'Why, are you jealous, Mum? No, they're just friends!' exclaimed Jessica. 'It is possible for a man and woman to be friends and not in a relationship, you know. Haven't you seen that vintage film *When Harry met Susan*?'

'*When Harry Met Sally!*' Jenny laughed, 'and yes, of course I've seen it – and they end up together, remember? No, of course I'm not jealous. I just wondered, that's all. And good luck to them anyway – it's no business of mine.' Privately, Jenny felt conflicted: if they were in a relationship, Jenny felt duty-bound to warn Sam about Mark, but on the other hand, she knew whatever she had to say would be rejected… What a conundrum.

Jenny realised that she knew very little about Sam. Nothing about her family, her past, not even who the father of her son was. She recalled the few times Sam had took him to the office over the years. He was a gorgeous little boy with auburn hair and dark eyes. Her heart dropped to the pit of her stomach. Could he be Mark's? Is that why Mark is cagey about being with Sam? Because they've been together all along? No, no… and what if he was. It was nothing to her now.

But, maybe she should ask Andy…? She gave herself a shake, she was being silly. Mark and her were over, so why did it matter who he shacked up with? She knew she should leave well alone but it was irresistible. Before she could stop herself, she texted Andy. It was like an obsession, the need to illuminate all the dark shadows that had surrounded her for so long, to uncover all the dirty secrets that haunted her.

The following day, a text pinged back. *Samantha Penbode's son's father is not named on the birth certificate. Her most recent ex was Roger Millstone, a solicitor in Bristol.* Not named eh? So, he could be Mark's son. Jenny felt like texting a million more questions but stopped herself. This need to expose Mark was becoming dangerously close to an addiction. She had to focus on the present, on what was going on right here, right now. Be mindful, that's what they called it.

Later that day, Jenny resolved to go and see George in his new luxury lodge.

'Hello, Dad' she said as she walked up the steps, finding him on the veranda in a wooden recliner, enjoying the afternoon sunshine.

'Jennifer. Didn't expect to see you here so soon. Coming to check up on me?'

'Yes! I wanted to see your new digs. Very nice too. How are you Dad?'

'Chipper, old thing. Chipper. Got myself a job mowing the lawns around the lodges on the ride-on mower. Great fun. And then tonight we have a meeting of shareholders to look at building a new indoor swimming-pool. I feel in the thick of it Jenny. It's great to be in business again.'

'Well you look good on it Dad. I'm pleased for you. By the way, Jessie asked me the other day what regiment you were in, in the Army, and I couldn't remember. What was it?'

'Why does she want to know?' he asked, suddenly defensive. 'Don't talk much about my Army days Jennifer. Let's leave it at that, eh?'

'But it was an important part of your life. We want to know, we really do,' Jenny replied.

'Well… I remember it like yesterday. Better than yesterday in fact,' he said, and she caught a gleam in his eye of the vigour and strength that he used to have. Once he was on a roll, he went on to tell her the highlights of his military career, such as being stationed in Germany during the 50s.

'Your mother wasn't too pleased,' he said with a chuckle. 'There was a bit of unrest amongst the troops, dissention in the ranks, as they say. One chap ended up being court-marshalled.'

'For what?' asked Jenny.

'Oh, it was such a scandal, brought shame on the whole base…' he stopped abruptly. 'Anyway, all a long time ago,' he said, signalling she should leave. 'I must wash and shave ready for the meeting tonight. Thanks for calling by.'

As she lay in bed that night, she thought about what George had said. How sad that someone was court-marshalled – for being gay, she assumed. Homosexuality was a crime in those days, she knew that. Her thoughts turned to the people she knew who had had the courage to come out. It was only 50 years ago, and how much things had changed, but her own brother Paul hadn't come out because of how her father would react, so discrimination still lingered on, even now. People having to live a lie because the truth is unacceptable to some.

What was it that Oscar Wilde had said? 'One's real life isn't the one one lives.' Suddenly, an image of her son's face popped into her mind. Her darling Marcus, her baby. She'd suspected he might be gay himself, for some time. No sign of a girlfriend and he always surrounded himself with his group of male friends, all single themselves. Should she ask him? She didn't mind, of course, but she wanted him to know that he was safe to come out, that he should be true to himself. Then, inevitably, she thought of Mark and how homophobic he had always been, despite being bi-sexual. *What a hypocrite!* She sighed, sinking down into the pillow. If it was the last thing she did, she'd make sure Jessica and Marcus were not afraid of their father's judgmentalism.

CHAPTER 9

The Raising of Dust and Loose Paper

Force Four on the Beaufort Scale

Jenny took a long drink of her white wine and looked around her. *What the hell am I doing here?* she asked herself. Right in the heart of the enemy camp. It was Sam's birthday party and somehow, she had found herself agreeing to go. Partly because she wanted to prove that she wasn't the social pariah that Mark had made her out to be, but mainly because she wanted to show that she wasn't scared of him. God knows why Sam had invited her though. If she wanted to pretend that they were all pally-pally then she wasn't going to stop her. It might give her a glimpse of what Sam was up to.

The party was at the opening night of a new wine-bar in town, so Jenny supposed that Sam saw it as a networking opportunity. Mixing business with pleasure as usual. Mark was there, Liz, Joy. It was heaving with people she wanted to avoid. She'd already had an excruciating exchange with Sam, who was all faux-concern for her, asking if she was coping okay on her own at Trethorne, and saying she'd heard about how unwell Jenny had been. Obviously, Sam looked a million dollars and Jenny felt shabby and old in comparison.

This was a stupid idea. She put down her glass, gathered up her bag and coat and started to walk to the exit but she felt a hand on her shoulder, stopping her.

'Stay,' came a male voice. Heart sinking, she turned, pasting a smile on her face. 'Don't go yet, Mum,' said Marcus.

Relief coursed through her. Her son. A friendly face amidst a nest of vipers.

'Marcus, how've you been?' she exclaimed.

'What? Since breakfast? Fine, thanks,' he replied.

'Right, yes. Sorry, I was on automatic small-talk mode,' she said. 'Are you having fun?'

'Not really, not my sort of crowd,' he said, nodding towards the throng of forty- and fifty-somethings.

'Old enough to be your parents, eh?

'Sorry, Mum. You know what I mean.'

'So, who is your crowd?' asked Jenny.

'Oh, you know, Ben, Dan, that lot,' replied Marcus, referring to the group of mates he always hung around with. 'I'm meeting them later, but I thought I'd show my face here first. Sam's been really good to me.'

'I'm sure she has,' said Jenny tightly. 'In what way?'

' Oh, she's helped me out a lot,' Marcus flushed. 'Helped me get my head round things…'

'Get your head round what? What is it, Marcus?'

'It's fine, Mum, it's nothing,' he said, flushing darker. His eyes were darting around the room as if he was looking to flee.

'You can tell me, Marcus.'

'Oh, it's just about… about me being…' Marcus trailed off.

'What? Being what?'

'Oh, you must have guessed by now!' He looked furiously at her.

'Are you trying to tell me you're gay, Marcus? Is that it?'

'Yes, Mum!' Marcus looked down at his beer bottle and started scratching the foil off the neck of it with his thumbnail, his mouth set in a line.

'Oh, Marcus, you could have told me any time, it's not a problem at all, in fact I'm pleased you've come out.' Marcus pulled a face. 'What? That's the right phrase, isn't it?'

'Yes, Mum but it just sounds odd you saying it.'

'Oh, you'll get used to it! Now, is it wrong of me to ask if you've got a boyfriend? Or should I say partner?'

'Mum, stop! Just telling you was bad enough…'

'Is that why you told Sam first? Because you were worried what I'd say?'

'Yes, well no, I don't know. She's just so chilled about everything.'

And I'm not, thought Jenny. She straightened the collar of his check shirt – she longed to hug him but she knew he wouldn't want her to in public; he wouldn't want to draw attention to himself. Marcus had always been very sensitive to how others viewed him, always on the look-out for any slight. And no wonder, with Mark as a father. Jenny shuddered to think how Mark would react to Marcus's news. She certainly wasn't going to tell him. 'So apart from Sam, who else knows?' she asked.

'Jessica, obviously. And a couple of friends. Not everyone. I've known since I was at junior school but I never felt I could say. I haven't told Dad...'

'No, I can understand that.' Mark was open about his homophobia. *Fucking hypocrite.* An image of his gay sex toys that she discovered flashed through her mind. And her dad's bigoted attitude was no better. It was unsurprising that Marcus hadn't felt safe enough to reveal his sexuality. Just like his Uncle Paul – another pattern running through the family.

Jenny looked around and accidentally caught Liz's eye, who waved. 'Shall we get out of here? Have a proper chat somewhere else?' she said quickly. She had managed to avoid speaking to Liz for weeks and she didn't want to break that habit now.

'Sorry, Mum, I'm meeting the boys at The Crown,' replied Marcus.

'Yes, you did say. Oh well, I'll walk there with you and grab a taxi from the rank.' Jenny made to start walking to the door but Marcus stopped her.

'One sec, I'll just say goodbye to Sam,' he replied. Jenny rued the fact she'd brought him up to be a polite boy, as Liz was advancing fast and she had nowhere to hide.

'Liz, hi, how are you?' she said coolly.

'Jen! Long time no see,' replied Liz, giving her friend a hug. 'What do you make of it here then?' She gestured to their surroundings.

'Nice, it certainly fills a gap in the market. This town is crying out for somewhere decent to have a glass of wine,' said Jenny, looking at the stylish glass lampshades and velvet seats in vibrant jewel tones.

'Yes, anywhere but The Crown. That carpet's been absorbing stains since the eighties. It must be well-marinated by now,' joked Liz. Jenny couldn't help but laugh. Despite their recent spat, she'd missed her old friend.

'The décor here's quirky and fun, isn't it?' replied Jenny. 'I wonder who did it?'

'Sam of course! I thought you knew…? She's done a good job, but she's not as good as you.'

Jenny found the compliment somewhat galling. *Is she just saying that to get back in my good books?*

'Maybe she should do the same for Joy and Tony's restaurant?' continued Liz, unaware of Jenny's cynicism. 'Mark's been bailing them out for umpteen years but I think a complete new refit would work wonders for them.'

Jenny took a sip of her wine, trying to hide her reaction. *Mark had been financing Tony and Joy's restaurant? This was news to her. And why did Liz know but not her?* Again, she felt like a mushroom – fed shit and kept in the dark. As these thoughts crossed her mind she just kept smiling but it was no good, as Liz detected her old friend's agitation. 'Oh, sorry… Am I not supposed to mention Mark?'

'Of course you can!' said Jenny, bristling.

'Then why the long face?' She'd forgotten that Liz knew her too well. 'Jen, honestly, you need to get over yourself, my lovely. Yes, I know you've been through the mill but you're out the other side now. Everyone's moved on – you're the only one obsessing about the past.'

'Have you forgotten what Mark did to me?' said Jenny, keeping her voice low.

'Are you still on about that? Look Jen, you know I think Mark is an arsehole, always did and always will, but do you seriously think he was trying to do away with you?' Liz raised her eyebrows. 'Darling, you've been through hell: you have MS, you're menopausal, you've had a painful divorce… if you put all those factors together it's no wonder you "lost it" a bit.'

Jenny was furious. 'I didn't "lose it,"' she hissed, imitating Liz's air-quotes. 'I know what he did. And he's still at it, and I can't believe you, of all people, are taking his side.' She looked desperately over her shoulder for Marcus. He was now talking to his dad and they were laughing together. *For God's sake, stop fraternising with the enemy and hurry up,* she willed him.

'What makes you think that? Your CCTV? Can you hear what you sound like, Jen? It's like you're obsessed or something. Why would Mark want to hurt you now you're divorced?'

'Why indeed, Liz? Anyway, I must just nip to the loo. MS and all that,' she said pointedly, and slipped away. In the cool of the ladies – with chic vintage tiles, she noted bitterly – Jenny reflected on the conversation. Liz was once her fiercest advocate, but now it was as if she didn't believe a word Jenny said. What had changed? How did Liz know about the CCTV? She hadn't mentioned it. Jenny dried her hands and left, finding Marcus at the door, looking for her. Swapping the fug of the bar for the fresh evening air was soothing. She found she was trembling. What a total over-load of information and emotions the evening had been.

Jenny was just dozing off when she heard the front door slam. *One of the kids coming home,* she thought sleepily. Then she heard loud sobbing and found herself upright and putting on her dressing gown before she had hardly opened her eyes. Old habits die hard. The kids may be grown up but once a mother, always a mother.

Marcus was sitting on the bottom step of the stairs, his head in his hands.

'What's wrong, darling?' she asked, stroking his hair. The aniseed fumes of Sambuca drifted off him.

'It's Dad…' he wept. *Mark? Has something happened to him?* Despite her loathing of him, she felt an intestinal lurch. 'He joined us in The Crown. It was fine at first but then I decided to tell him… I thought, "Bite the bullet" and all that. You took it so well, Mum but…' Marcus thumped his temple with his fist, 'I'm such a fucking idiot! Why did I tell him?'

'You told Mark you're gay?'

'Yes. Apparently, I'm a queer, a poofter, a faggot. That's what he called me,' her son sobbed. 'Can you believe it, Mum? He's sacked me, disowned me. "You're no son of mine," he said.'

'Oh Marcus,' she said, 'that's so cruel.' She took him in her arms and just let him cry. As she held him, she thought back to all the times Mark had been so hard on him as he grew up. So mean with the birthday bike all those years ago. And before that the 'mysterious bruises' of the leukaemia scare that Jenny had always felt uneasy about. Their beautiful, delicate boy had never been good enough for Mark. He wasn't the macho son he'd hoped for. Marcus was a disappointment to him. Her heart ached for her son.

After a few minutes, Marcus staggered off towards the bathroom and she heard him being sick. She put a glass of water by his bedside and went back to bed. *Fucking Mark. What a total hypocrite. When will his toxic impact end?*

Jenny forced herself to think it over. Mark's own sexuality was obviously so precarious to him that he felt threatened even by his own son. It also gave Mark the motive for fathering a boy with Sam – a son to mould into a 'real man' when the first one failed to come up to scratch. To Jenny, it was all just another example of how single-minded Mark was, and how ruthless.

The next day Jenny was lingering over her coffee when Marcus walked into the kitchen looking awful. His eyes were bloodshot and his face a pale grey.

'How are you feeling, love?' she asked Marcus, who was slumped at the table.

'Not great, Mum. I can't decide whether I need to throw up again or have a huge fry-up.'

'Shall we take it gently with egg on toast?'

'Please,' he said gratefully. As she flicked on the kettle, she didn't know whether to broach his argument with Mark or not, so she stayed silent.

'What a total balls-up I made,' Marcus groaned, head in his hands. 'Biggest mistake of my life, telling Dad.'

'You did what you felt was right; you were just being honest with your father. There's nothing wrong with being gay. It's not your fault if Mark can't accept that.'

'Well it obviously wasn't right, was it? I'm unemployed and my dad's disowned me. Great result,' croaked Marcus, near to tears. 'I wish I could turn the clock back.'

Don't we all, thought Jenny, *then I would never have married the bastard in the first place.*

'Oh, love, don't worry, you can work for me,' said Jenny.

'What doing? Being your carer?' Marcus flushed. 'Sorry, Mum, I didn't mean that. It was just something Dad said; that all I was good for was taking care of you. But that's bollocks, I know it is. You're doing brilliantly. It's me who's the weak one.'

'Who's weak?' It was Jessica, bounding in the back-door from a run, looking fresh-faced and healthy, the polar opposite to her brother.

'Nothing, no one,' mumbled Marcus.

'Come on, you can tell me,' she persisted.

'Jessica, that's enough,' said Jenny.

'Fine, suit yourself,' said Jessica, grabbing a glass of water and giving Marcus a glare as she headed for her room.

Later that day Jenny had another meeting with Andy.

'I've been doing some more digging,' he said, 'and there are a lot of military connections in this case, Jenny. Every lead I follow ends there.'

'Well, I know my dad was in the Army. Oh, and Sam's father too, apparently,' replied Jenny, recalling a comment Jessica had made about it recently – although at the time, it meant nothing to her.

'And Mark's,' added Andy.

'Really? Mark's dad? I never knew that… I only knew he'd left when Mark was little.'

'That's one way of putting it. Mark's mother actually divorced his father.'

'Wow, Mark never mentioned that.'

'It doesn't surprise me – there was a stigma attached to it then so maybe his mother never told him that they'd divorced – maybe it was easier to say he deserted them? Anyway, I think the military connection is a promising lead and I'm going to pursue it. I'll let you know if anything comes of it, ASAP.'

'Great, thanks. But when you find out, don't send anything to me by post – phone me instead. There's a problem with my mail again.' Jenny'd had a few letters delivered wrapped in Royal Mail plastic bags as they'd been mysteriously ripped or the seal had come open. In years gone by, she'd just thought this was a normal occurrence, but now she realised that they'd obviously been tampered with. Someone was still sticking his nose in. It was incredible the lengths he went to.

When Jenny got back home, Jessica was watching TV.

'Hi, darling,' she called but her daughter didn't reply. She went through to the lounge. 'What are you watching?'

'A film on Netflix. It's called *Getting Away With It*. Dad recommended it when we had lunch today,' Jessica said flatly, not looking away from the screen.

'You okay? Anything wrong?'

'No, I'm fine,' Jessica replied, still in a monotone. She obviously wasn't, but Jenny felt tired and couldn't face delving deeper so she went into her room. Immediately she noticed that her desk was in a mess.

'Have you been looking through my paperwork?' she asked, going back into the living room.

'What makes you think that?' said Jessica.

'My bank statements have moved.'

'Mum, you're so paranoid. Why would I look at your bank statements?'

Jenny noticed that her daughter was answering a question with a question, a classic way of dodging the truth. She hated the fact that she could identify this sort of thing now. Once upon a time she trusted everyone, believed what they said, but now she was hard-wired to be suspicious.

Jenny knew Mark had put Jessica up to it, and that he would couch the snooping in such terms that her daughter would think there was nothing wrong with doing so. He wouldn't be able to resist nosing into her affairs, seeing her cash flow. He could even have found out about the old painting she'd discovered, and the cool fortune it had made at auction. That would make him seethe with rage, but what could he do with the information? They were divorced now and he couldn't touch her money; a fact that was wonderfully reassuring to Jenny.

For the first time in years she was truly self-sufficient, supporting herself financially. It made her shudder to remember how he used to use money as another way of humiliating her – throwing a few pounds at her here and there, always leaving her overdrawn and struggling whilst he was making a mint. But not any longer. She knew this would make Mark hopping mad, and a smile crept over her face. He wanted to strip away everything from her again, grind her back into the ground, but he couldn't. He didn't have that power over her any more.

Although her daughter was being very rude, Jenny decided to leave it. She had noticed that whenever Jessica spent prolonged time with her father, she always returned out of sorts. It must be difficult having divided loyalties at the best of times, but nigh-on impossible with someone like Mark for a dad, who was all about point-scoring and manipulation. Now Mark no longer had easy access to Jenny, he had to resort to controlling her indirectly through their daughter. He just couldn't stop himself; he was obsessed. She wondered what he had said to convince Jessica to spy on her. Probably some rubbish about still caring for her, despite them being divorced, and needing to keep an eye on her. She expected he included a line about her being hopeless with finances, to lay it on thick. She could practically hear him saying it: *You know your mum, Jessie, she's a spendthrift, buying shiny trinkets with no thought to balancing the books. You need to be her sentinel, taking care of her like I did.*

She could just imagine the drip-drip-drip of lies until Jessica totally believed him. And because Jenny wasn't doing the same about Mark, Jessica had no reason to challenge him. So much for the moral high-ground. She knew it was doing the right thing not to enter into a slanging match but not doing so meant her children didn't respect her. They didn't know the half of what he'd done. She felt a pang of sadness in her heart for how Mark had damaged their relationships with her. Marcus had felt that he couldn't confide in her about being gay and Jessica felt comfortable about rifling through her things. Not how she ever wanted her children to be.

One thing she hadn't reckoned on was the damage Mark was doing to the children's relationship with each other too, as she discovered later when she heard Jessica and Marcus talking in the hall.

'Oh my god, when will you ever learn?' said Jessica.

Marcus's voice was quieter, indistinct. Then Jessica spoke again: 'Oh, you're such an idiot. You don't deserve to work for Dad anyway. What a moron!'

Jenny leapt out of her chair and rushed out into the hall.

'Jessica, do not EVER speak to your brother like that again, do you hear me?' Jessica span round, her eyebrows raised in shock.

'Keep your hair on, mother!'

'That language is completely unacceptable. If you're living in my house, I expect, no I DEMAND that you speak respectfully to everyone in it, including Marcus. Do you understand?'

Jessica stood there, her mouth hanging open in surprise. It was the first time Jenny had ever spoken so forcefully to her.

'Yes, Mum,' she replied quietly. 'Sorry, Marcus.'

Jenny stood there quivering, as Jessica slowly walked upstairs into her bedroom and shut the door. Marcus did the same. Jessica's words, her tone of voice were an exact replica of Mark's. But now Jenny was finding her own voice, maybe some of her personality would make an impact on them too. Jenny had always believed that it was never too late.

Returning to her own room, Jenny picked up her journal and began to write the latest entry. *You couldn't make this up,* she mused. She looked back over the pages and felt shocked at the rollercoaster ride she'd been through. When she came to the revelation about being poisoned, the paper was slightly ridged with dried tears. She felt a sudden wave of fury and frustration. *No one should have that done to them without any consequences.* She'd nearly died, and she would have if Mark'd had his way – and yet she was expected to put it behind her and give up wanting justice. She was continually being told this by her so-called friends, and even the police didn't want to touch her allegations with a barge-pole. Mark had managed to charm them all enough to make them believe him rather than her. He had turned gaslighting into a fine art. It was easier and more palatable for people to explain away Mark's actions by blaming it on her mental health, rather than accepting the truth. It was fine for her life to be ruined and her relationships shattered, to be labelled 'mentally unstable' so long as the status quo wasn't disrupted. Even if it meant a psychopath was living in their midst.

What was the name of the film Jessica was watching? *Getting Away With It* – another coded message from Mark. She felt like screaming. He was so damn smart and he knew exactly how to get to her without it being used as evidence. She was being toyed with, like a cat toys with a mouse. What could she do that was equally clever? She hated to reduce herself to his level but what was the alternative? Rise above it, as Joy would say? That would mean he'd won.

She looked down at her lap and saw her journal – and then it dawned on her. This could be her secret weapon. If she turned her life story into a novel she could tell the world what had happened. She could change names and counties to protect herself and her children, but she could still write about every last detail of Mark's evil ways. At last she could reveal her story to the world so that the truth of what had happened to her could help other women in a similar situation. She picked up her pen and continued with renewed vigour, the writing process suddenly becoming incredibly cathartic. This would be her way of getting even.

The next morning Jenny tried to peel her eyes open but they felt glued together; she was exhausted and felt emotionally wrung out. She'd had an awful night – hours staring into the darkness, her racing thoughts not settling enough to sleep, and then when she did manage to, she was plagued by recurring nightmares. Somehow, deciding to write the novel had unlocked a whole new level of anxiety in her. Rationally, she knew Mark couldn't touch her as long as she made the book unidentifiable – and that if he did make a fuss about it or tried to sue her for libel then it would be tantamount to admitting his guilt – but still, she felt very vulnerable. She rang Marie from Women's Aid.

'Recovering from domestic abuse takes a very long time, Jenny,' she said. 'You may be physically safe now but the psychological damage is harder to heal. Writing down your experiences is an excellent form of therapy; it's proven to help ease post-traumatic stress disorder. A lot of clients also benefit from a course of counselling – is this something you'd consider?' she asked.

More counselling, she thought, recalling her time with the psychotherapist, but then she reflected on her relationship with Marie. 'Well, talking to you has been an absolute lifeline. You were the one person who believed me – so perhaps counselling would help…'

'I'm so glad to hear that, Jenny. You've come such a long way and you should feel very proud of yourself. But there's only so much I can do. I'm not a professionally trained therapist, so I can't help with the deeper issues that are surfacing for you.'

When Jenny put down the phone she wondered if Marie could be right. She researched local therapists and found one who specialised in domestic abuse based in a neighbouring village, would you believe. *It must be fate,* Jenny thought.

She got an initial assessment the next day and it was like opening the floodgates. The psychotherapist, Kathryn, just sat listening as Jenny poured out everything that had happened. She brought her journal with her but didn't need to refer to it, it was all etched in her memory. When she spoke about it, again she thought it sounded fantastical; the abuse, the poisoning, her phone being monitored, her post being intercepted and she said as much.

'You feel that what has happened to you is unbeliev-able?' asked Kathryn.

'Yes – well, no – more that I can understand why people think I'm losing it. I can't prove it's Mark – it's all so compli-cated and the monitoring is all tied up with his network of cronies. So, there's nothing to connect the poisoning to him. It feels like he's got everyone working for him, like he's set everyone against me, even the postman! God, I do sound paranoid, I really do,' exclaimed Jenny.

'I'm not here to judge,' said Kathryn, 'I'm here to help you process your feelings.'

Her perspective was a comfort and it helped clear Jenny's head from the jumble of defensiveness and self-doubt. The 50 minutes were over in a flash and Jenny left the session deep in thought.

Waiting at the nearby bus stop, she glimpsed a figure heading up the path to the house she'd just left. She looked familiar. It was Rachael. Rachael from the office. What was she doing going to a psychotherapist? Jenny's hyper-vigilance kicked-in and she worried that Rachael was in cahoots with the therapist, but then Jenny remembered how Kathryn had taken pains to reassure her that their meetings would be entirely confidential. Jenny took a closer look and saw Rachael's coat was buttoned over a large bulge. She was pregnant. Immediately Jenny thought of Mark. She'd always suspected them of having an affair. All those secret meetings, the giggling in the stock cupboard. But whatever had happened, Rachael obviously wasn't happy now and she would certainly be in the 'geriatric mother' category. Jenny calculated that she must easily be in her early forties. What she'd give to be a fly on the wall at her appointment.

And then Jenny understood something as if for the first time: Liz was right. Jenny did suspect everyone. First Sam and her child, now Rachael and her unborn baby. But the world was bigger than Mark Damerell and not everyone fell for his charms. Their stories were not hers; their pain was not her pain. It felt like a letting go. It was a very slight, almost imperceptible feeling, but was this the start of Jenny moving on? How she hoped so. How she longed to never be within Mark's gravitational pull ever again.

That evening Jenny was flicking through the channels on the TV when she came across a programme about internet crime. Organised crime rings targeted online dating sites, luring people in with fake identities and swindling them out of their money. Jenny felt sorry for the victims; innocent souls just hoping for love. She found herself welling up at the thought of others like her, so trusting, only to be slapped in the face for their gullibility. But then she remembered how Mark was always glued to his laptop. Tapping away late at night in the office. Could Mark be involved with something like that – either as a victim or a perpetrator? She wouldn't put it past him. Not content with having affairs with colleagues and secret liaisons with men, he also needed to sate his dark, twisted sexuality on the internet. He'd be perfectly at home there, in the maelstrom of vice and immorality. But then another thought came to her: she'd read recently that most antisocial or extreme behaviour had its roots in abuse of some sort or another. This was not the first time that she'd suspected that Mark himself could have been a victim of abuse and that he was enacting what he'd learned as a young child. She would never know whether Mark's father or another family member had himself perpetrated horrendous crimes on the young boy, nonetheless, this did not exonerate Mark from his own behaviour.

The following week she had another appointment scheduled with Andy, having received a text from him saying '*I have some new information*'. She was getting used to hopping on and off trains and was enjoying the sense of freedom this brought, and it would not be long now before her own licence would be renewed, because – surprise, surprise – she hadn't had another seizure since Mark had left; since she'd stopped drinking the iced water.

They met in a hotel lobby and Andy ushered her to a discreet booth. Jenny couldn't help but feel a burst of excitement, she was enjoying the suspense – what had he unearthed this time?

'Jenny, I was right about the military connection,' he began. 'Mark's father was in the army for nearly 20 years, but he ended up being court-marshalled...'

'Court-marshalled? What for?' replied Jenny.

'Read this: it's all here in black and white,' said Andy, showing her a photocopy of an official-looking form. In the box marked 'Charge', in typed letters, were the words *Sexual Indecency*.

'Sexual indecency? What does that mean?'

'It's military parlance for homosexual behaviour, which was, of course, illegal then,' replied Andy.

'Mark's dad was gay?' Jenny was speechless. 'So that's why his mother divorced his father?'

'Probably, but since same-sex adultery wasn't grounds for divorce – not then and not now either – we'll never be entirely certain,' said Andy, 'but I don't think this is the end of the story. I'm sure there's something else I'm missing. I'm going to keep hunting and don't worry, I won't give up until I find it,' he said.

CHAPTER 10

Small Trees Begin to Sway

Force Five on the Beaufort Scale

Jenny put the key in the ignition and turned it. As the car purred into life, she felt magnificent. Finally, a year after her seizure, she'd had the all-clear and was allowed to drive again. The sense of freedom was incredible; no more begging for lifts, no more waiting at chilly bus stops and train stations. And she certainly wouldn't miss shelling out for taxis all the time, although she'd got to know the local taxi driver so well they were on first-name terms now. Jenny had already enjoyed a few trips to the beach on her own and it was glorious just sitting in the cliff top car park completely alone, feeling the wind buffet the car and gazing out at the shimmering dark blue horizon. Jenny manoeuvred the car around to the front of the house and beeped the horn. After a few moments, Jessica emerged and hopped in to the passenger seat. 'And we're off!' she joked, as Jenny pulled out of the drive. They were heading to Bristol to go to the Harbour Festival and Boat Show. Neither of them was particularly interested in boats but it was a good excuse for a jolly.

As they pootled along the lanes towards the dual carriageway, Jenny thought about Andy's last revelation. So, Mark's dad was thrown out of the army for being gay. What a humdinger of a skeleton in the closet. She thought of the impact that must have had on his family. His mother had divorced him, surely, because of this. Mark had grown up never knowing his father. Such was the shame at the time, the public judgement and condemnation that tore families apart and ruined careers. Marcus had experienced a flavour of this, but the big question was: Did Mark know? Was this at the root of his hypocritical and complicated sex life – homophobic yet attracted to men? Did he loathe that aspect of himself because he was repeating his father's behaviour? Delving deeper, did his psychopathy stem from there? All her reading on the subject suggested that it can be caused by separation from a parent in the early years. Mark's father left without a backward glance on his fourth birthday. It all added up.

Jenny glanced over at Jessica, who was tapping away at her mobile, earphones plugged in as usual. There was no way she could tell her about this, not yet anyway. Jenny felt she was already treading on eggshells, trying to negotiate her way around her daughter's relationship with Mark. Throwing in this bombshell would be destructive. Tempting, but ultimately destructive. She'd already seen how her children could be put in the firing line when she'd tried her experiment with Joy passing information to Mark, and she didn't want to do that again.

One good thing about this discovery is that it helped her understand Mark's motives. The more she learnt about him, the less she felt like a powerless victim. Being controlled and abused by Mark for so many years had had a devastating effect on Jenny's self-esteem. Gaining a glimpse at why he felt the need to crush her helped her claw back some sense of pride. She wasn't weak, as she'd been brainwashed into thinking, she was trusting, as any normal, loving person is. Mark had taken advantage of this and used it to dominate her.

As the countryside flashed by, Jenny's thoughts turned to her own family. Hadn't her father said something about an incident whilst he was in the Army…? Her foot lifted off the accelerator slightly as something occurred to her. The car started to slow down and Jessica raised her eyes from her phone.

'Mum? What is it? Why are you stopping?' Jenny had turned white and her heart was pounding. A layby was up ahead and Jenny pulled into it, grateful to stop.

Jenny became aware that she was breathing very shallowly and consciously took a deep breath to steady herself.

'Are you okay, Mum? Do you feel sick or something?' asked Jessica. 'Hang on, I've got a bottle of water somewhere…'

'I'm fine. Sorry, darling, I just remembered something…' replied Jenny, taking a swig of the water to moisten her dry mouth. *Could her father have anything to do with Mark's dad's court-marshal…? Don't be stupid, Jennifer! I'm putting two and two together and making five, again.*

'What? What have you remembered?'

'Oh nothing, really. It's not important,' she replied. 'I'm just being silly. It's all ancient history anyway, nothing for you to worry about. Now, we'd better get going, we don't want to miss the first flotilla, do we?'

'Oh no, Mum. I'm longing to see the flotilla,' answered Jessica with heavy sarcasm. 'What's a flotilla again?' and they both laughed.

They got home at dusk the next day, the boot loaded with shopping bags. As Jessica had observed, a trip to Bristol wouldn't be right without swinging by Cribbs Causeway. It was a treat for both of them to wander around the shining glass and steel shopping centre after the rather limited rows of shops in their local towns. The car crunched over the gravel drive and Jessica got out.

'I'm just popping over to see granddad for a while,' Jenny said nonchalantly.

'Okay Mum.' Jess slammed the car door, then opened it again. 'It was nice to spend some "quality time" with you, Mum,' she said, making air quotes with her fingers. She smiled and slammed the door even harder. The vigour of youth.

Jenny drove over to her father's lodge in the nearby country club.

After knocking several times to no avail, she opened the front door to see George sitting in his lounge chatting to someone. Whoever it was sat in the armchair opposite so she couldn't see a face. She walked around to see an old, balding man holding a glass of whiskey.

'Hello there, I'm Jenny, George's daughter,' she said, extending her hand.

'Hello Jenny,' he replied sheepishly. 'Sorry, I should get up but I may have had a little too much of this,' he said, gesturing to the glass.

'Jenny? I didn't hear you knock? This is Malcolm, an old friend from my Army days,' said George. 'He's a solicitor now in Bristol.'

Jenny immediately wondered if he could be linked with the court martial too, but realised she was jumping to far too many conclusions. They'd clearly been stuck into the whiskey for some time. In the kitchen, dirty lunch plates were abandoned on the table, joined by empty wine glasses and bottles.

She had been hoping to ask her father about his time in the military again, to perhaps gently probe for more details but Malcolm was here, and anyway they were both far too drunk to hold a sensible conversation with. It would have to wait for another day.

Jenny made her excuses, saying she'd just popped around on the spur of the moment to see if he was alright, but that it was obvious he most certainly was – and she left.

Sinking down into the bubbles of a hot bath she'd been promising herself all day, Jenny reflected on the weekend.

It had been lovely to spend time with Jessica, one-to-one. It had been a long time since they'd done that. She felt so proud of her confident, self-assured daughter, but part of her worried about how vulnerable she was too. She was working closely with Mark now as part of his ever-expanding team, and to Jenny this seemed dangerous, because if she put a foot wrong, Mark would inevitably punish her, like he did with Marcus, with everyone around him. Jenny shivered despite the warmth of the water. Mark only had people around him who served a purpose and she knew full-well that Jessica's purpose, though the girl didn't know it, was to gather information about her. It was horrendous that both Jessica and Marcus still didn't know the truth about Mark. Jenny wanted to protect them but she couldn't do so for much longer; they were adults, with minds of their own. At least Jessica had her boyfriend Ben to confide in. But then Ben seemed to be getting a little too cosy with Mark, joining his gang of cronies, neatly replacing the ostracised Marcus. Jenny sighed and sank under the water, letting her head fully submerge until all around her was muted.

Jenny drove back round to see her father the next morning after ringing first to see if Malcolm had left.

'Coffee, dear?' her father asked as she walked through his front door.

'Sounds just the ticket. Feeling slightly under par today, are you Dad?' she asked.

'Not at all. Don't know what you mean,' he huffed.

'So, who was Malcolm?' Jenny asked lightly.

'Oh, just an Army pal, like I said. It was good to catch

up. He works in the same firm as Mark's solicitor, funnily enough.

What a surprise, Jenny mused. 'He wasn't involved in the court-marshal you told me about, was he?'

'Good lord, no! Why are you dredging all that up again?'

'I'm not Dad – I just want to know a bit more about your Army days, that's all...'

'Oh, I suppose it doesn't matter now – nothing really matters that much, does it?' George looked deflated, realising that the moments of his life that once held such importance to him were now hardly worth talking about.

Jenny held her breath. What was her father about to tell her?

'It was a Private Jenkins who was involved.'

Jenny's heart sank; nothing to do with Mark's dad then... She decided to risk it. 'You don't remember anyone called Damerell do you?'

'But that's Mark's surname! No, I'd definitely remember that. Why are you asking?' he looked at her sharply.

'Oh, no reason.' Now wasn't the time, as George was hunched over his cup, nursing what was obviously a nasty hangover.

'No, my girl. It was a ghastly business, brought discord amongst the ranks; shame on us all to be honest...'

'Go on, Dad.'

'Nothing more to say really. Water under the bridge. Truth be told I am feeling rather peaky Jennifer – maybe too much of the old grape and grain yesterday. Going to retire. Do you mind?'

'No Dad, off you go. I'll let myself out.' Jenny glanced out of the window. The sun was just peeping over the beech tree in George's garden and the sky was a pale blue. Skylarks were already soaring high up above and she could see the sea glittering like a sapphire in the distance.

She decided to spend a day at the beach. *Time for some 'me-time'*, she thought.

She returned to Trethorne to pick up a beach towel and make a flask of tea. Rummaging at the back of her craft cupboard, she unearthed some oil pastels and a sketch book and packed these up, together with a rudimentary picnic of bread and cheese. She would be perfectly happy with this simple lunch. It felt good to not have to think about anyone else or have to anticipate their requests for choccy bars and crisps. She chose a beach a few miles away, just off the coastal path. It was often deserted and this early in the year, she knew she would have the beach to herself.

Leaving the car at the top of the track, Jenny walked down the path to the beach. It was uneven and she was glad of the handrail, but she made it. The tide had just gone out and the beach gleamed in the sun, a few shells and pebbles dotting the otherwise smooth, shimmering sheet of sand. Jenny picked a sheltered spot up by the dunes and laid out her picnic blanket. She drank in the pure sea air and enjoyed the breeze ruffling her hair. Heaven, it was absolute heaven. She felt her senses coming back alive; her creativity blossoming again. She took out the pastels and began to draw, sketching the headlands fading into mist around the bay. Several blissful hours passed with Jenny simply bathing in the solitude and the beauty of her surroundings.

Finally, as the scudding clouds started to cover the sun and the breeze picked up to a gusty wind, Jenny gathered her belongings and made her way to the car. As she walked back up the path, her phone began to ping. There must've been no signal at the beach and these were delayed messages. Jenny decided to check them all at the car but as she continued to trudge, her phone was going mad, pinging constantly as message after message came in. She unhooked her backpack from her shoulder and reached into the front pocket to retrieve her phone.

'Oh shit!' she exclaimed as she looked at the screen. 21 missed calls. 12 messages. She hurriedly opened her message folder. *Mum, ring me right away,* from Jessica. *Mum, where are you? Call me,* from Marcus. The rest were versions of the same, getting more and more agitated. She jogged the last few hundred yards to the car – and despite her aching joints she smiled to herself that she was actually able to jog – and put her phone on speaker to call Jessica as she drove.

'Mummy, thank god you've called,' said Jessica.

'What is it, darling?' *Mummy, she never calls me Mummy. It must be bad...*

'It's Granddad. I went over to see him and found him collapsed in his bedroom. He's in hospital...' Jessica's voice thickened. 'Come quickly.'

'I'll be there as soon as I can,' replied Jenny and put her foot down on the accelerator. It was a 50-minute drive to

Barnstaple hospital and Jenny wished, not for the first time, that they weren't quite so remote. She swore when she got stuck behind a tractor, and pulled out to overtake before she could really see the road ahead. During the journey, she couldn't help but be reminded of the awful drive along these same roads when she and her father had followed the ambulance to hospital after her mother's heart attack. 'Please God let him be okay,' she willed.

After finding out where he was, she rushed up to her father's ward and was escorted into a side room. George was lying there motionless, hooked up to monitors and drips. Jessica and Marcus were sitting either side of him, holding his pale, papery hands. They turned when Jenny entered the room and rushed towards her.

'My darlings,' she said, hugging them both. 'I'm so sorry I wasn't here. What's happened to Granddad?'

'He's really ill. He's been unconscious all day,' replied Marcus. 'They've done millions of tests. I can't remember all of them…' he faltered and a tear ran down his cheek. Just then, a nurse in a dark blue uniform came into the room and took Jenny aside.

'You're Mr Truscott's daughter?'

Jenny nodded.

'Your father has had a severe stroke. At the moment, we can't tell the amount of damage it has caused, but it's on the left side of his brain, the area that controls speech and movement.'

'Is there anything you can do? Medication or an operation?' pleaded Jenny.

'We've done everything we can and the next 24 hours are critical as to whether he'll pull through. You need to prepare yourself,' she finished, looking directly at Jenny.

'Thank you for being straight with me,' Jenny replied. The nurse went over to monitor her father and Jenny followed her. She looked down at him, his face waxy against the white pillow. Wires and tubes emerged from under the covers. He looked so small, so lost. A tiny frame in a big bed. She kissed his forehead and adjusted his oxygen mask slightly. Jessica and Marcus were sitting back in their chairs, looking very young and pensive.

'I'm so sorry I wasn't here for you,' Jenny repeated. 'I was at the beach, no signal. I should have thought… I feel terrible.'

'It's all right, Mum,' said Jessica. 'You weren't to know.' She pulled up a chair next to her and they sat, watching the old man's chest slowly rise and fall again, the only sign that he was alive.

After a few hours, Jenny and her children made their way back home. She stopped at the nurses' station on her way out.

'Please can you ring me if there's any change? I'll make sure my phone is on this time,' she said, smiling awkwardly. She began to wonder why it was that the first time she allowed herself to relax and just focus on herself, it seemed like she was being punished for it? It felt like the universe was against her, as Joy would say. But then she stopped herself as her counselling sessions kicked-in. *I am not being punished. This is not about me. I am not responsible for this.*

At home in bed after a quick meal of pasta, Jenny allowed the tears to come for the first time. *Dear old Dad.* She thought of him all alone in that dimly-lit side ward. Once he was such a powerful man, now he was reduced to a frail figure in a hospital gown. And the nurse had sounded very foreboding – would she ever get a chance to speak to her father again? Jenny eventually drifted off and was woken by her phone ringing. She glanced at the time – 6.10am. It was the hospital.

'Your father has passed away peacefully,' said the nurse.

'Oh no!' Jenny gasped. He's gone…?' She broke down in tears. She managed to listen to the nurse's instructions and then let her head flop back on the pillow. Her heart was aching with loss. She felt so alone; first her mother died, then her father, and her brother was on the other side of the world. Her family seemed to shrink before her. For the first time in a long time, she missed Mark and how he would've taken over the situation and sorted everything out. But then she shook herself out of her reverie: Mark was evil and her father would've sold her inheritance down the river if he could've. George was a hard-hearted bigot of a man and no amount of eulogising would change that. But he was her father and despite everything, she still loved him.

After a while, she forced herself to get up and splash her face with water. Then she went and broke the news to her children.

When they arrived at the ward, the nurses had taken away all the monitors and tubes and a rose had been placed on his pillow. Her father looked strangely at peace, his noble profile still strong, an echo of his handsome younger days. They spent a few moments saying their goodbyes, then returned home, muted and shaken.

George's funeral 10 days later was well-attended and it reminded Jenny just how popular he had been; an influential businessman and member of the community. Over the past few years she'd forgotten this side to him. So many people came up to her to shake her hand and tell her how her father had helped them in some way. The day before the funeral, Jessica had asked if Mark and Sam could come and she'd been too tired and wrung out to object, and after all, Mark had known George for years. He'd been his son-in-law. As she walked to the front of the church to take her seat, she could see the back of Mark's smart black overcoat as he sat in a pew. She looked more carefully. His shoulders were shaking and his head was bent. He was sobbing his heart out and seeing his sadness made tears well in her own eyes. Sam reached out and stroked his back, and Jenny's sympathy turned to sadness for herself – she had no man to comfort her. She grabbed Jessica and Marcus' hands and took a deep breath. *No disguising the fact that they're definitely an item now,* she said to herself. *Come on Jen, no wallowing in self-pity.* It was exactly what her father would have said.

After a week or two had passed, Jenny decided to tackle her father's things – sorting out what were keepsakes and what needed to go to the charity shop. Marcus could have his pocket watch and medals, Jessica would like the leather writing case and fountain pen. Jenny's heart melted when she found a bundle of letters between her parents. It was lovely to read how much they loved each other when they were courting, and she decided to keep them. Amongst George's papers, she discovered a battered old rent book in the name of E. Cliff. *Who can that be?* She wondered. The only Cliff she knew was Liz' ex-husband, but Clifford was his first name, not his surname. The payments went back to 1996, over 20 years ago, and the last payment had been a month ago. She couldn't make sense of it. Her father had a lot of property that he had rented out but all the paperwork for these were kept at the office and handled by his accountant. He'd relinquished responsibility for them years ago. What was he doing with this one? Jenny had another meeting with Andy, so she decided to take it along and see what he could find out about it.

Despite having her own transport again, Jenny took the train to meet Andy, as she enjoyed the journey and she felt it was not so easy to be followed on a train – because after all this time, she was still wary of Mark and his warped agenda. Plus, it gave her a chance to write more of her book.

When they'd got settled with a coffee, Andy produced a file of papers.

'That woman, Samantha Penbode who you mentioned. I've accessed her son's medical records and discovered that the father's name is Lesley. Lesley Montrose.'

'Hah! And I bet Mark thought *he* was the father. Excellent work! Any other good news?'

'Well, I found out some more about your father's regiment. One of the court-marshalled privates was called Albert Jenkins.

'Jenkins! I know that name! My dad mentioned him before he died,' replied Jenny.

'Well it turns out this Jenkins was married with a son, and after he was thrown out of the army he got divorced.'

'Married with a son? Then divorced? Just like Mark's dad…?'

'You're right. And sadly, after the divorce he committed suicide. I actually believe that this man was Mark's father. I hadn't investigated Mark's mother's family much until now, but I've found out that Damerell was her maiden name. She changed her name back after she got divorced.'

'Back from… Jenkins?'

'Yes.'

Jenny could hardly believe it. 'Do you think Mark knows of this?'

'He must do. Jenkins was on his birth certificate.' Andy dug in his folder and showed her a photocopy of Mark's birth certificate. Jenny realised that she had never seen this, only his passport. Even when they got married, it had never appeared. He was registered as Mark Albert Jenkins.

'My hunch when you first told me about Mark was that he was driven by revenge. Well, if he knew that his father had killed himself after being publically disgraced for being a homosexual, that would certainly be reason enough.'

'But revenge against whom?'

Andy looked at her quietly. He busied himself stirring his coffee. 'Now, I don't want to upset you, because I know your father died recently, but…' Jenny's heart felt like it was going to burst out of her chest. 'But, I think the other soldier involved was your father.'

'…? You're wrong, you must be! It absolutely can't be true…, it's completely far-fetched.' Jenny felt her cheeks burning.

'I'm sorry, Jenny, it's just my instincts. I don't have definitive proof, but your father was an officer in the same regiment and they enjoyed much higher privileges than privates, including the hushing-up of certain behaviours.'

'Behaviours?' echoed Jenny faintly.

'And your own father left the Army at much the same time as Private Jenkins, but not under such a cloud. It adds up Jenny. Think about it. Mark plotted revenge against the Truscott family from day one for besmirching his own family's name.'

'But… even before we were married? Mark knew about his father and my father? No… It can't be true – even Mark wouldn't go that far, would he? And anyway, Mark got on well with my father. He was at the funeral, grieving. That couldn't be an act, surely?'

'You know what lengths Mark will go to, Jenny. And who's to say that Mark hasn't found a way to blackmail your father, to buy his silence?'

'No, no. no. I'm sorry, Andy, but I'm finding this very hard to take in. I'm going to go now, I can't think straight.

Can we be in touch again when I've had a chance to absorb all this? I don't think... I can't... I'm sorry.' Jenny sobbed and picked up her things, walking out of the hotel foyer and into the sunlight, tears spilling from her eyes.

She couldn't believe what she'd just heard, she didn't want to either. She was coming to terms with her father's death, and she didn't want all these dark secrets revealed about him. She had thought that Andy would help her get to the bottom of Mark's motives, not sully her own family's name.

On the train home, the information slowly sank in. She wouldn't have become Mrs Damerell at all, she would have been Jenny Jenkins. All these years, and now she had discovered the seeds of Mark's cruel, sadistic ways. Underneath that calculating, manipulative façade was a man hell-bent on revenge. Revenge for his father's death. The self-control, the willpower it must have taken to systematically track down her family, marry her and proceed to crush her... it was inconceivable. He had obviously approached Paul at university first, and when that didn't work out, he moved on to her. He would stop at nothing – taking over the family empire, attempting to steal the ancestral home, and even trying to murder the daughter.

Jenny turned her head to the window, trying to control her shaking. The tears began to fall again. Her father had died never knowing that his beloved son-in-law was a psychopathic monster. He had been duped into believing Mark was a doting husband and father, doing the best for his family. How would her father have reacted if he'd known

Mark was the son of his lover? His lover... So, her father was bi-sexual too... But this fact mattered to her far less than that of Mark's war on the Truscotts. She wondered if her mother knew any of this. *Poor Mum... I wonder if she forgave him?*

When Jenny got home she went straight to her room. She had a pounding headache and just wanted to sleep. But Jessica tapped lightly on the door.

'Hey Mum, how are you?'

'Fine,' said Jenny, feeling far from it.

'I've just been to a lunch with Dad and Sam and guess what? He's proposed to her! They're going to get married.'

'Really?' replied Jenny. *Poor Sam.* Nothing would surprise her about him now.

'Yes, I think it makes so much sense. They're perfect together. He gave her a gorgeous ring – opals and pearls, really stylish.' *Pearls eh? Just like my necklace,* thought Jenny.

'And a bottle of perfume – Chanel No. 5. Isn't that the one you used to wear, Mum?'

'You're right, it was.'

And so it begins again. History is repeating, same modus operandi and all.

'Weird,' Jessica said half to herself as she pulled the door closed, 'Sam's going to be my stepmother!'

Jenny wondered not for the first time, if she should say something to Sam, to warn her. But she knew from previous experience she wouldn't be believed or thanked. She was perceived as weak, jealous, mentally unstable Jenny. How ironic that she'd be dismissed when she was trying to save the woman's life. What about the police? Should they know Mark may have begun poisoning again? She could just imagine them laughing at her – of how the bitter and twisted ex is now fabricating stories about the new wife. But wasn't it morally wrong to ignore what she knew to be the truth? Jenny glanced over at her handbag and saw the rent book poking out. *Damn*. She didn't have a chance to ask Andy about it. She wasn't sure she wanted to know now, either. She felt sickened by recent revelations. She pulled the covers up tightly around her neck and clamped her eyes shut. She'd had enough of this day.

At 3.04am Jenny's eyes popped open again, a jolt of adrenalin making her completely alert. Something had suddenly occurred to her in the depths of her sleep. E. Cliff on the rent book. That's got to be Elizabeth and Clifford. She'd forgotten her dad had always called Liz, Elizabeth. She tried to think back to what had happened in 1996. Had Clifford left Liz by then? She couldn't remember. Was she overthinking this? There had to be a logical reason that her father would have a rent book for her friend Liz.

At 9am she went straight round to Liz's house.

'Hi Jen, how've you been since the funeral? It's good to see you,' said Liz. 'Come in. Would you like a coffee?'

'Yes, please,' Jenny replied, stepping over the threshold. She sat at the kitchen table and put her handbag down, the corner of the rent book clearly visible. 'I'm doing okay. Tidying up lots of loose ends at Dad's house, you know...' Jenny dabbed her handkerchief at the involuntary tear that had trickled down her face.

'It must be hard for you babe.' said Liz, bringing the cafetiere to the table, and taking a seat. 'Hey, this is just like old times, isn't it!' she smiled, giving Jenny's hand a squeeze.

'Yes, it is. Talking of old times, I found this in Dad's things. Do you know anything about it?' She brought out the rent book and on seeing it, Liz jerked her coffee cup down with a thud. She sighed and put her head in her hands.

After some time, she said, 'Well... I suppose I can tell you now your dad's passed away.'

'Tell me what?' said Jenny, her blood running cold.

'Do you remember when me and Clifford broke up? 1996 it was.'

'Yes. I remember you came round and we sat talking for hours,' answered Jenny.

'Yes, that's right. Well, what I didn't tell you was that I'd actually been round a couple of days before to see you, and you were out. I couldn't find you in the house so I went round to the office.'

'Oh yes?' Jenny couldn't imagine where this was going.

'The thing is... Oh Christ, this is hard... I found... Well, I found your dad and Mark, together...' said Liz.

'What do you mean, together? said Jenny, staring at Liz. The two women sat in silence, Liz not able to meet Jenny's eyes. After a while, Jenny eventually said: 'You mean, *together* together?'

'Yes,' croaked Liz. '*In flagrante*, I think they call it.'

'Stop! I don't want to hear any more!'

'Please let me tell you, Jen. I've been living with this for

20 years and the times I've wanted to tell you, I can't count how many they were. The thing is, they saw me.'

Jenny put her hands to her mouth. Abruptly she got up from the table and was sick in the kitchen sink. Liz rushed over to her and passed her a box of tissues.

'Why the fucking HELL didn't you tell me?' raged Jenny as she rinsed her mouth out.

'I'm so so sorry. I wanted to, but you were pregnant with Marcus...'

'That's even more reason why you should have told me!'

'I know, I know. As soon as they saw me, I tried to leave, but Mark came running over to the car. I told him that what they were doing was disgusting and wrong and he begged and pleaded with me not to say anything. He said you'd lose the baby with the shock.'

'And you *bought* that? Christ Liz, I thought you saw through him.'

'I do, believe me, I do. I hate Mark, and your father was a weak man who was charmed and manipulated by your husband... but there was something else. The next day, I was trying to think how to break it to you when your father came round. He offered to pay me £200 a month to keep quiet. That was a lot of money back then, especially since I was a single mum. Joe needed so much extra care and I was in dire straits financially as Clifford never paid a penny in maintenance... So, I took the money. I'm so sorry, Jenny. I've never forgiven myself.'

'Why didn't you ask me for the money? I would've given it to you in a heartbeat,' said Jenny.

'How could you have, Jen? Mark had such a hold over you, you never had any cash. All these years I've regretted keeping Mark's dirty secret, believe me. They blackmailed me to keep quiet, and I did, I kept quiet – but I've always hated myself for doing so, and I've never trusted Mark since.' Liz was crying, begging her to understand.

'So, the rent book wasn't for the receipt of money, it was a record of the money paid to you? Well, it must've mounted up over the years Liz. I hope it was worth the price of our friendship.'

'Oh please, Jen! Please don't hate me. I was desperate and I thought, what good would it do you to know that the two men in your life were cheating on you, together? With everything that you were going through at the time, I thought it would kill you. And I thought I may as well take some money from the bastards as that was one thing that would really hurt them.'

'But now, all these years later? Joe died, Clifford's gone, you've got a good job… Why take the money?'

'I told myself I would tell you after your dad had passed away – and so I am. And once I got back on my feet, I saved all the money to give back to you. It's in a savings account, every penny. I can get the book now and show you. You can have it – it's thousands. I didn't know what to do for the best, Jen.' Liz pleaded with her friend. 'Jen?'

'Oh Liz, it's all right, I forgive you.'

'You do? I wouldn't forgive me.'

'I do though, because we've both been manipulated by those two men, and we've both lived under a cloud of their making. We have to be strong. We have to forgive and forget, otherwise they've won,' Jenny sobbed and the two women hugged. 'Christ knows, if there's anyone who understands about getting wrapped up in Mark's mind games, it's me.'

'Thank you, Jenny. And Mark's taken over the direct debit – he's paying me now,' said Liz, 'so we can let him just keep paying. He doesn't know that you know, and unless you tell him, you can use the money to take yourself on a world cruise!'

'Christ, that is priceless. I hope he keeps paying until the day he dies!' exclaimed Jenny. 'Let him think you're protecting him for the rest of his life.'

'Don't worry I will,' said Liz. 'It will be my pleasure.'

'Maybe you can come with me on the cruise? Thelma and Louise, remember!'

They both laughed. Liz stood up and made more coffee. 'It's so good that you finally know. I can't tell you what a relief it is. The times I've agonised over this, especially when you divorced Mark and found out how he'd been manipulating you. But knowing that about George… your father… I just couldn't do it. I'm truly sorry, my friend. You are my dearest friend Jen, I hope you know that. Anyway, as my Great Aunt Miriam used to say: "The truth comes out like oil on water."'

When Jenny left a couple of hours later, she was still reeling. Was there no end to Mark's depravity? Seducing her father? She could hardly take it in. She desperately wanted to confront Mark, to announce to the world what he had been up to, but she knew she wouldn't get very far before Mark shut her down, one way or another. And the children... How could she do that to them? How could they live with the truth about their father and grandfather? They would probably ostracise her forever, just for telling them. She felt so tired and small. Mark would continue getting away with it, wreaking havoc with all around to satisfy the darkness within him, and she was powerless to stop him. He shouldn't be allowed to walk on God's green earth, let alone run wild on it, leaving a trail of destruction behind him. The frustration she felt was overwhelming; she couldn't get justice – nobody except Liz believed her, and Liz was implicated in the debacle up to her eyeballs. She just had to watch him starting to crush Sam whilst she stood by, helpless. It felt morally wrong to see another human being having to go through what she had, but what could she do? She could present Andy's findings to the police, but where was the incontrovertible proof? Albert Jenkins and George and Eleanor Truscott were dead. Mark Damerell covered his tracks like a hunter in the desert and had poisoned the community against her. And Jenny – well, Jenny had no fight left in her. She had to just accept that he'd won and put it behind her.

Then she had a better idea.

A year later, Jenny was in Exeter Castle Art Gallery. Resplendent in a glorious sage-coloured Oska dress. She had never felt more alive or beautiful. She was at a Private View – of her own paintings. Almost all of her seascape sketches had little red 'sold' dots on them. She was waiting for her guests to arrive and her mind wandered. She thought of her children, grown adults now, who would soon join her at tonight's celebration. Marcus had got himself a place at the Eden Project training to be a Landscape Designer, and he was in his element. He had grown strong and so handsome and was living with his partner, Simon, in Charlestown, a beautiful little fishing port on the south coast of Cornwall. Jess was still working with Mark and Sam and had been promoted to Office Manager taking over Rachael's old role, Rachael having left to have her baby and move nearer to her parents in Oxfordshire. Jess, who was once manipulated by Mark to spy on Jenny, now inadvertently kept Jenny abreast of the Damerell empire. It seemed it was not doing so well, after all. Mark had to sell a lot of assets to keep the business afloat, and Sam, who was now pregnant with her second child and Mark's third, was off work with constant morning sickness. *I bet he loves that,* Jenny chuckled. She wondered if Mark's skeletons would ever come out of the closet, but from the little she could glean, it seemed that he hadn't changed his controlling ways much and that he had the new marriage sewn-up much like the last.

On the day of Sam's hen night, Jenny had dropped Jessie off at the spa hotel near Padstow where a dozen hens were spending a glamorous 'pamper weekend.' Jenny dropped her daughter at the gate but then parked the car opposite and waited. When she saw Sam arrive in her sleek little Mini, Jenny locked her car and walked over to the bride-to-be.

'Hello Sam.'

'Oh… Hello Jenny.'

'I've just dropped Jess off, and I wanted to offer you my very best wishes for your future.'

'Thank you. That's kind of you.'

Then, catching Sam's eye, Jenny said, 'If you ever need to talk – ever – I'm here for you.'

Sam's eyes dropped and a shadow crossed her face. Without looking up, she squeezed Jenny's hands, held on to them for dear life, then let them drop and walked into her future.

Jenny looked up when the gallery door opened. It was her friend Cassandra who had come down from London to visit.

'Oh Jen, I'm so proud of you!' she said, enveloping her in a hug. 'And guess what I saw in Waterstones at Paddington station?' She whipped out the signature black carrier bag. 'Only a copy of your novel – it was in a massive display in the front window.'

'Oh wow!' said Jenny, eyes glittering, still not able to get over the fact that her book had been published. 'My "novel".' She glanced at her friend, who understood implicitly the irony of that word, then looked admiringly at the stylish paperback, *Hearts of Ice*. 'It's been such a crazy few months since I finished it. My agent said there's a bidding war for the film rights. Can you believe it!'

'Wow,' echoed Cassandra. 'You couldn't make it up.'

'That's right,' replied Jenny. 'You couldn't make it up.'

Printed in Great Britain
by Amazon